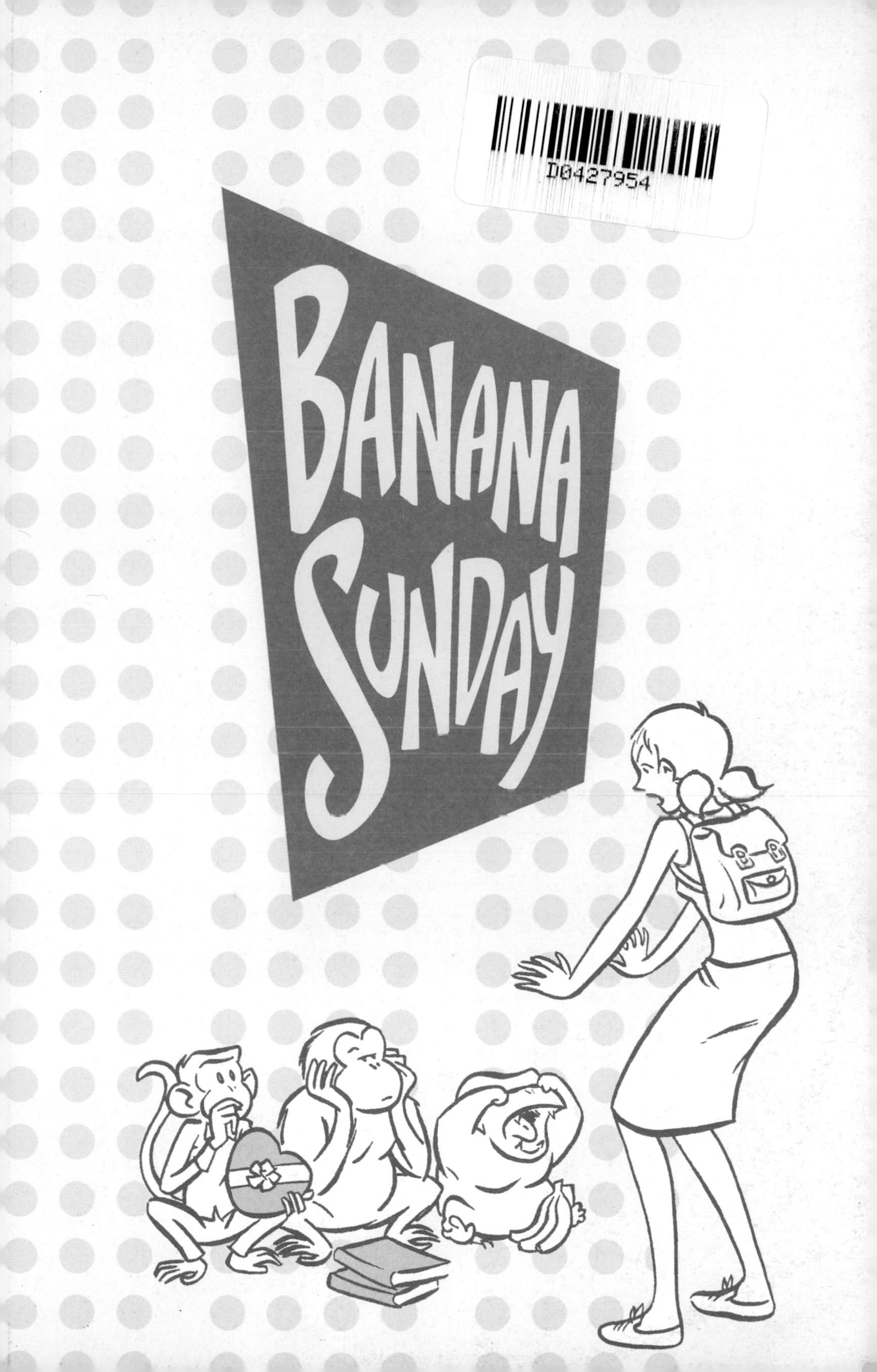
BANANA
SUNDAY

Written by
PAUL TOBIN

Illustrated and lettered by
COLLEEN COOVER

Colored by
RIAN SYGH

Tobin, Paul, 1965-
Banana Sunday /
2018.
33305243862426
ca   10/30/18

BANANA SUNDAY

...zZz

ONI PRESS

AN ONI PRESS PUBLICATION

Designed by Kate Z. Stone
Original edition edited by James Lucas Jones
New edition edited by Ari Yarwood

PUBLISHED BY ONI PRESS, INC.

JOE NOZEMACK	founder & chief financial officer
JAMES LUCAS JONES	publisher
CHARLIE CHU	v.p. of creative & business development
BRAD ROOKS	director of operations
MELISSA MESZAROS	director of publicity
MARGOT WOOD	director of sales
SANDY TANAKA	marketing design manager
AMBER O'NEILL	special projects manager
TROY LOOK	director of design & production
HILARY THOMPSON	senior graphic designer
KATE Z. STONE	graphic designer
SONJA SYNAK	junior graphic designer
ANGIE KNOWLES	digital prepress lead
ARI YARWOOD	executive editor
SARAH GAYDOS	editorial director of licensed publishing
ROBIN HERRERA	senior editor
DESIREE WILSON	associate editor
ALISSA SALLAH	administrative assistant
JUNG LEE	logistics associate
SCOTT SHARKEY	warehouse assistant

onipress.com
facebook.com/onipress
twitter.com/onipress
onipress.tumblr.com
instagram.com/onipress

1319 SE Martin Luther King, Jr. Blvd.
Suite 240
Portland, OR 97214

Paultobin.net / @PaulTobin
Colleencoover.net/ @ColleenCoover
Riansygh.com / @RianSygh

First Edition: October 2018
ISBN: 978-1-62010-541-2 • **eISBN:** 978-1-62010-542-9

1 3 5 7 9 10 8 6 4 2

Library of Congress Control Number: 2018940470

Printed in China.

Banana Sunday, October 2018. Published by Oni Press, Inc. 1319 SE Martin
Luther King, Jr. Blvd., Suite 240, Portland, OR 97214. Banana Sunday is ™ &
© 2006, 2018 Paul Tobin and Colleen Coover. All rights reserved. Oni Press
logo and icon ™ & © 2018 Oni Press, Inc. Oni Press logo and icon artwork
created by Keith A. Wood. The events, institutions, and characters presented
in this book are fictional. Any resemblance to actual persons, living or dead,
is purely coincidental. No portion of this publication may be reproduced, by
any means, without the express written permission of the copyright holders.

Welcome to the remastered and revamped *Banana Sunday,* in color for the first time!

This book was, I think, the first truly major project that Colleen and I ever worked on together, and I remember that it took us several tries to get it right. There are dusty portfolios in my closet, for instance, filled with the forgotten pages of far more manga-inspired versions, pages that Colleen insisted NOT be included in this book's extra material, because of that thing where the art is old and Colleen doesn't want to cringe every time she picks up this collection. I can easily understand it on her part; there are parts of this story that I ACHE to rewrite, and in fact there are a few bits that we did nudge around, because the times have changed since we created this work, and we've definitely changed with them. Plus those early versions were, from I think both our parts, homages to the work of Rumiko Takahashi, rather than Colleen and I speaking with our own voices the way I feel we eventually accomplished with this version of *Banana Sunday.*

I absolutely adore this book. How could I not? With all this gorgeous Colleen Coover art? And there's a gorilla, after all, and for me gorillas will always be the King of Beasts. In addition to that, there's an orangutan, a creature that I grew to love while watching those *Every Which Way But Loose* movies with Clint Eastwood. Plus there's a spider-monkey, which is the first type of monkey I ever met, way back when one stole my sunglasses from me at a zoo in Mason City, Iowa, after country life had insufficiently prepared me to be wary of monkey thieves.

In addition, this time *Banana Sunday* is finally under my own name, rather than the "Root Nibot" pseudonym I originally used, for some reason I no longer remember.

And seeing the work in color for the first time, thanks to the genius efforts of Rian Sygh, has been eye-opening. I get to look at the work fresh, and be proud of it in other ways. I'm really happy that editor Ari Yarwood and Oni Press provided this opportunity to get the work back in print. I think it's important for creators to stop every now and then, to look backward, to take a look at some of our first works. It's grounding. It's like seeing pictures from your childhood. Sure, you're dressed in funny clothes and your hair looks like a bowl of spaghetti just exploded in a zero-gravity situation, but... dang... you can also see the roots of what you were putting down. You can key back into paths that you may have wandered away from. You can hear the laughter you've forgotten to keep laughing. There's nothing like taking a trip back to where you're from, in order to help stabilize the path you want to travel.

So, yes, sometimes you can come home again. And sometimes you can do it in color.

Paul Tobin
January 30, 2018

CHAPTER ONE

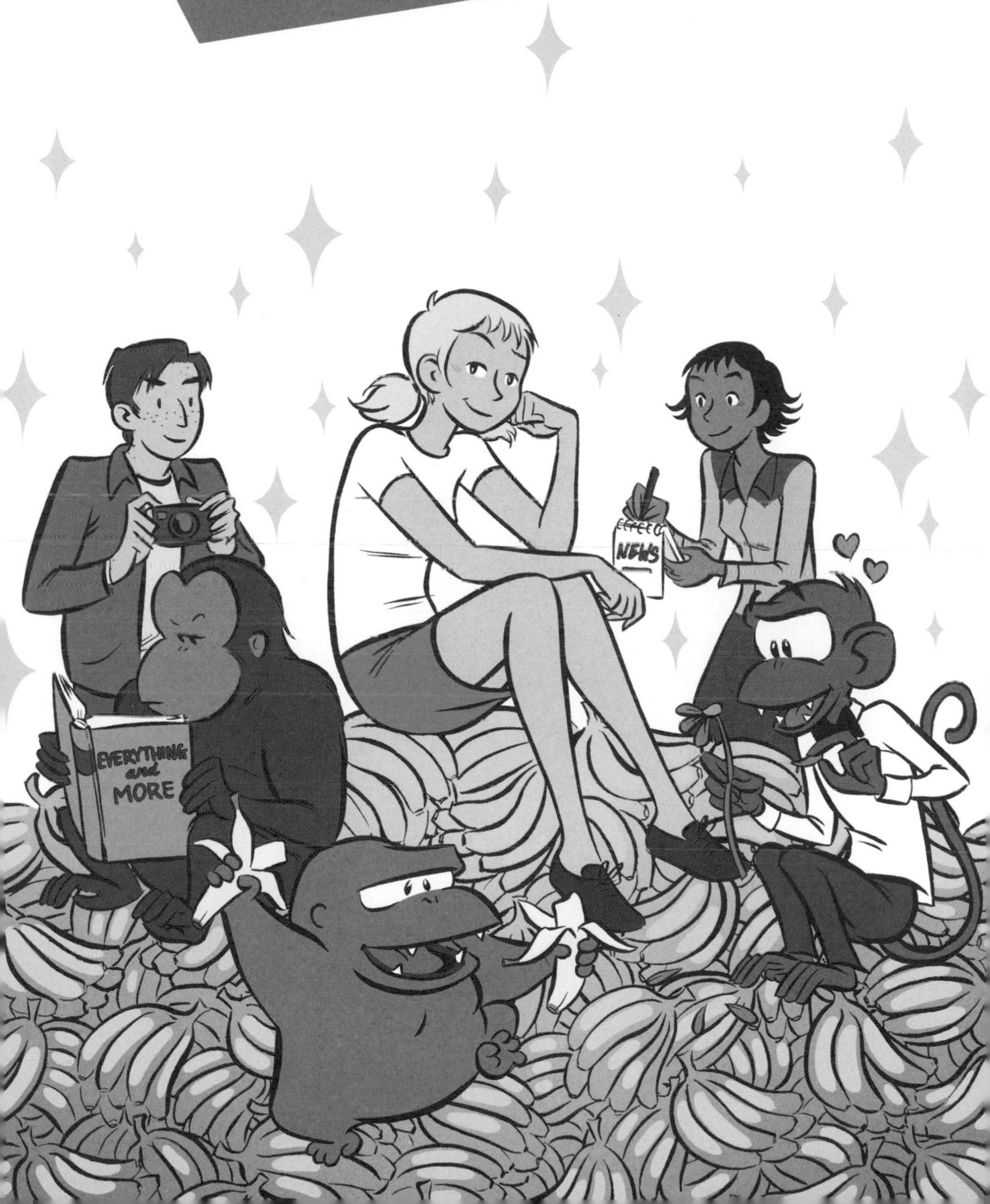
NEWS
EVERYTHING and MORE

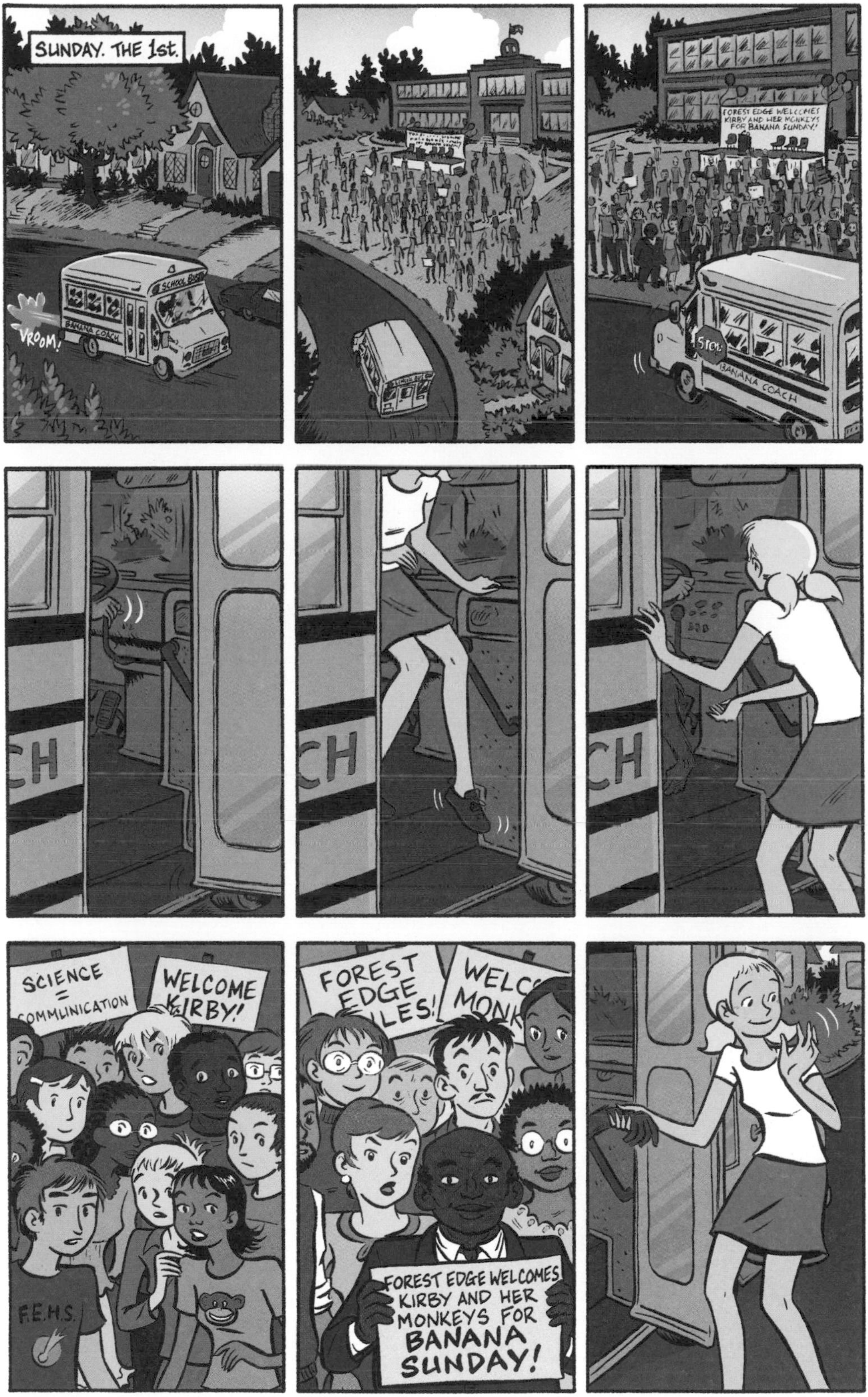
SUNDAY. THE 1st.
SCHOOL BUS
BANANA COACH
VROOM!
FOREST EDGE WELCOMES KIRBY AND HER MONKEYS FOR BANANA SUNDAY!
STOP
BANANA COACH
CH
CH
CH
SCIENCE = COMMUNICATION
WELCOME KIRBY!
F.E.H.S.
FOREST EDGE
FOREST EDGE WELCOMES KIRBY AND HER MONKEYS FOR BANANA SUNDAY!

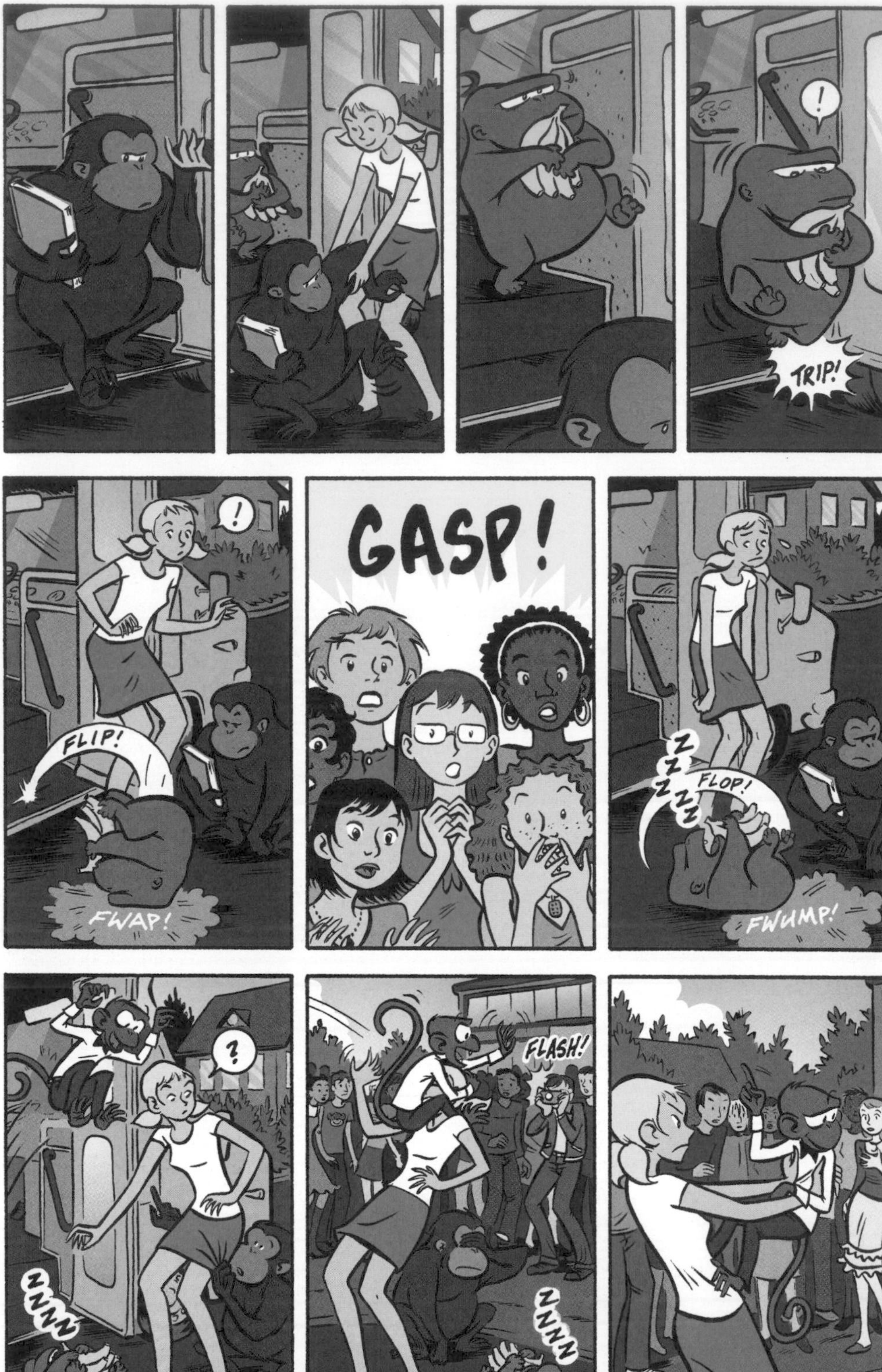
!
TRIP!
!
FLIP!
FWAP!
GASP!
ZZZZZ
FLOP!
FWUMP!
?
ZZZZ
FLASH!
ZZZZ

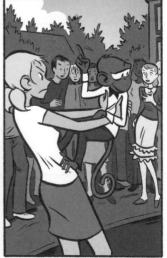

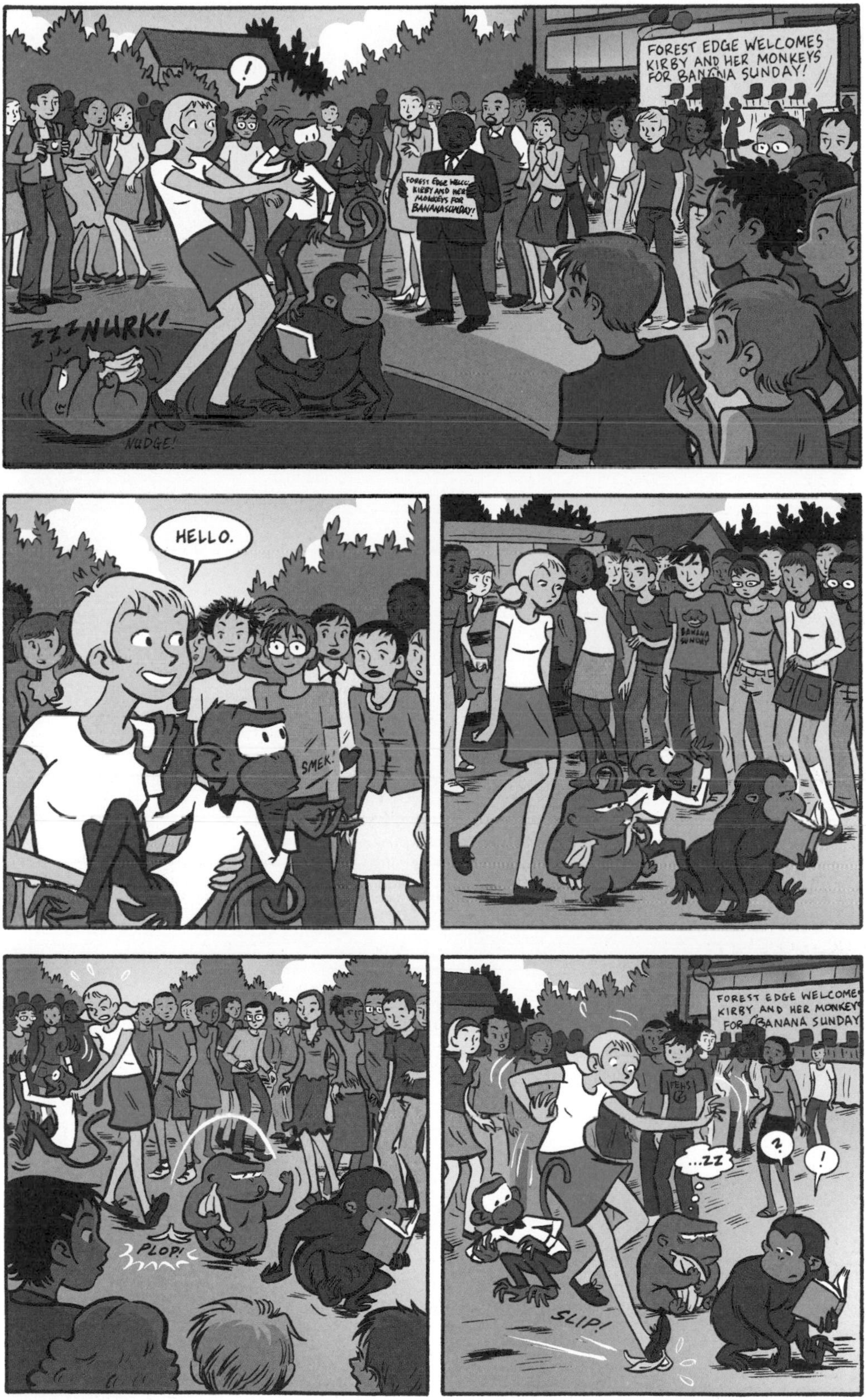
FOREST EDGE WELCOMES KIRBY AND HER MONKEYS FOR BANANA SUNDAY!
!
ZZZNURK!
NUDGE!
HELLO.
SMEK!
BANANA SUNDAY
PLOP!
FOREST EDGE WELCOMES KIRBY AND HER MONKEYS FOR BANANA SUNDAY
...ZZ
?
!
SLIP!

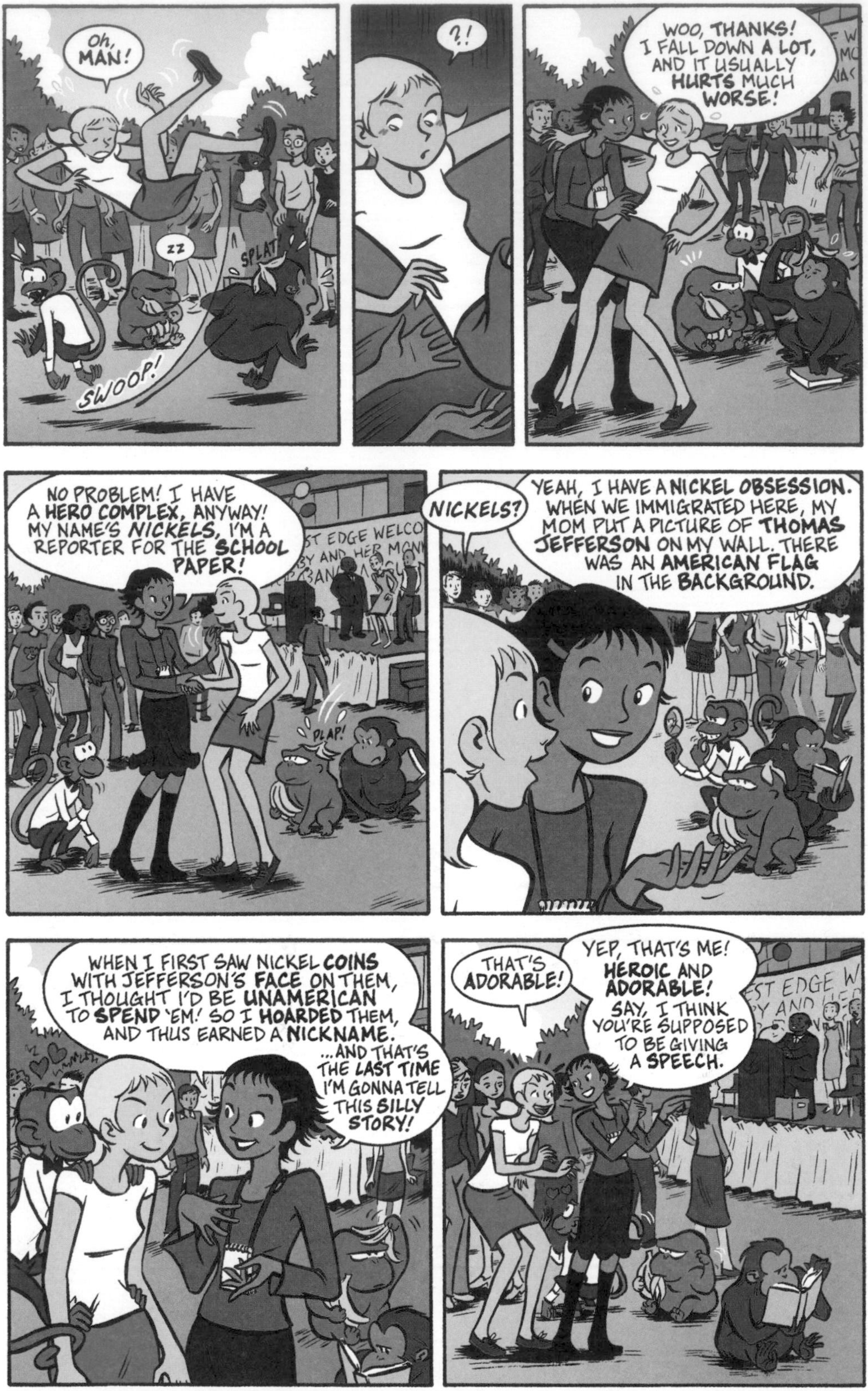

Oh, MAN!
ZZ
SPLAT
SWOOP!
?!
WOO, THANKS! I FALL DOWN A LOT, AND IT USUALLY HURTS MUCH WORSE!
NO PROBLEM! I HAVE A HERO COMPLEX, ANYWAY! MY NAME'S NICKELS, I'M A REPORTER FOR THE SCHOOL PAPER!
PLAP!
NICKELS?
YEAH, I HAVE A NICKEL OBSESSION. WHEN WE IMMIGRATED HERE, MY MOM PUT A PICTURE OF THOMAS JEFFERSON ON MY WALL. THERE WAS AN AMERICAN FLAG IN THE BACKGROUND.
WHEN I FIRST SAW NICKEL COINS WITH JEFFERSON'S FACE ON THEM, I THOUGHT I'D BE UNAMERICAN TO SPEND 'EM! SO I HOARDED THEM, AND THUS EARNED A NICKNAME.
...AND THAT'S THE LAST TIME I'M GONNA TELL THIS SILLY STORY!
THAT'S ADORABLE!
YEP, THAT'S ME! HEROIC AND ADORABLE! SAY, I THINK YOU'RE SUPPOSED TO BE GIVING A SPEECH.

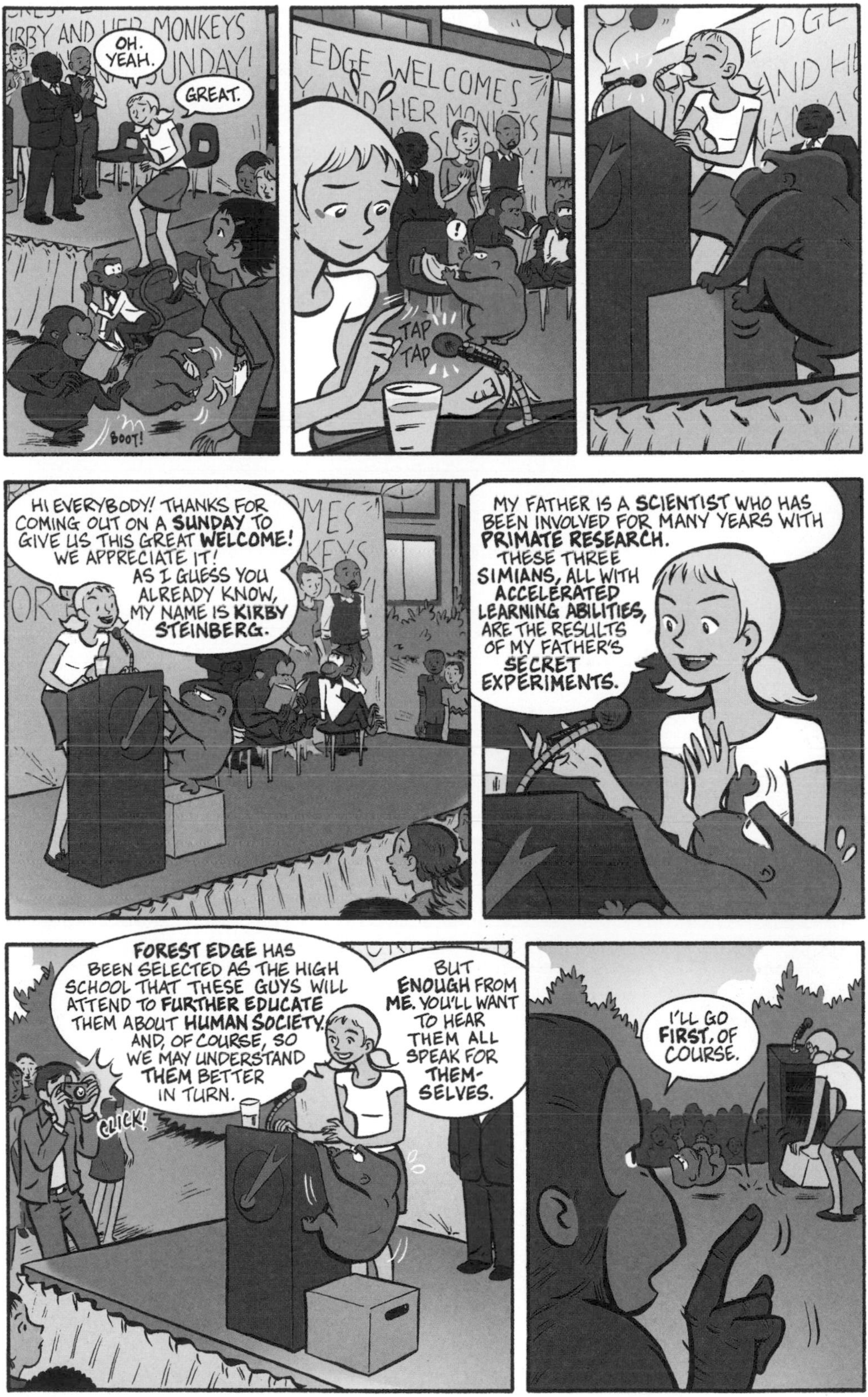
KIRBY AND HER MONKEYS
SUNDAY!
OH. YEAH.
GREAT.
BOOT!
EDGE WELCOMES
AND HER MONKEYS
TAP TAP
EDGE
AND H
HI EVERYBODY! THANKS FOR COMING OUT ON A SUNDAY TO GIVE US THIS GREAT WELCOME! WE APPRECIATE IT!
AS I GUESS YOU ALREADY KNOW, MY NAME IS KIRBY STEINBERG.
MY FATHER IS A SCIENTIST WHO HAS BEEN INVOLVED FOR MANY YEARS WITH PRIMATE RESEARCH.
THESE THREE SIMIANS, ALL WITH ACCELERATED LEARNING ABILITIES, ARE THE RESULTS OF MY FATHER'S SECRET EXPERIMENTS.
FOREST EDGE HAS BEEN SELECTED AS THE HIGH SCHOOL THAT THESE GUYS WILL ATTEND TO FURTHER EDUCATE THEM ABOUT HUMAN SOCIETY. AND, OF COURSE, SO WE MAY UNDERSTAND THEM BETTER IN TURN.
BUT ENOUGH FROM ME. YOU'LL WANT TO HEAR THEM ALL SPEAK FOR THEM-SELVES.
CLICK!
I'LL GO FIRST, OF COURSE.

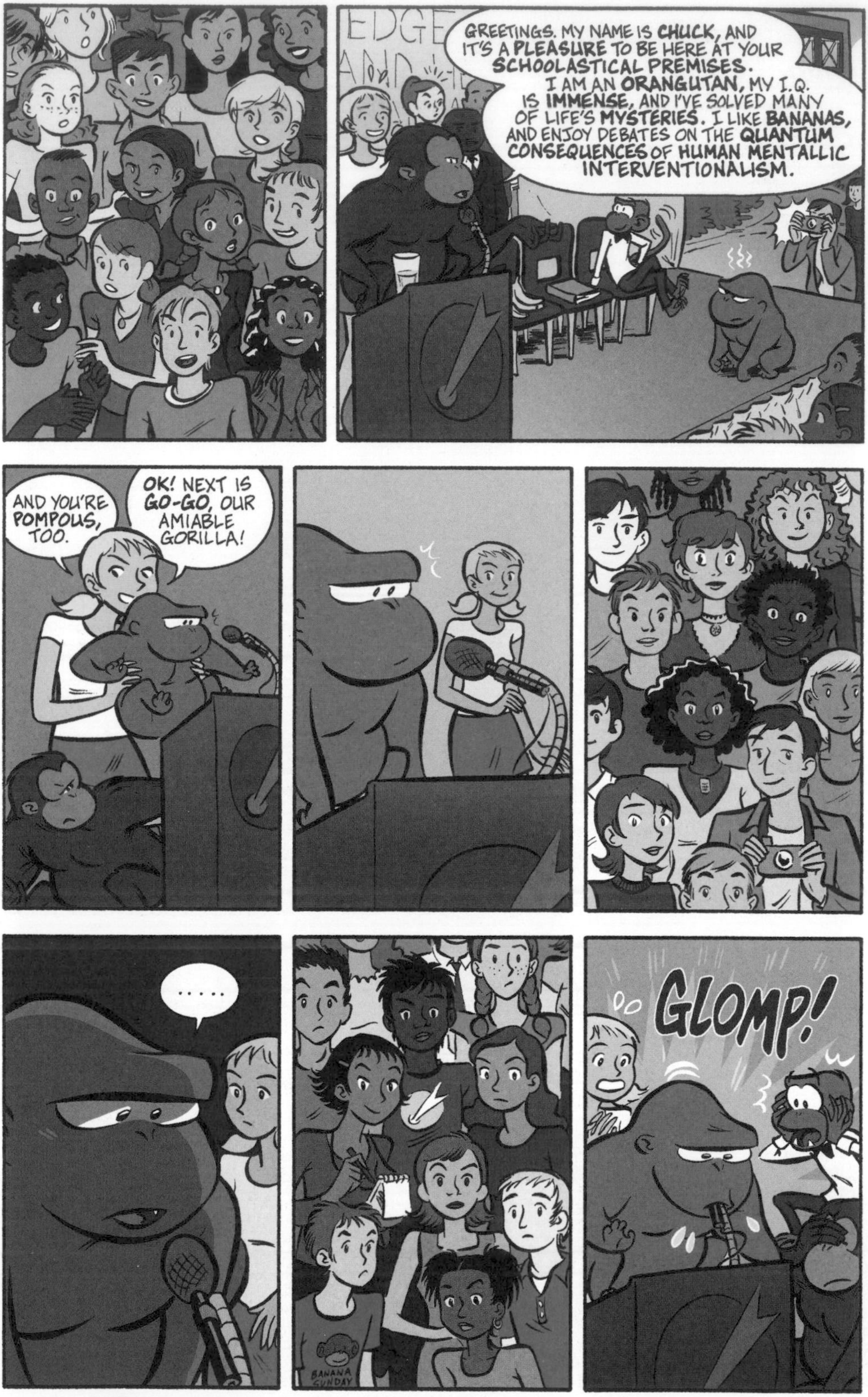
GREETINGS. MY NAME IS CHUCK, AND IT'S A PLEASURE TO BE HERE AT YOUR SCHOOLASTICAL PREMISES. I AM AN ORANGUTAN, MY I.Q. IS IMMENSE, AND I'VE SOLVED MANY OF LIFE'S MYSTERIES. I LIKE BANANAS, AND ENJOY DEBATES ON THE QUANTUM CONSEQUENCES OF HUMAN MENTALLIC INTERVENTIONALISM.
AND YOU'RE POMPOUS, TOO.
OK! NEXT IS GO-GO, OUR AMIABLE GORILLA!
......
BANANA SUNDAY
GLOMP!

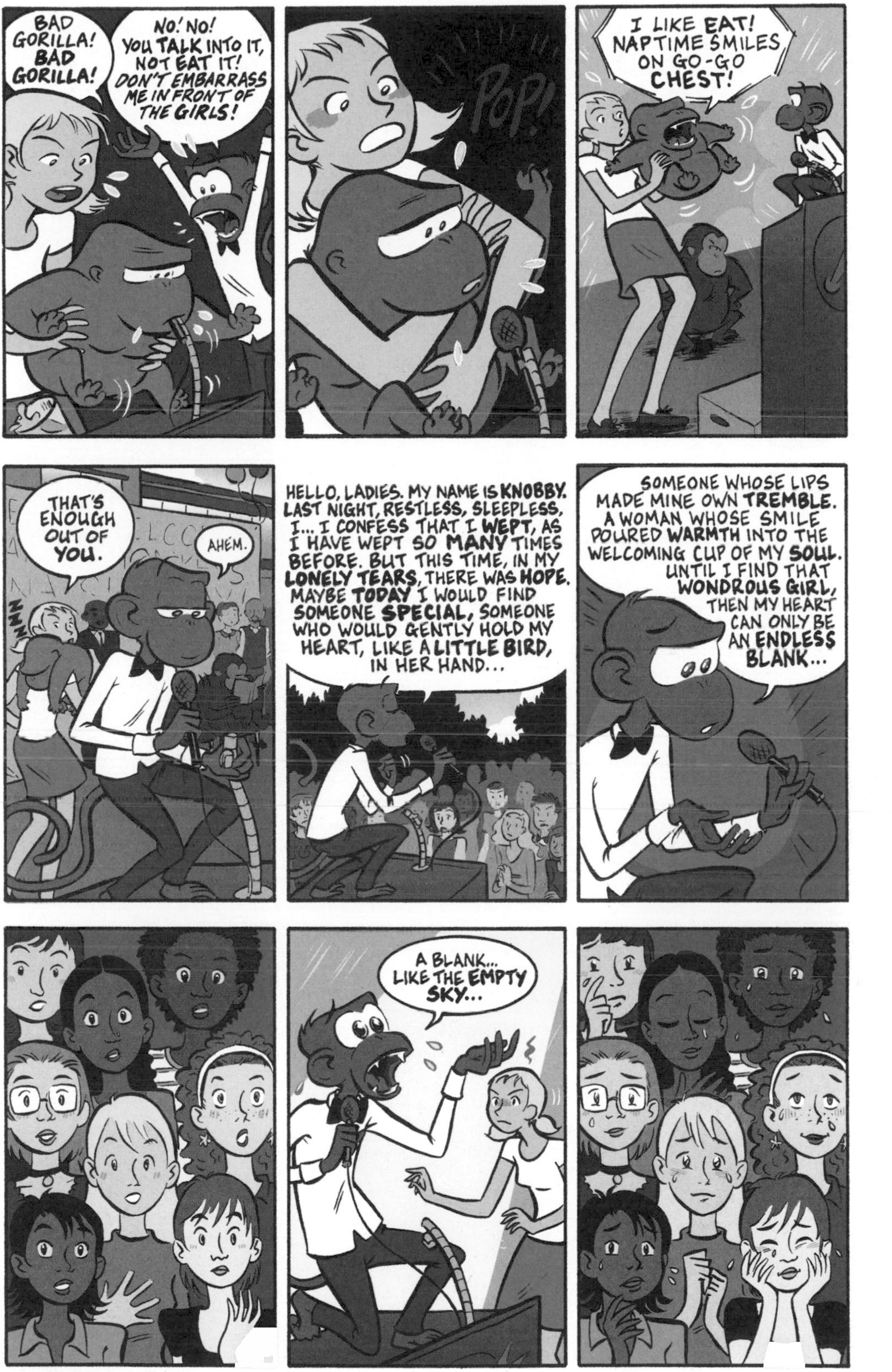
BAD GORILLA! BAD GORILLA!
NO! NO! YOU TALK INTO IT, NOT EAT IT! DON'T EMBARRASS ME IN FRONT OF THE GIRLS!
POP!
I LIKE EAT! NAPTIME SMILES ON GO-GO CHEST!
THAT'S ENOUGH OUT OF YOU.
AHEM.
HELLO, LADIES. MY NAME IS KNOBBY. LAST NIGHT, RESTLESS, SLEEPLESS, I... I CONFESS THAT I WEPT, AS I HAVE WEPT SO MANY TIMES BEFORE. BUT THIS TIME, IN MY LONELY TEARS, THERE WAS HOPE. MAYBE TODAY I WOULD FIND SOMEONE SPECIAL, SOMEONE WHO WOULD GENTLY HOLD MY HEART, LIKE A LITTLE BIRD, IN HER HAND...
SOMEONE WHOSE LIPS MADE MINE OWN TREMBLE. A WOMAN WHOSE SMILE POURED WARMTH INTO THE WELCOMING CUP OF MY SOUL. UNTIL I FIND THAT WONDROUS GIRL, THEN MY HEART CAN ONLY BE AN ENDLESS BLANK...
A BLANK... LIKE THE EMPTY SKY...

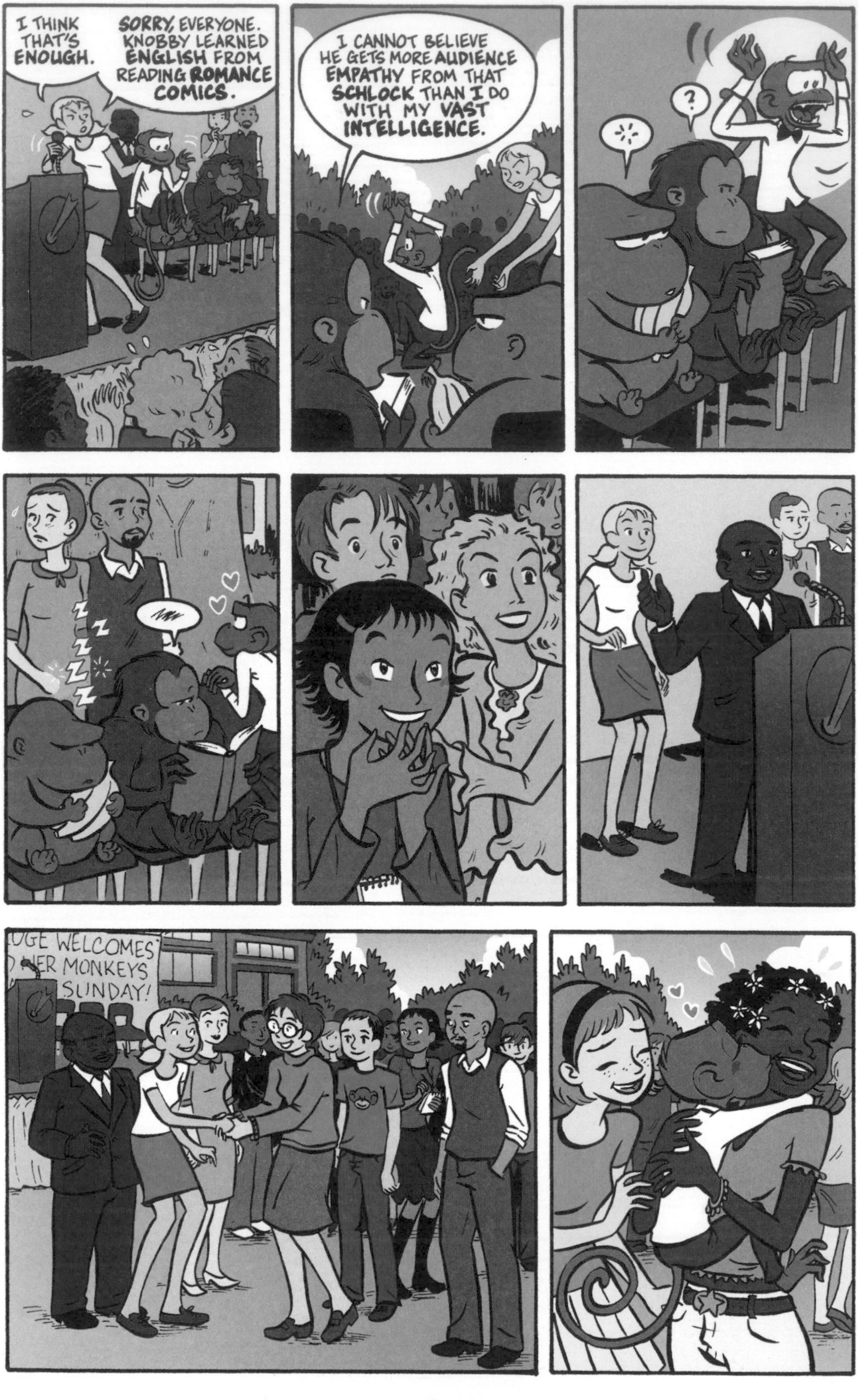

I THINK THAT'S ENOUGH.
SORRY, EVERYONE. KNOBBY LEARNED ENGLISH FROM READING ROMANCE COMICS.
I CANNOT BELIEVE HE GETS MORE AUDIENCE EMPATHY FROM THAT SCHLOCK THAN I DO WITH MY VAST INTELLIGENCE.
?
UGE WELCOMES
ER MONKEYS
SUNDAY!

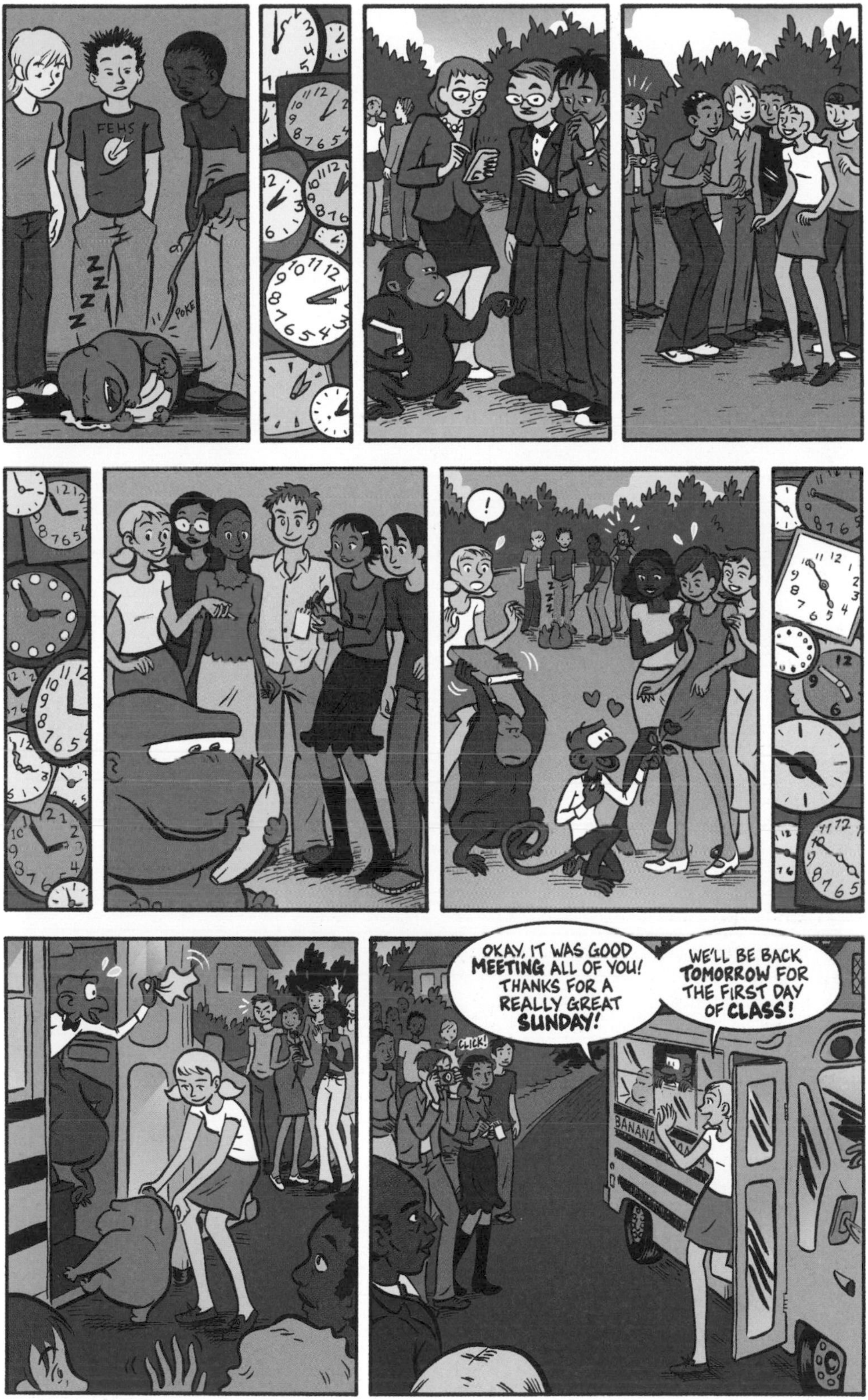
FEHS
ZZZZ
POKE
!
CLICK!
BANANA
OKAY, IT WAS GOOD MEETING ALL OF YOU! THANKS FOR A REALLY GREAT SUNDAY!
WE'LL BE BACK TOMORROW FOR THE FIRST DAY OF CLASS!

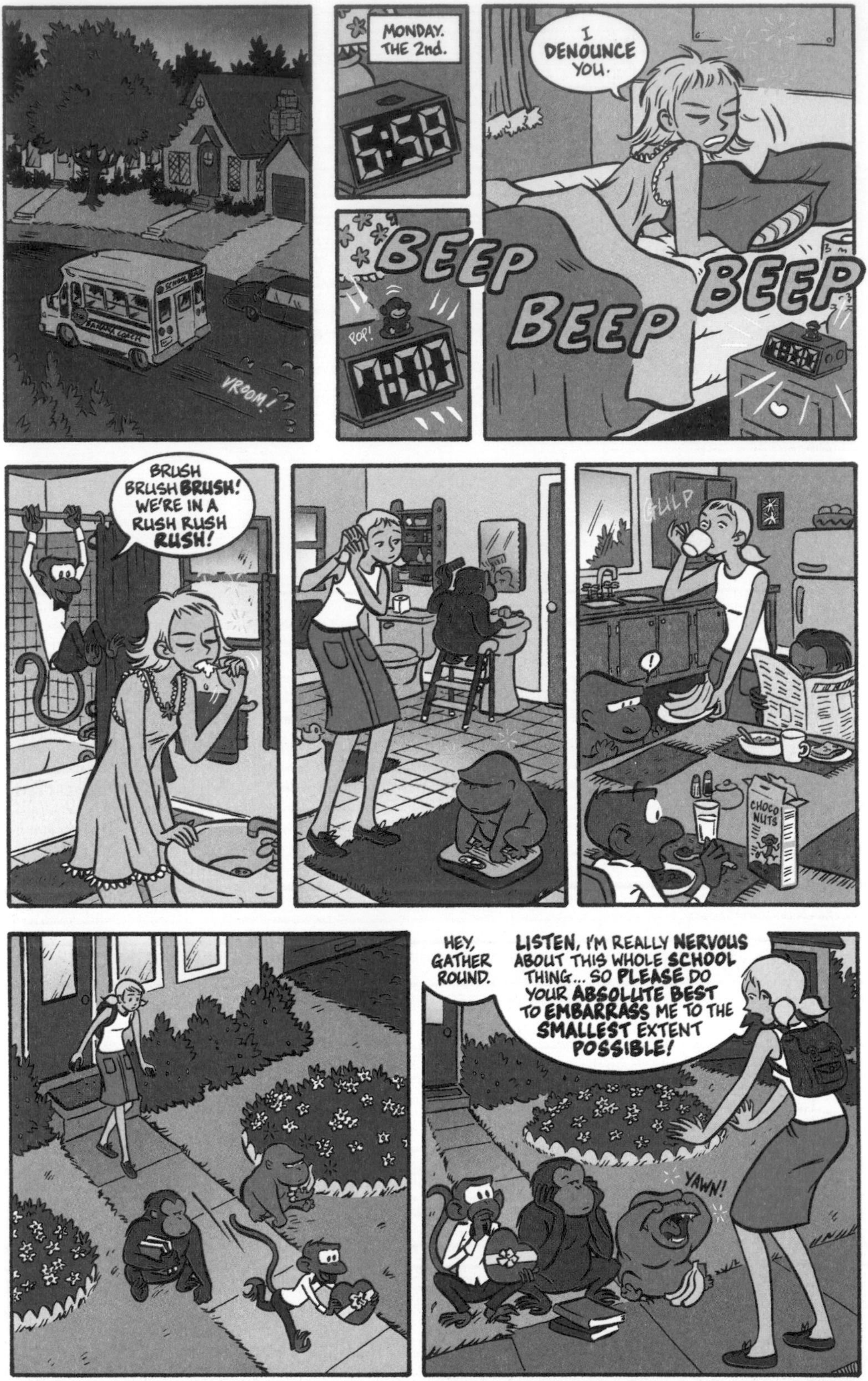

SCHOOL BUS
BANANA COACH
VROOM!
MONDAY. THE 2nd.
6:58
I DENOUNCE YOU.
POP!
7:00
BEEP
BEEP
BEEP
BRUSH BRUSH BRUSH! WE'RE IN A RUSH RUSH RUSH!
GULP
!
CHOCO NUTS
HEY, GATHER ROUND.
LISTEN, I'M REALLY NERVOUS ABOUT THIS WHOLE SCHOOL THING... SO PLEASE DO YOUR ABSOLUTE BEST TO EMBARRASS ME TO THE SMALLEST EXTENT POSSIBLE!
YAWN!

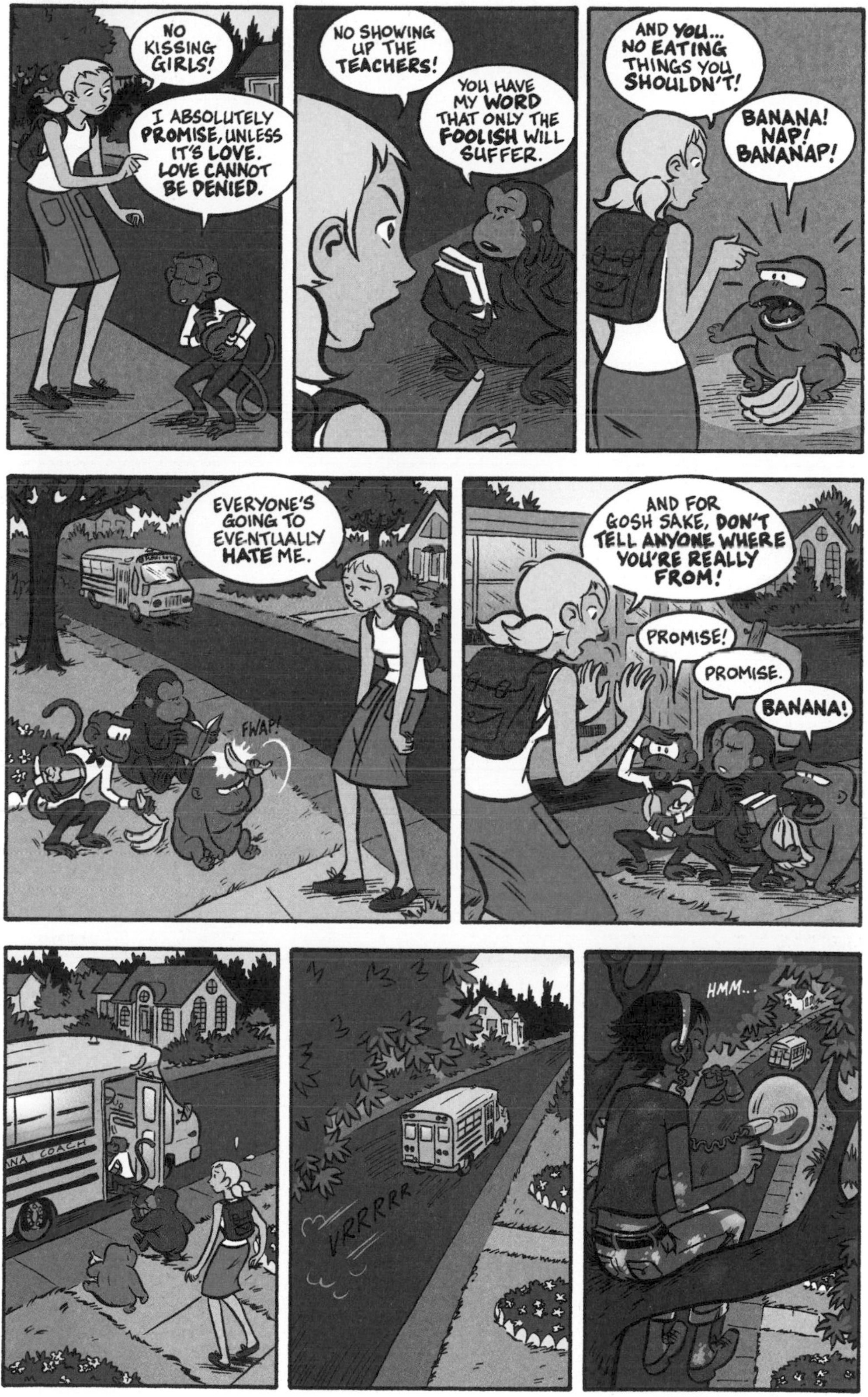
NO KISSING GIRLS!
I ABSOLUTELY PROMISE, UNLESS IT'S LOVE. LOVE CANNOT BE DENIED.
NO SHOWING UP THE TEACHERS!
YOU HAVE MY WORD THAT ONLY THE FOOLISH WILL SUFFER.
AND YOU... NO EATING THINGS YOU SHOULDN'T!
BANANA! NAP! BANANAP!
EVERYONE'S GOING TO EVENTUALLY HATE ME.
FWAP!
AND FOR GOSH SAKE, DON'T TELL ANYONE WHERE YOU'RE REALLY FROM!
PROMISE!
PROMISE.
BANANA!
VRRRRR
HMM...

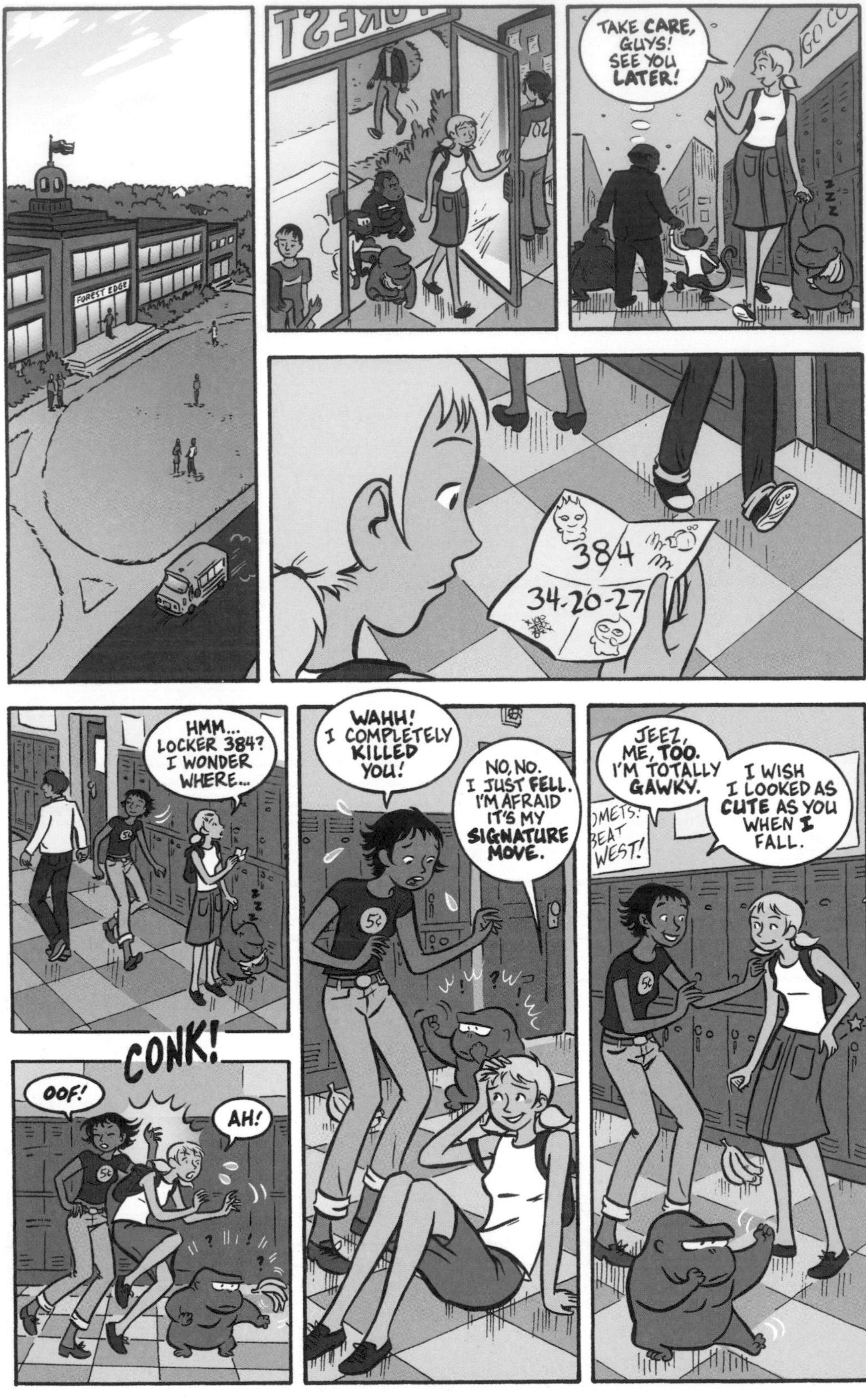
FOREST EDGE
TAKE CARE, GUYS! SEE YOU LATER!
384
34-20-27
HMM... LOCKER 384? I WONDER WHERE...
CONK!
OOF!
AH!
WAHH! I COMPLETELY KILLED YOU!
NO, NO. I JUST FELL. I'M AFRAID IT'S MY SIGNATURE MOVE.
JEEZ, ME, TOO. I'M TOTALLY GAWKY.
I WISH I LOOKED AS CUTE AS YOU WHEN I FALL.

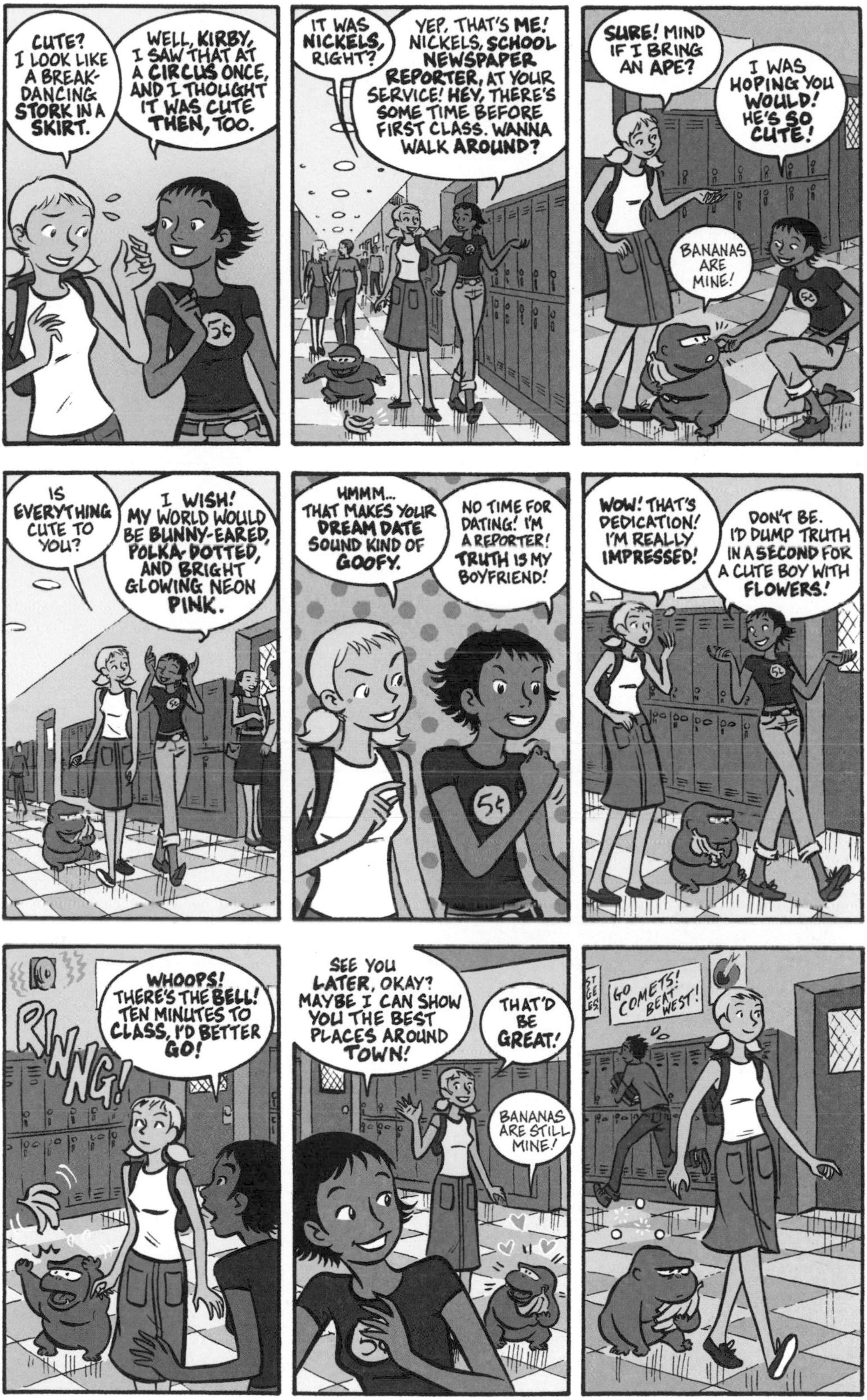
CUTE? I LOOK LIKE A BREAK-DANCING STORK IN A SKIRT.
WELL, KIRBY, I SAW THAT AT A CIRCUS ONCE, AND I THOUGHT IT WAS CUTE THEN, TOO.
IT WAS NICKELS, RIGHT?
YEP, THAT'S ME! NICKELS, SCHOOL NEWSPAPER REPORTER, AT YOUR SERVICE! HEY, THERE'S SOME TIME BEFORE FIRST CLASS. WANNA WALK AROUND?
SURE! MIND IF I BRING AN APE?
I WAS HOPING YOU WOULD! HE'S SO CUTE!
BANANAS ARE MINE!
IS EVERYTHING CUTE TO YOU?
I WISH! MY WORLD WOULD BE BUNNY-EARED, POLKA-DOTTED, AND BRIGHT GLOWING NEON PINK.
HMMM... THAT MAKES YOUR DREAM DATE SOUND KIND OF GOOFY.
NO TIME FOR DATING! I'M A REPORTER! TRUTH IS MY BOYFRIEND!
WOW! THAT'S DEDICATION! I'M REALLY IMPRESSED!
DON'T BE. I'D DUMP TRUTH IN A SECOND FOR A CUTE BOY WITH FLOWERS!
RINNNG!
WHOOPS! THERE'S THE BELL! TEN MINUTES TO CLASS, I'D BETTER GO!
SEE YOU LATER, OKAY? MAYBE I CAN SHOW YOU THE BEST PLACES AROUND TOWN!
THAT'D BE GREAT!
BANANAS ARE STILL MINE!
GO COMETS! BEAT WEST!

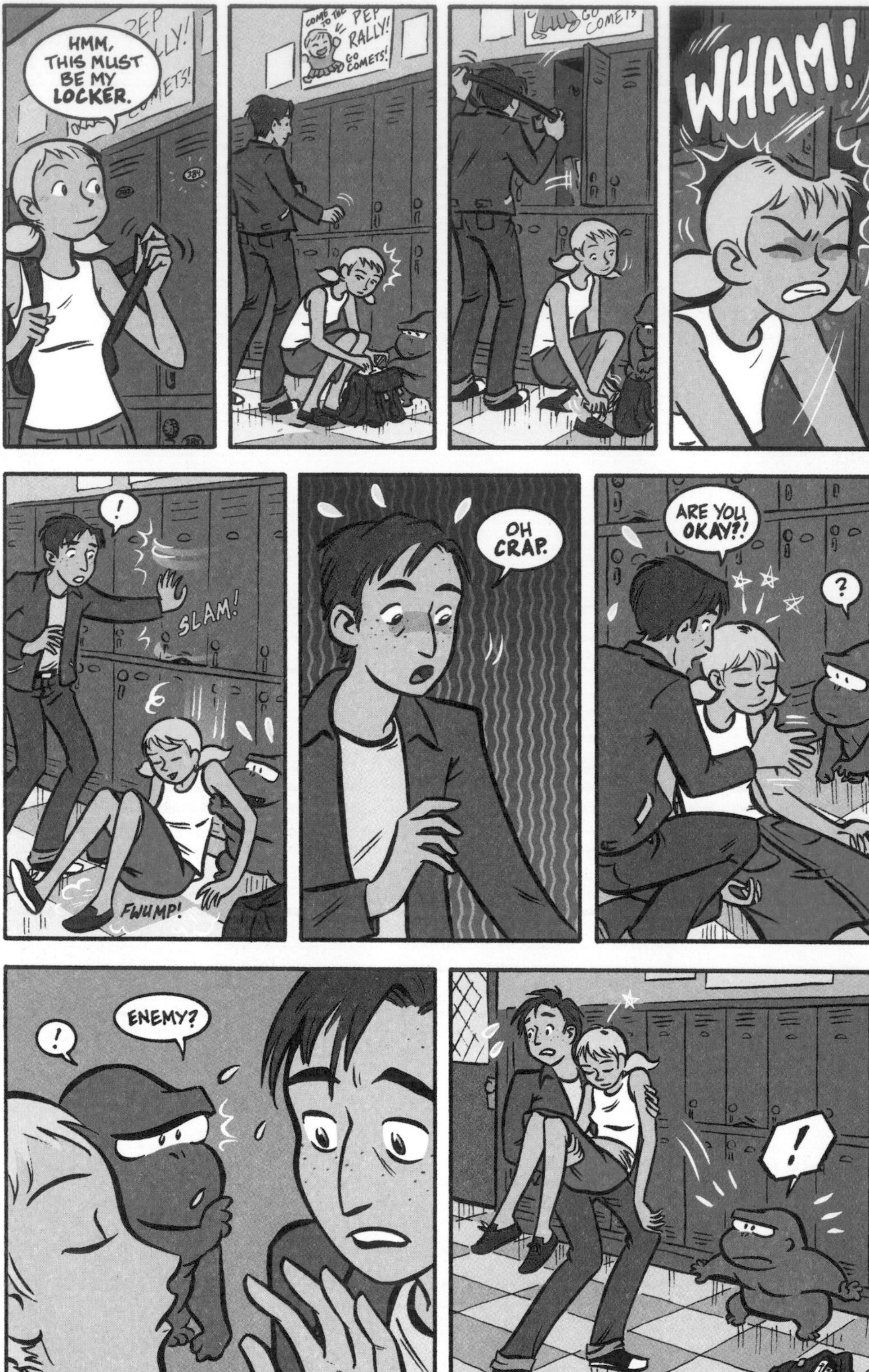
HMM, THIS MUST BE MY LOCKER.
COME TO THE PEP RALLY! GO COMETS!
WHAM!
!
SLAM!
FWUMP!
OH CRAP.
ARE YOU OKAY?!
?
!
ENEMY?
!

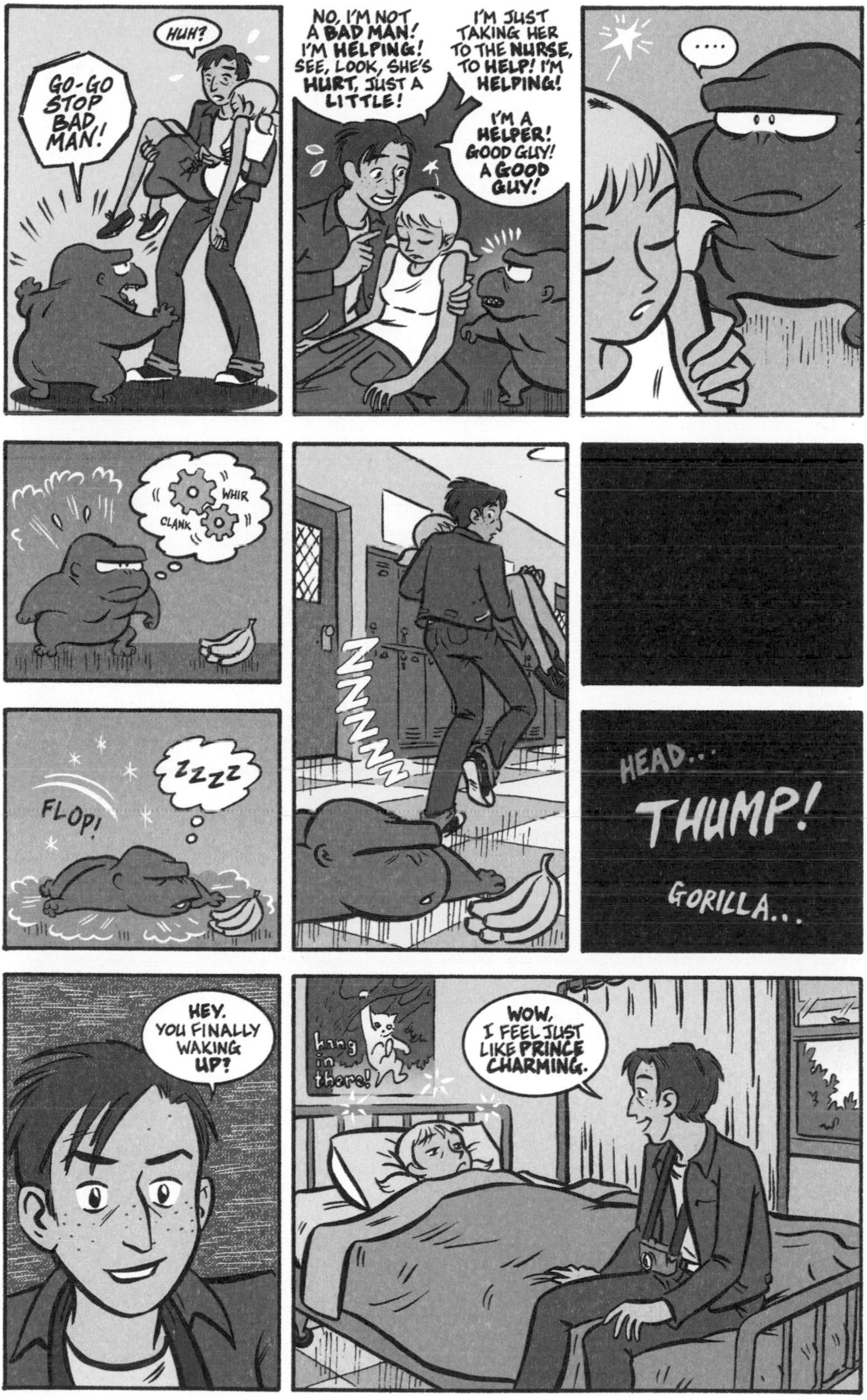
HUH?
GO-GO STOP BAD MAN!
NO, I'M NOT A BAD MAN! I'M HELPING! SEE, LOOK, SHE'S HURT, JUST A LITTLE!
I'M JUST TAKING HER TO THE NURSE, TO HELP! I'M HELPING!
I'M A HELPER! GOOD GUY! A GOOD GUY!
....
WHIR
CLANK
FLOP!
ZZZZ
ZZZZZZ
HEAD...
THUMP!
GORILLA...
HEY. YOU FINALLY WAKING UP?
hang in there!
WOW, I FEEL JUST LIKE PRINCE CHARMING.

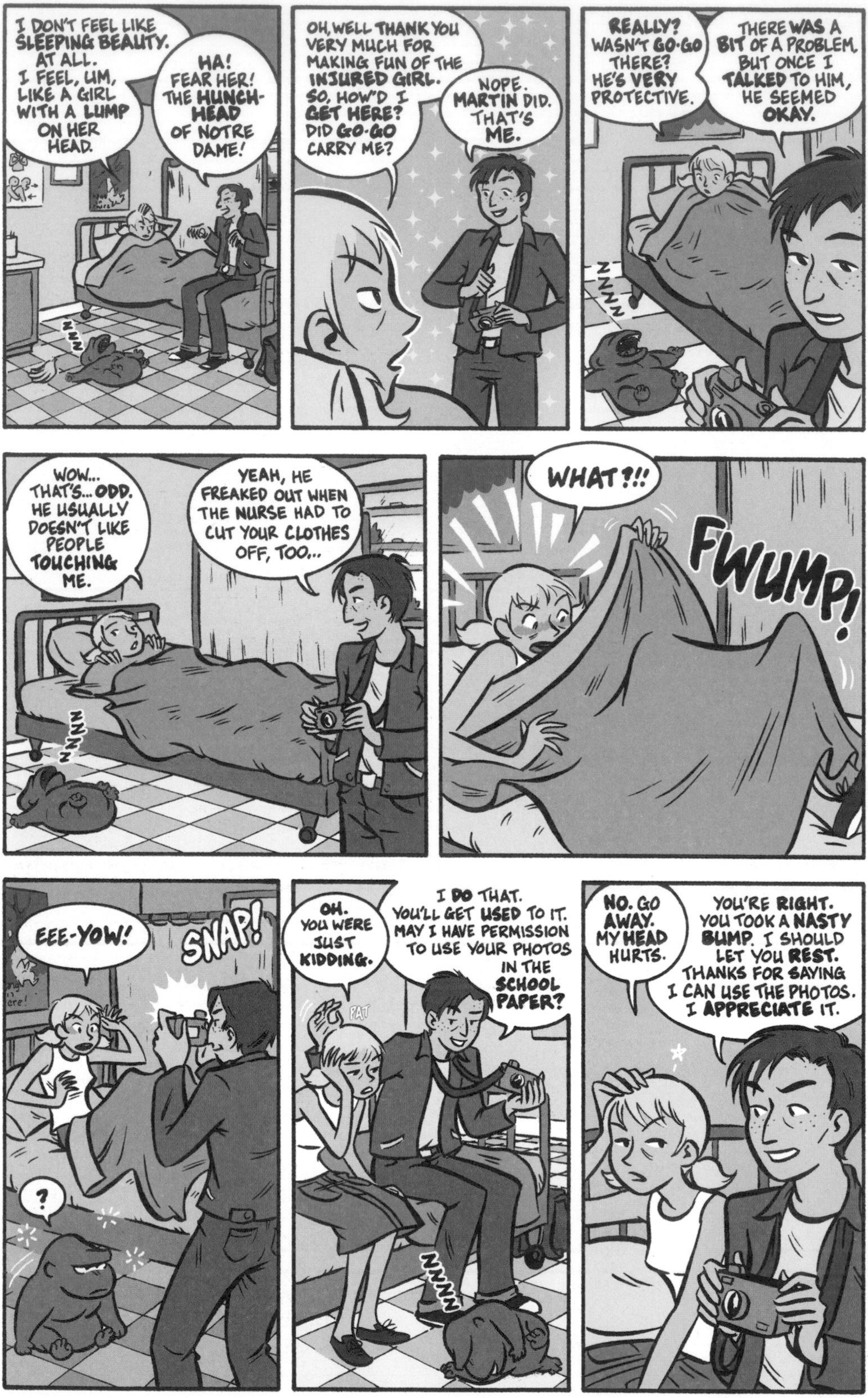
I DON'T FEEL LIKE SLEEPING BEAUTY. AT ALL. I FEEL, UM, LIKE A GIRL WITH A LUMP ON HER HEAD.
HA! FEAR HER! THE HUNCH-HEAD OF NOTRE DAME!
OH, WELL THANK YOU VERY MUCH FOR MAKING FUN OF THE INJURED GIRL. SO, HOW'D I GET HERE? DID GO-GO CARRY ME?
NOPE. MARTIN DID. THAT'S ME.
REALLY? WASN'T GO-GO THERE? HE'S VERY PROTECTIVE.
THERE WAS A BIT OF A PROBLEM, BUT ONCE I TALKED TO HIM, HE SEEMED OKAY.
WOW... THAT'S... ODD. HE USUALLY DOESN'T LIKE PEOPLE TOUCHING ME.
YEAH, HE FREAKED OUT WHEN THE NURSE HAD TO CUT YOUR CLOTHES OFF, TOO...
WHAT?!!
FWUMP!
EEE-YOW!
SNAP!
?
OH. YOU WERE JUST KIDDING.
I DO THAT. YOU'LL GET USED TO IT. MAY I HAVE PERMISSION TO USE YOUR PHOTOS IN THE SCHOOL PAPER?
PAT
NO. GO AWAY. MY HEAD HURTS.
YOU'RE RIGHT. YOU TOOK A NASTY BUMP. I SHOULD LET YOU REST. THANKS FOR SAYING I CAN USE THE PHOTOS. I APPRECIATE IT.

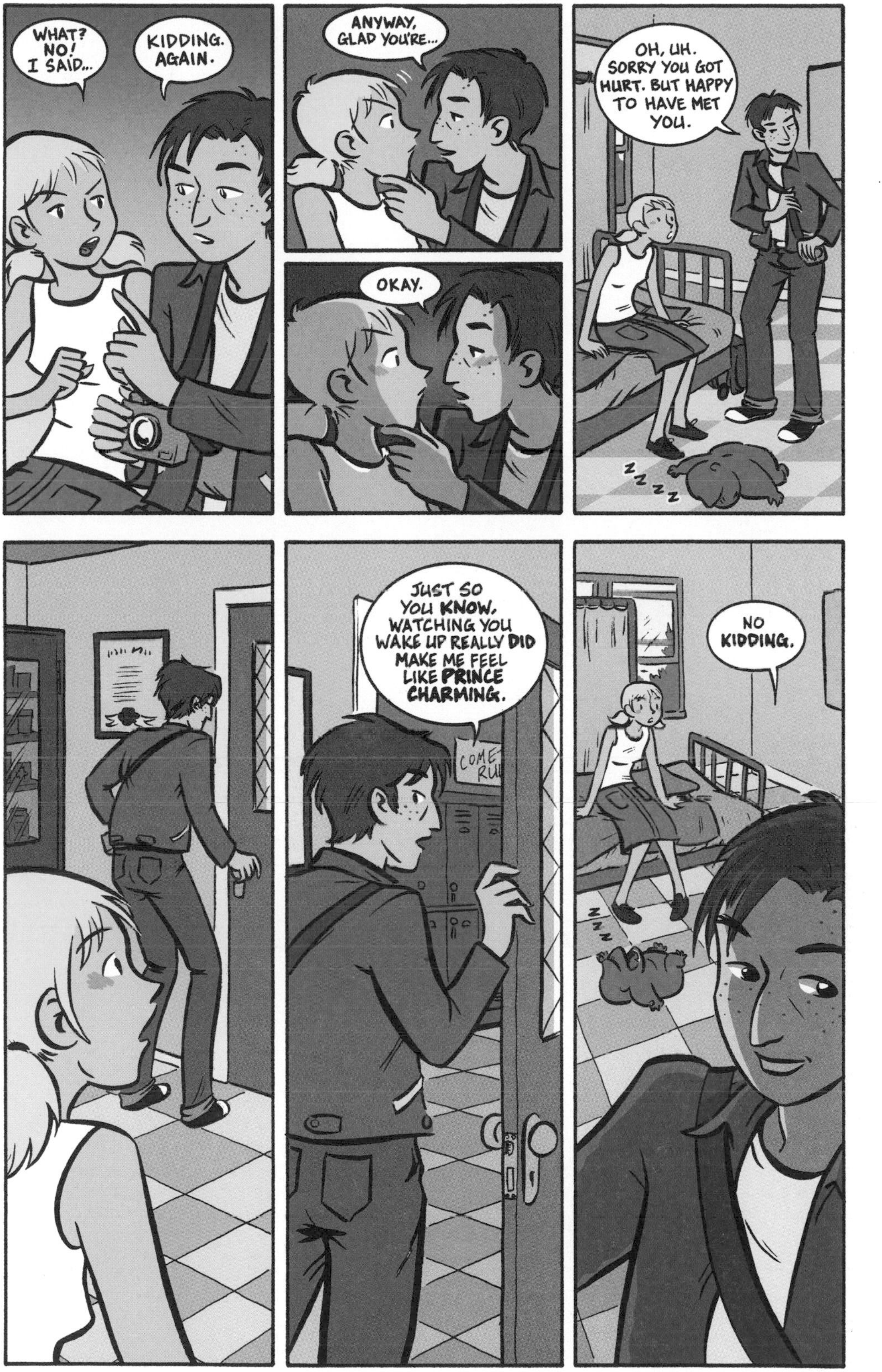
WHAT? NO! I SAID...
KIDDING. AGAIN.
ANYWAY, GLAD YOU'RE...
OKAY.
OH, UH. SORRY YOU GOT HURT. BUT HAPPY TO HAVE MET YOU.
Z Z Z Z
JUST SO YOU KNOW, WATCHING YOU WAKE UP REALLY DID MAKE ME FEEL LIKE PRINCE CHARMING.
NO KIDDING.
Z Z Z

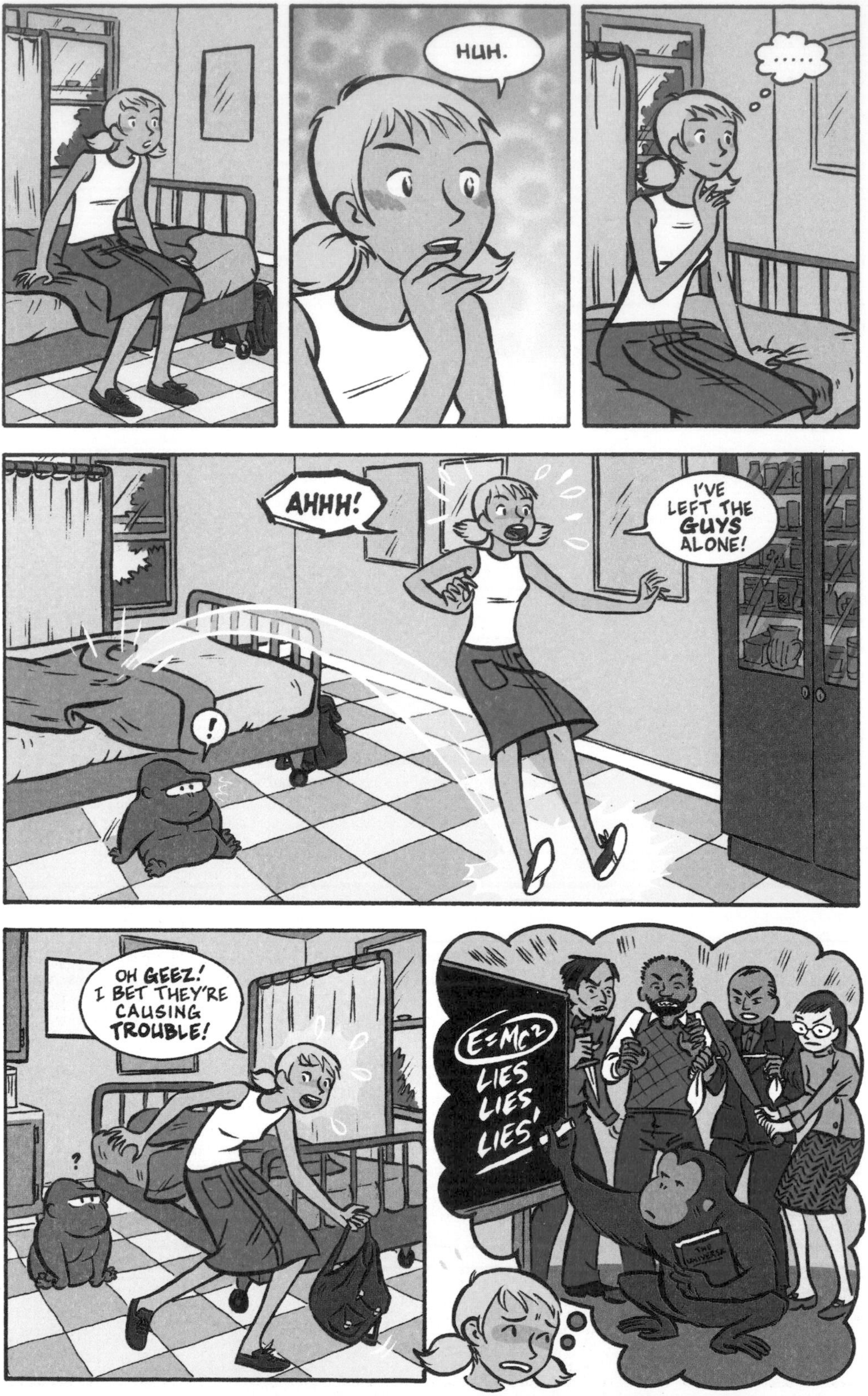
HUH.
......
AHHH!
I'VE LEFT THE GUYS ALONE!
!
OH GEEZ! I BET THEY'RE CAUSING TROUBLE!
?
E=MC²
LIES LIES LIES!
THE UNIVERSE

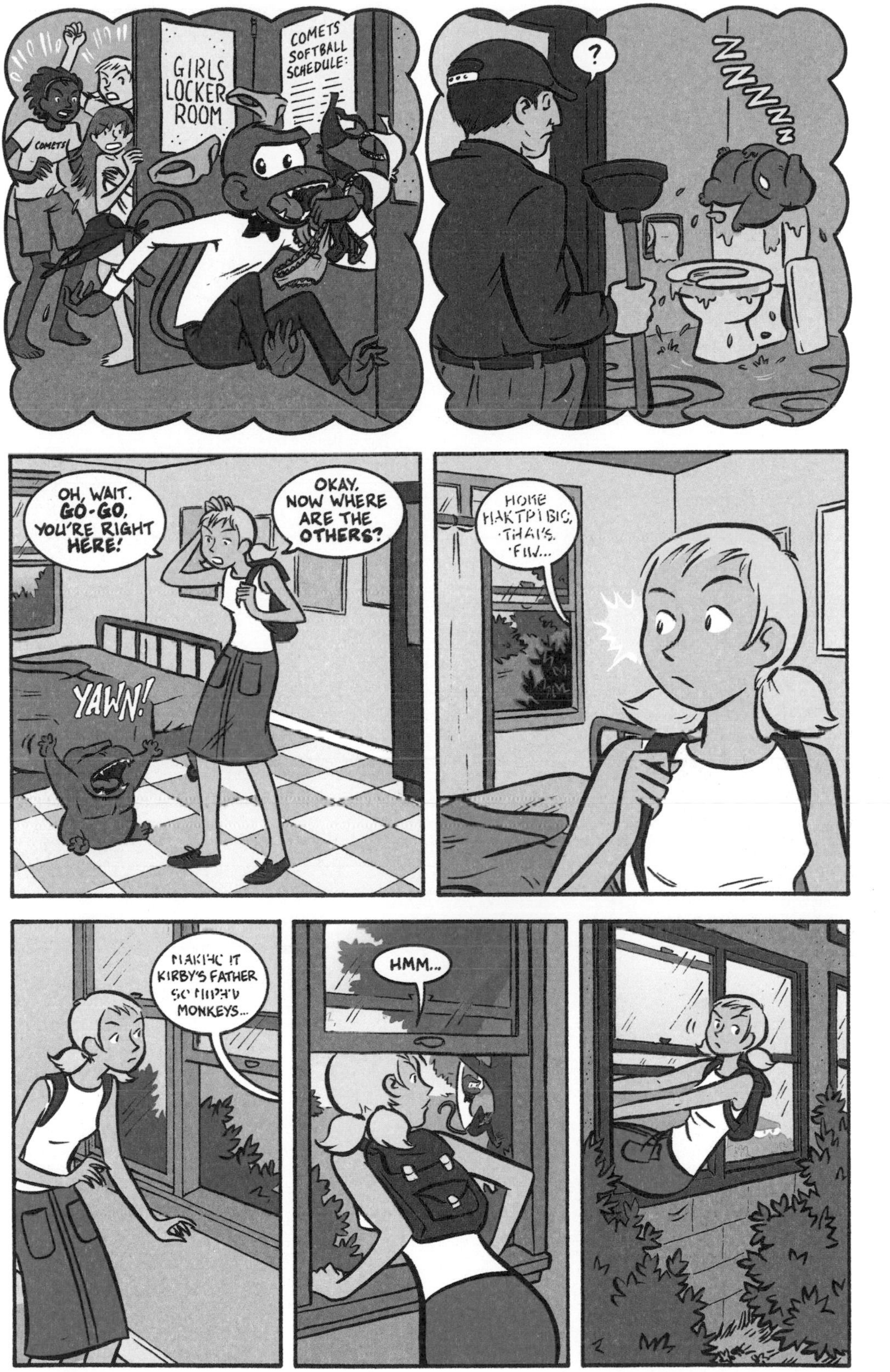
COMETS
GIRLS LOCKER ROOM
COMETS SOFTBALL SCHEDULE:
?
ZZZZZ
OH, WAIT. GO-GO, YOU'RE RIGHT HERE!
OKAY. NOW WHERE ARE THE OTHERS?
YAWN!
IT
KIRBY'S FATHER
MONKEYS...
HMM...

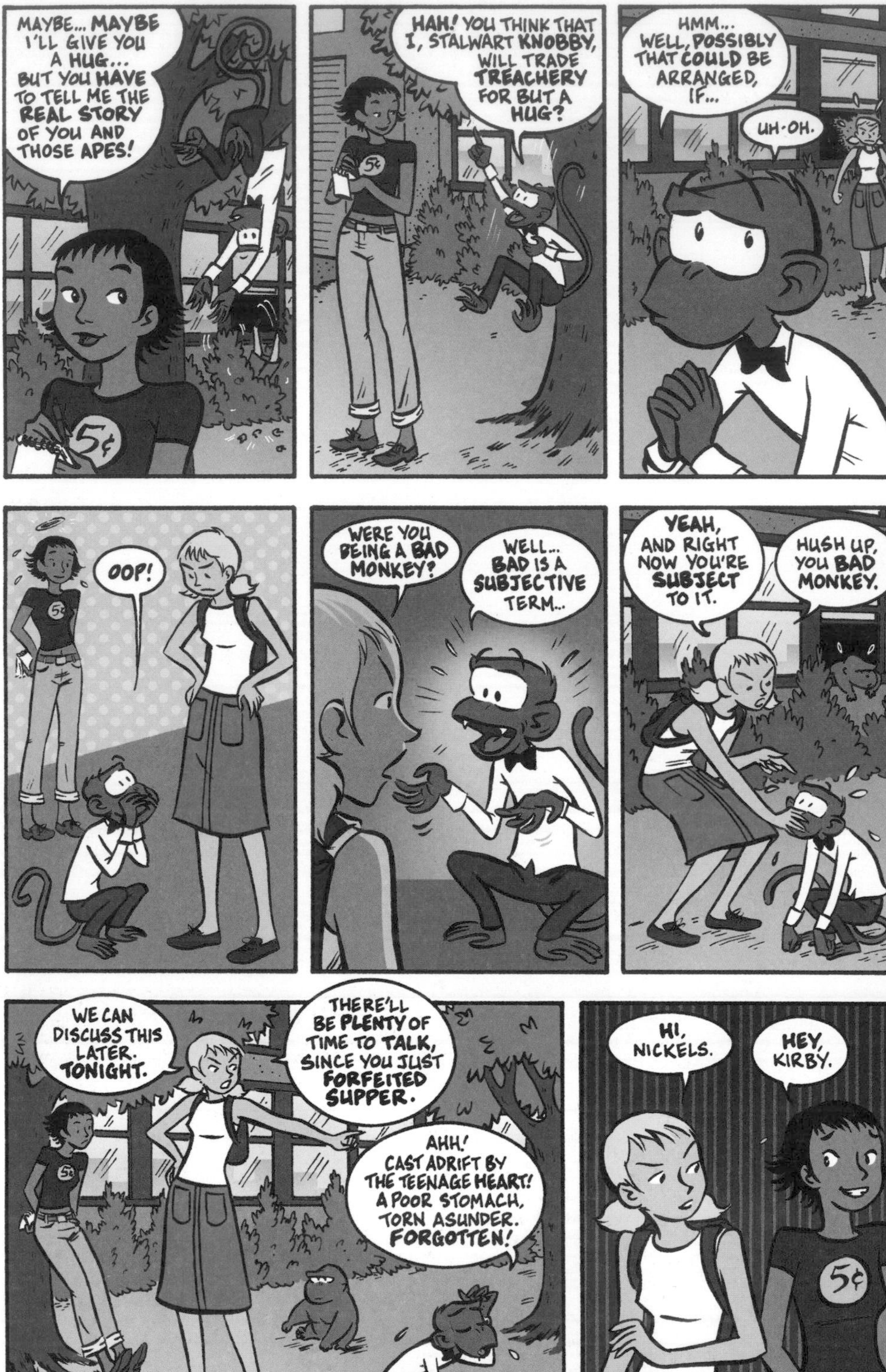
MAYBE... MAYBE I'LL GIVE YOU A HUG... BUT YOU HAVE TO TELL ME THE REAL STORY OF YOU AND THOSE APES!
HAH! YOU THINK THAT I, STALWART KNOBBY, WILL TRADE TREACHERY FOR BUT A HUG?
HMM... WELL, POSSIBLY THAT COULD BE ARRANGED, IF...
UH-OH.
OOP!
WERE YOU BEING A BAD MONKEY?
WELL... BAD IS A SUBJECTIVE TERM...
YEAH, AND RIGHT NOW YOU'RE SUBJECT TO IT.
HUSH UP, YOU BAD MONKEY.
WE CAN DISCUSS THIS LATER. TONIGHT.
THERE'LL BE PLENTY OF TIME TO TALK, SINCE YOU JUST FORFEITED SUPPER.
AHH! CAST ADRIFT BY THE TEENAGE HEART! A POOR STOMACH, TORN ASUNDER. FORGOTTEN!
HI, NICKELS.
HEY, KIRBY.

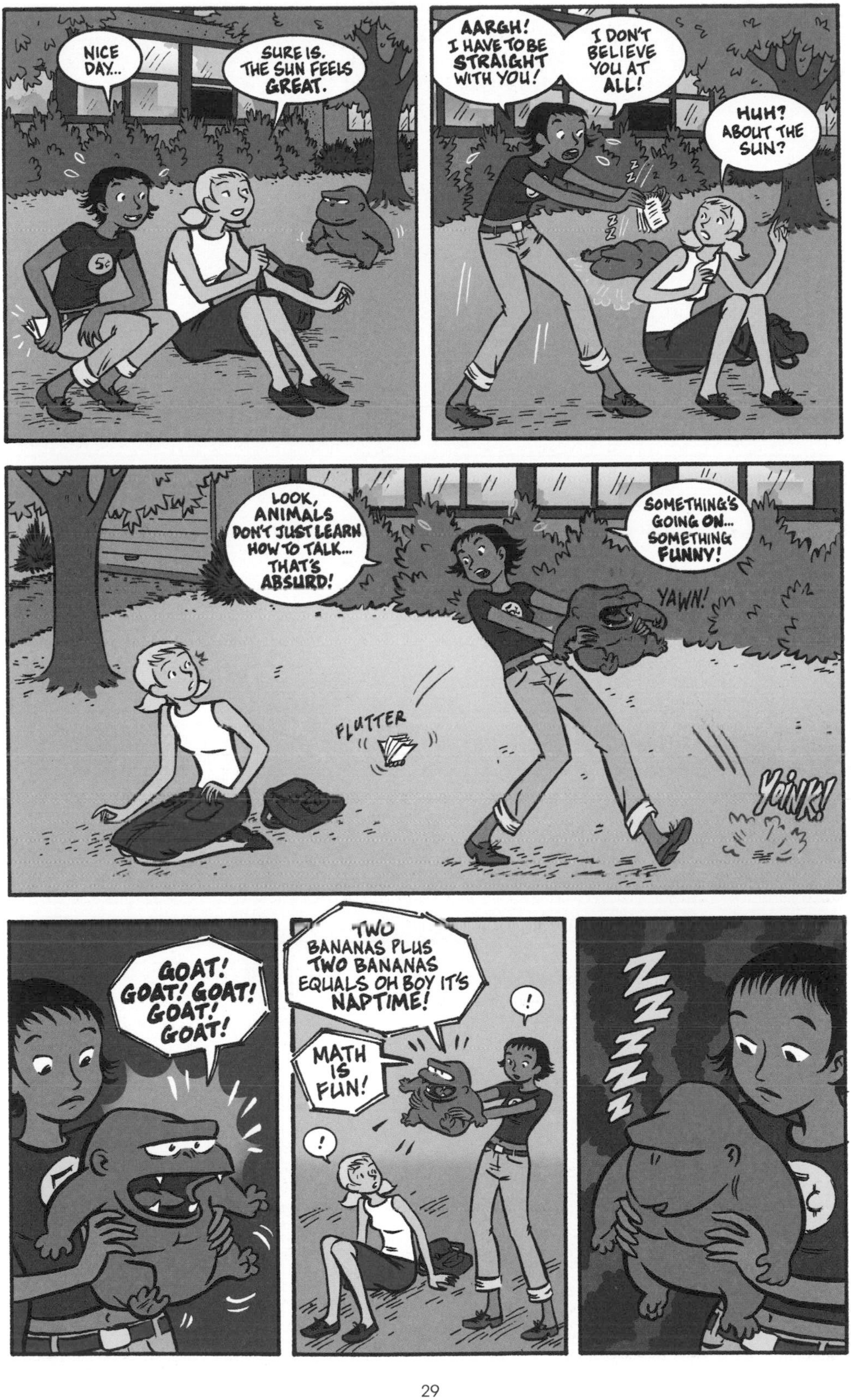
NICE DAY...
SURE IS. THE SUN FEELS GREAT.
AARGH! I HAVE TO BE STRAIGHT WITH YOU!
I DON'T BELIEVE YOU AT ALL!
HUH? ABOUT THE SUN?
LOOK, ANIMALS DON'T JUST LEARN HOW TO TALK... THAT'S ABSURD!
SOMETHING'S GOING ON... SOMETHING FUNNY!
YAWN!
FLUTTER
YOINK!
GOAT! GOAT! GOAT! GOAT! GOAT!
TWO BANANAS PLUS TWO BANANAS EQUALS OH BOY IT'S NAPTIME!
MATH IS FUN!
!
!
ZZZZZ

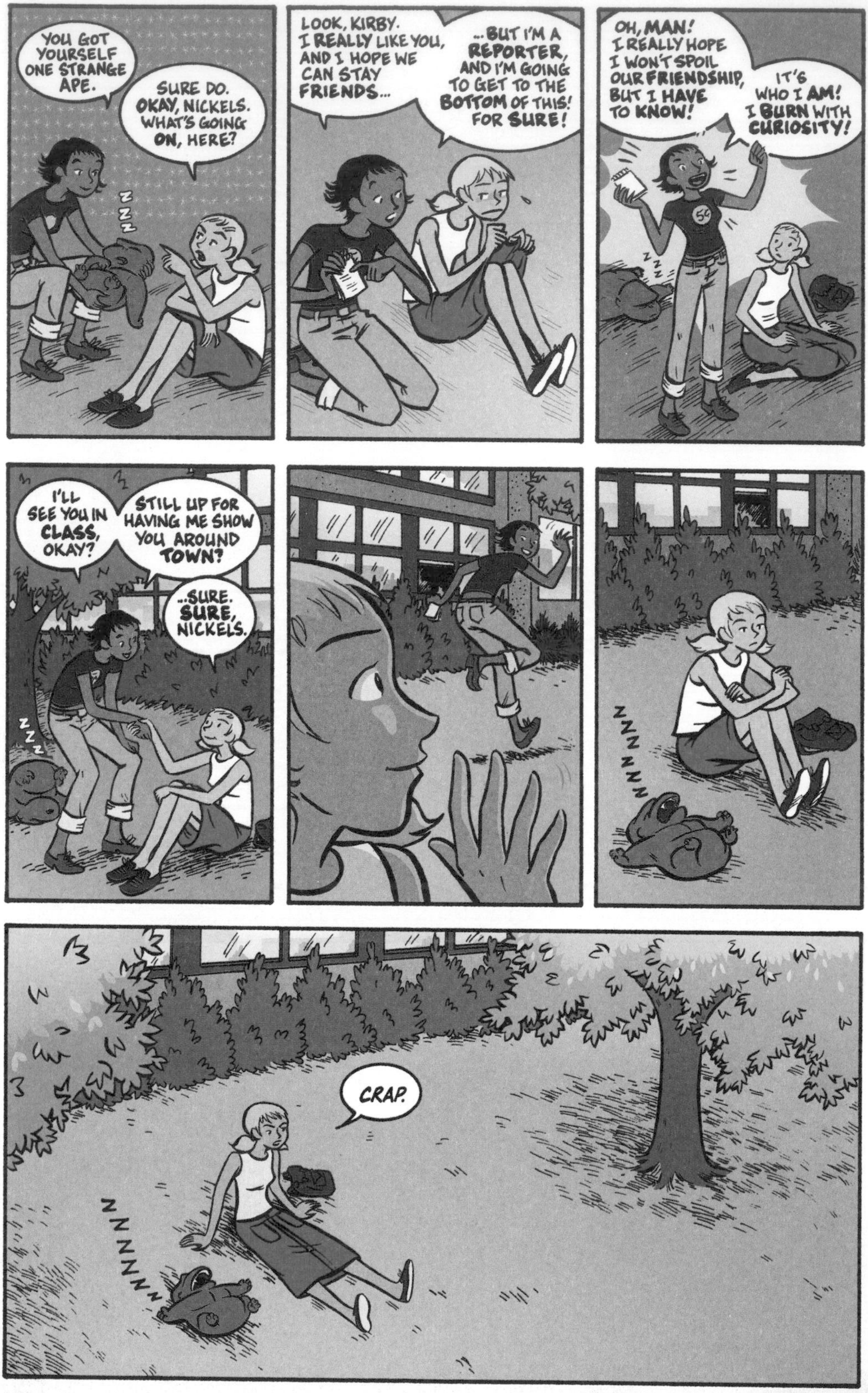

YOU GOT YOURSELF ONE STRANGE APE.
SURE DO. OKAY, NICKELS. WHAT'S GOING ON, HERE?
Z Z Z
LOOK, KIRBY. I REALLY LIKE YOU, AND I HOPE WE CAN STAY FRIENDS...
...BUT I'M A REPORTER, AND I'M GOING TO GET TO THE BOTTOM OF THIS! FOR SURE!
OH, MAN! I REALLY HOPE I WON'T SPOIL OUR FRIENDSHIP, BUT I HAVE TO KNOW!
IT'S WHO I AM! I BURN WITH CURIOSITY!
Z Z Z
I'LL SEE YOU IN CLASS, OKAY?
STILL UP FOR HAVING ME SHOW YOU AROUND TOWN?
...SURE. SURE, NICKELS.
Z Z Z
Z Z Z Z Z
CRAP.
Z Z Z Z Z

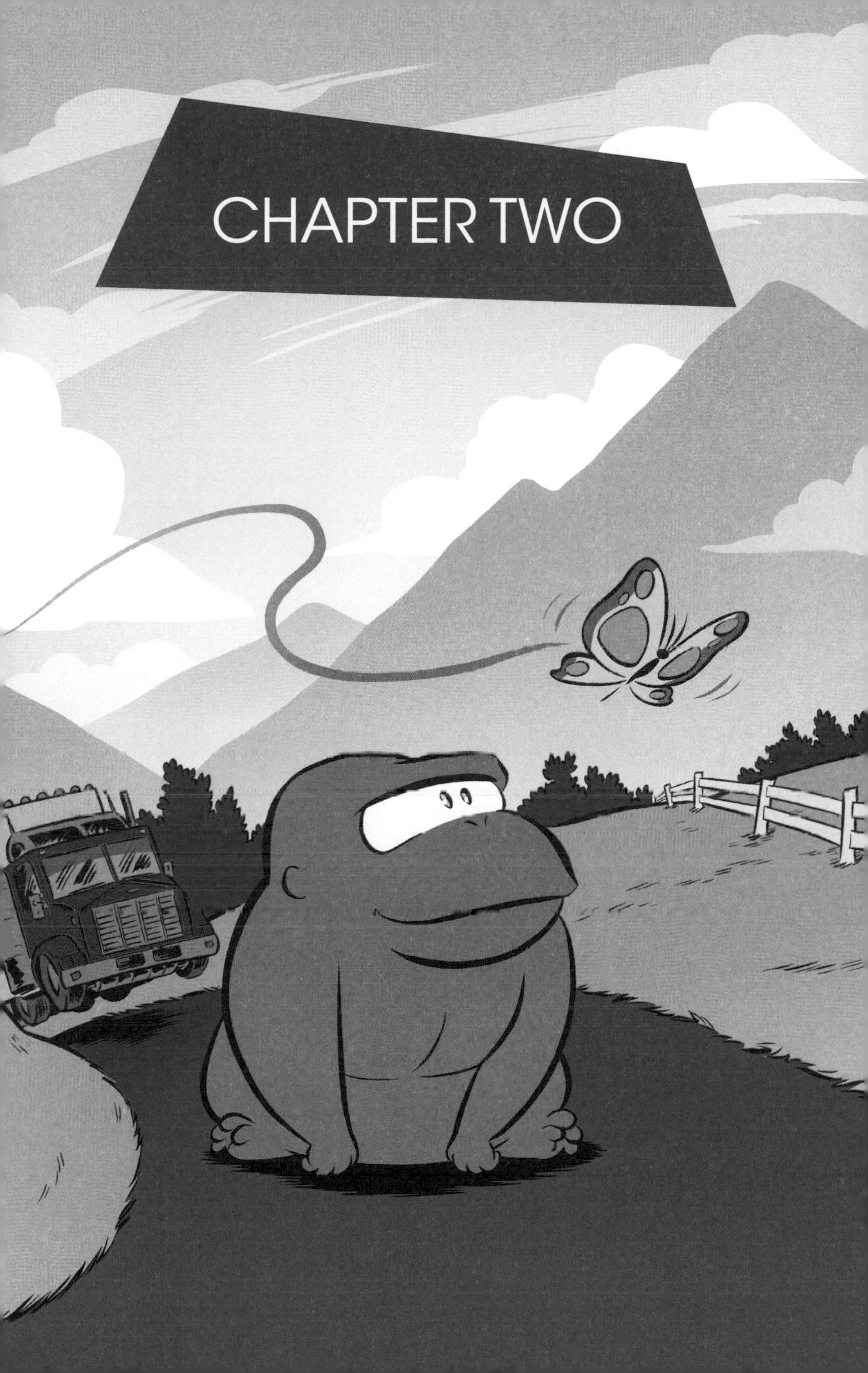
CHAPTER TWO

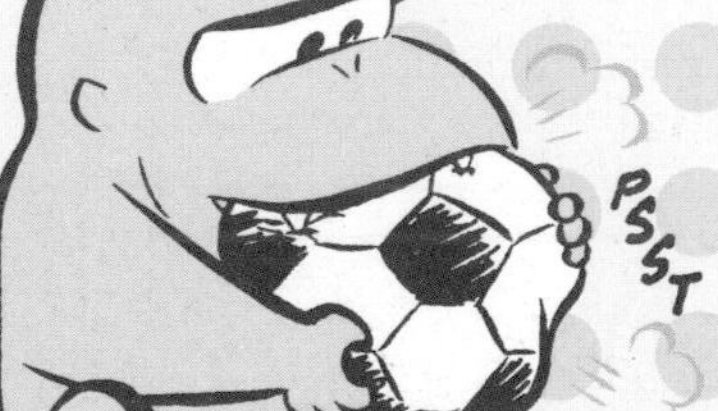
PSST

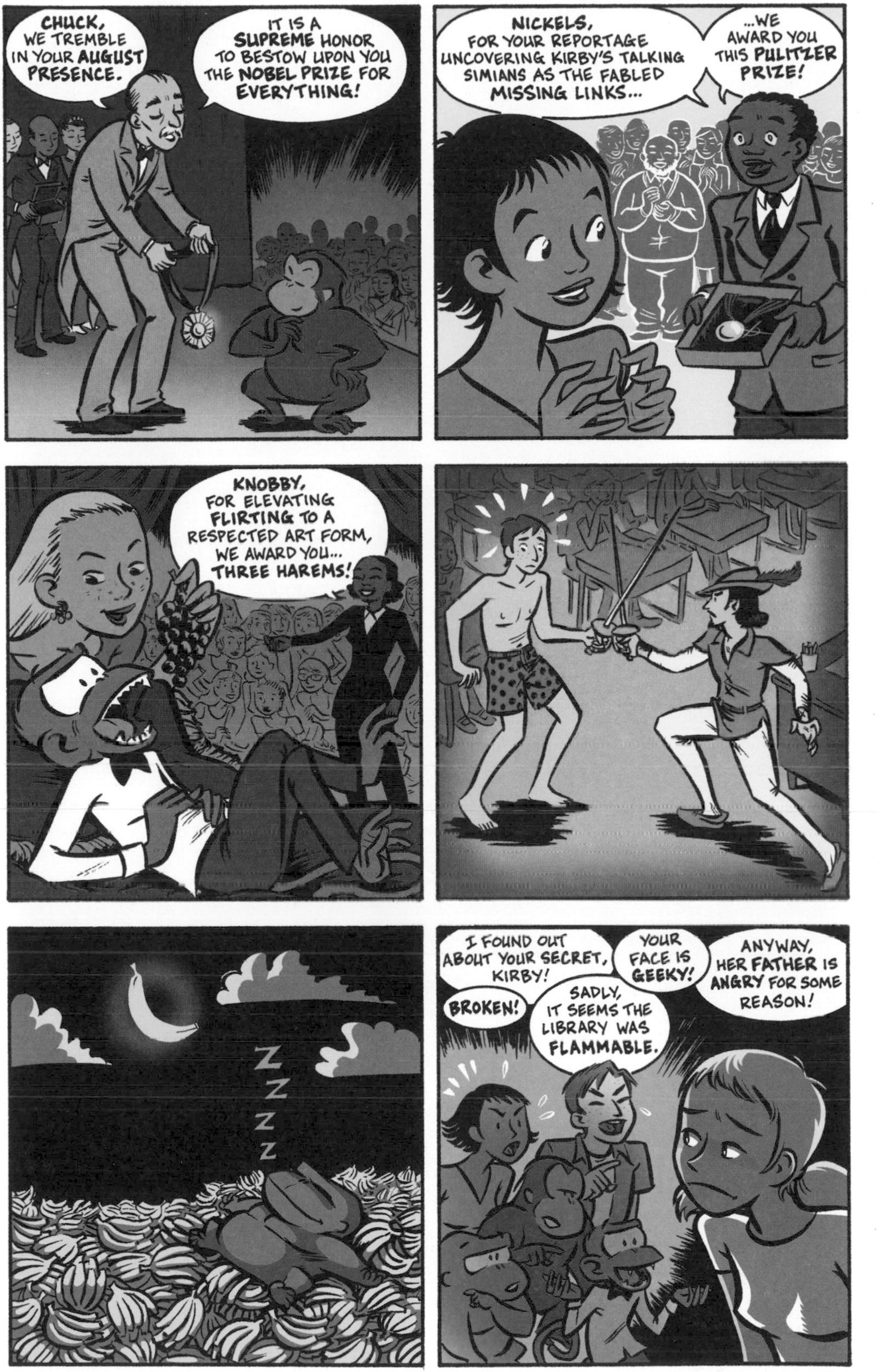
CHUCK, WE TREMBLE IN YOUR AUGUST PRESENCE.
IT IS A SUPREME HONOR TO BESTOW UPON YOU THE NOBEL PRIZE FOR EVERYTHING!
NICKELS, FOR YOUR REPORTAGE UNCOVERING KIRBY'S TALKING SIMIANS AS THE FABLED MISSING LINKS...
...WE AWARD YOU THIS PULITZER PRIZE!
KNOBBY, FOR ELEVATING FLIRTING TO A RESPECTED ART FORM, WE AWARD YOU... THREE HAREMS!
Z Z Z Z
I FOUND OUT ABOUT YOUR SECRET, KIRBY!
YOUR FACE IS GEEKY!
ANYWAY, HER FATHER IS ANGRY FOR SOME REASON!
BROKEN!
SADLY, IT SEEMS THE LIBRARY WAS FLAMMABLE.

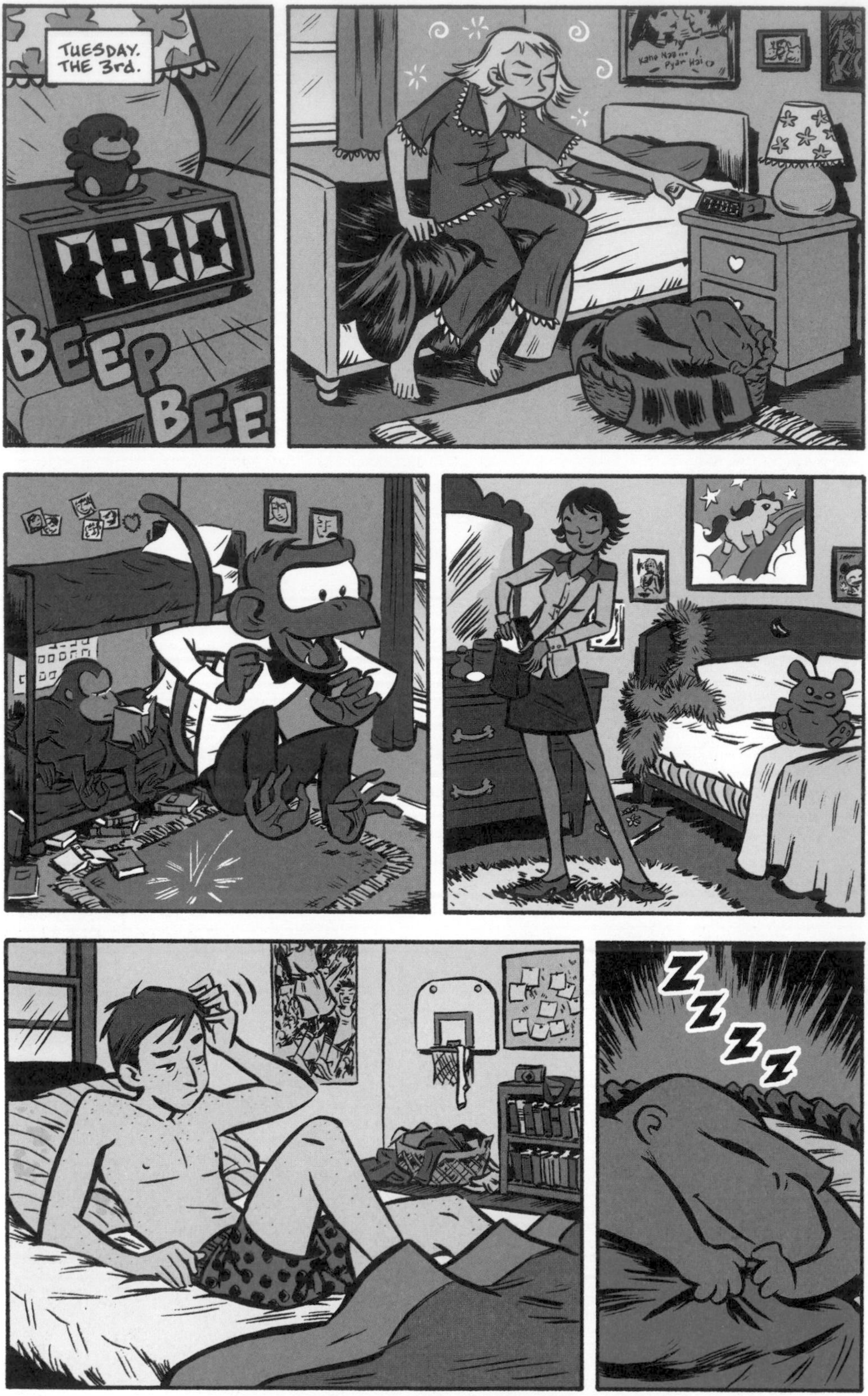
TUESDAY. THE 3rd.
BEEP
BEE
Z Z Z Z

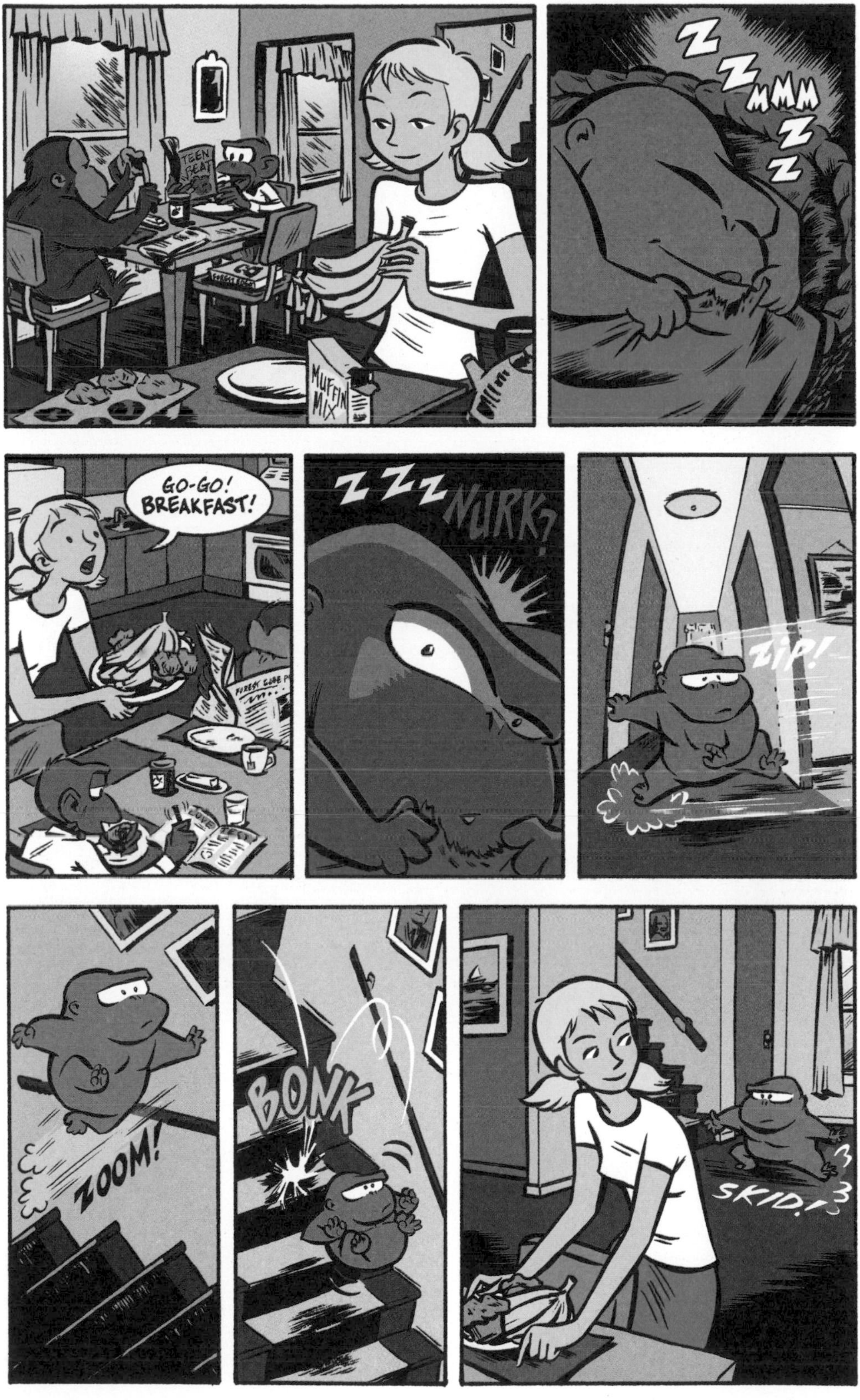
TEEN BEAT
MUFFIN MIX
ZZMMMZZ
GO-GO! BREAKFAST!
ZZZNURK
ZIP!
ZOOM!
BONK
SKID!

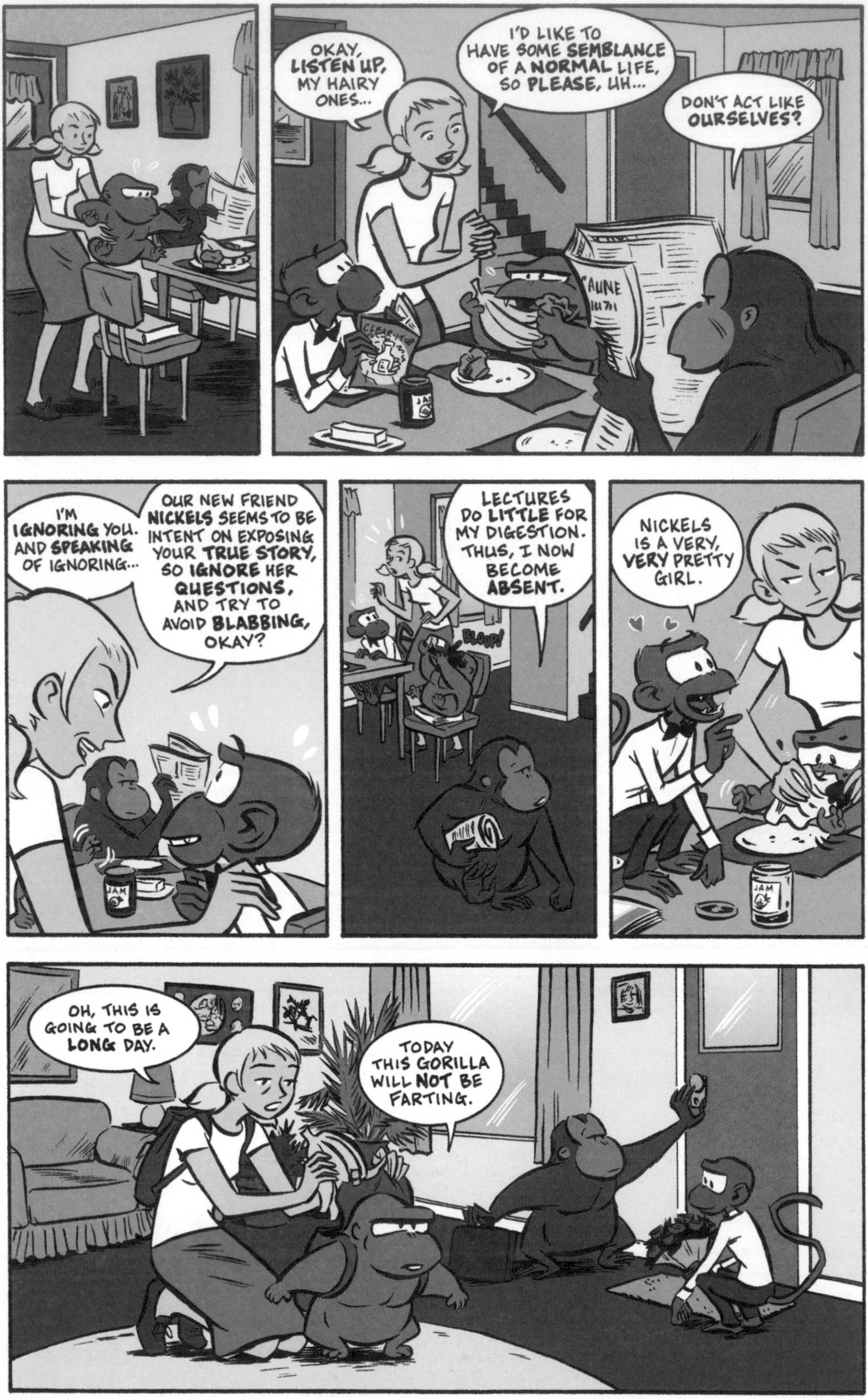
OKAY, LISTEN UP, MY HAIRY ONES...
I'D LIKE TO HAVE SOME SEMBLANCE OF A NORMAL LIFE, SO PLEASE, UH...
DON'T ACT LIKE OURSELVES?
I'M IGNORING YOU. AND SPEAKING OF IGNORING...
OUR NEW FRIEND NICKELS SEEMS TO BE INTENT ON EXPOSING YOUR TRUE STORY, SO IGNORE HER QUESTIONS, AND TRY TO AVOID BLABBING, OKAY?
LECTURES DO LITTLE FOR MY DIGESTION. THUS, I NOW BECOME ABSENT.
BLOOP!
NICKELS IS A VERY, VERY PRETTY GIRL.
OH, THIS IS GOING TO BE A LONG DAY.
TODAY THIS GORILLA WILL NOT BE FARTING.

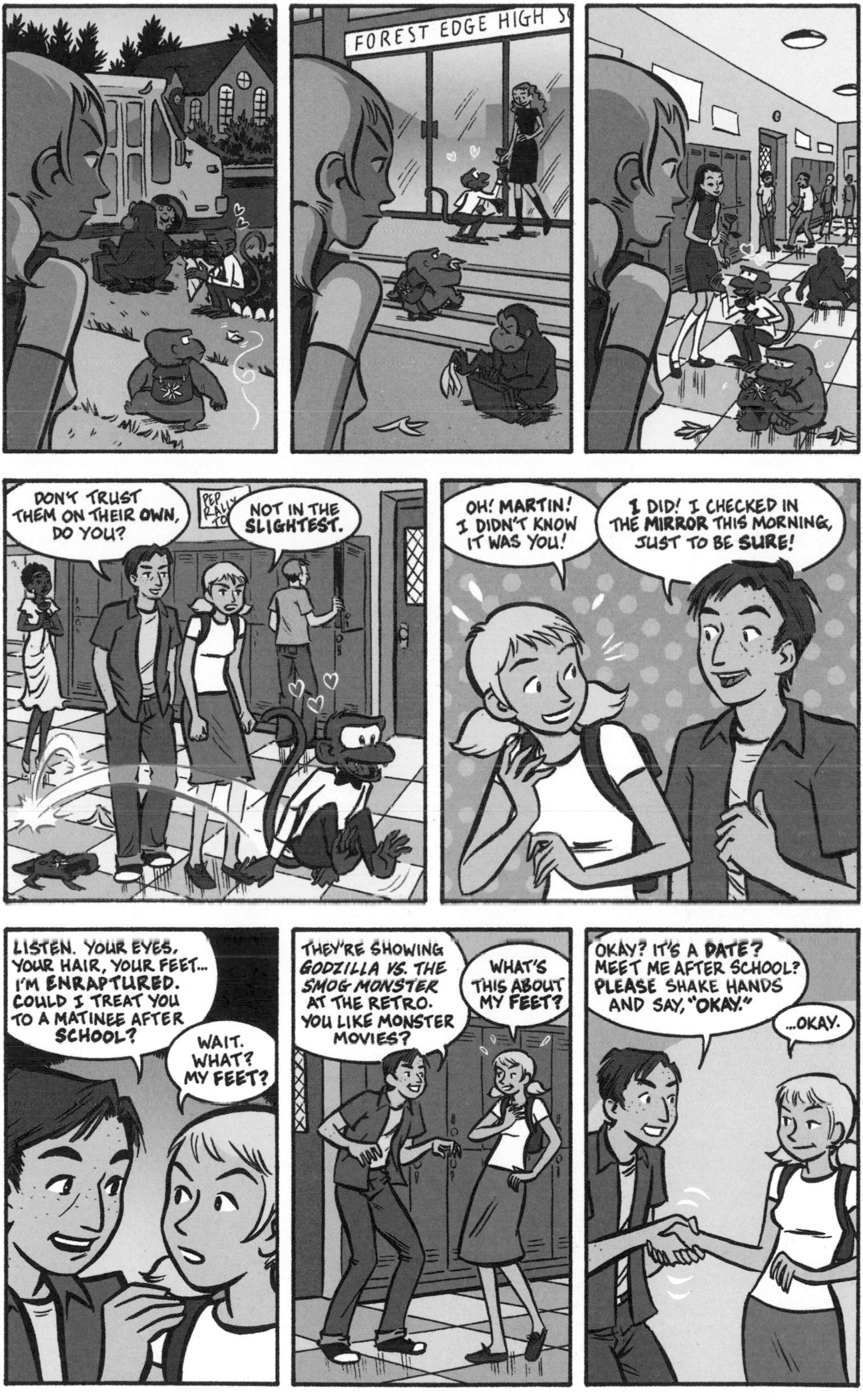
FOREST EDGE HIGH S
DON'T TRUST THEM ON THEIR OWN, DO YOU?
PEP RALLY TO
NOT IN THE SLIGHTEST.
OH! MARTIN! I DIDN'T KNOW IT WAS YOU!
I DID! I CHECKED IN THE MIRROR THIS MORNING, JUST TO BE SURE!
LISTEN. YOUR EYES, YOUR HAIR, YOUR FEET... I'M ENRAPTURED. COULD I TREAT YOU TO A MATINEE AFTER SCHOOL?
WAIT. WHAT? MY FEET?
THEY'RE SHOWING GODZILLA VS. THE SMOG MONSTER AT THE RETRO. YOU LIKE MONSTER MOVIES?
WHAT'S THIS ABOUT MY FEET?
OKAY? IT'S A DATE? MEET ME AFTER SCHOOL? PLEASE SHAKE HANDS AND SAY, "OKAY."
...OKAY.

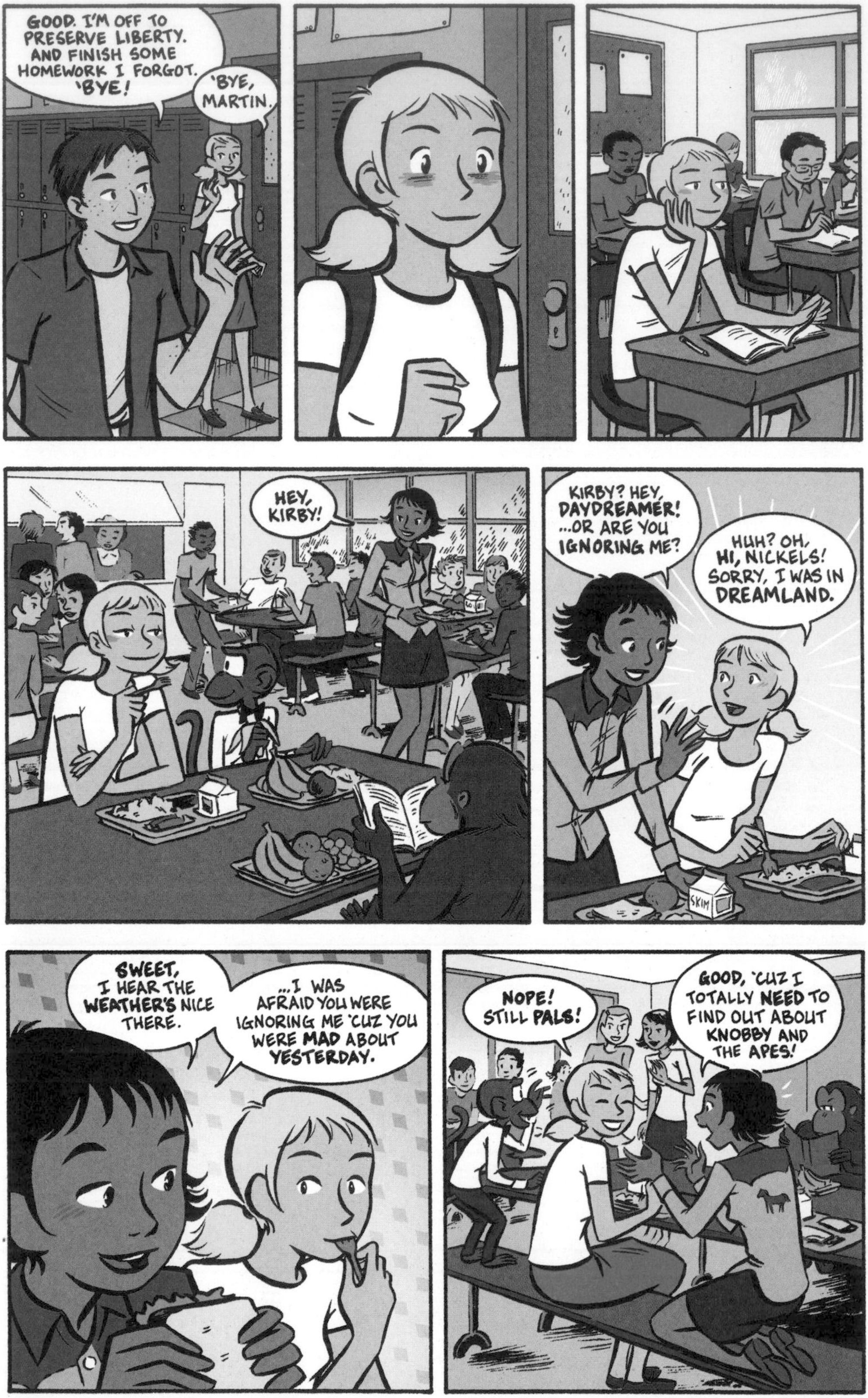
GOOD. I'M OFF TO PRESERVE LIBERTY. AND FINISH SOME HOMEWORK I FORGOT. 'BYE!
'BYE, MARTIN.
HEY, KIRBY!
KIRBY? HEY, DAYDREAMER! ...OR ARE YOU IGNORING ME?
HUH? OH, HI, NICKELS! SORRY, I WAS IN DREAMLAND.
SKIM
SWEET, I HEAR THE WEATHER'S NICE THERE.
...I WAS AFRAID YOU WERE IGNORING ME 'CUZ YOU WERE MAD ABOUT YESTERDAY.
NOPE! STILL PALS!
GOOD, 'CUZ I TOTALLY NEED TO FIND OUT ABOUT KNOBBY AND THE APES!

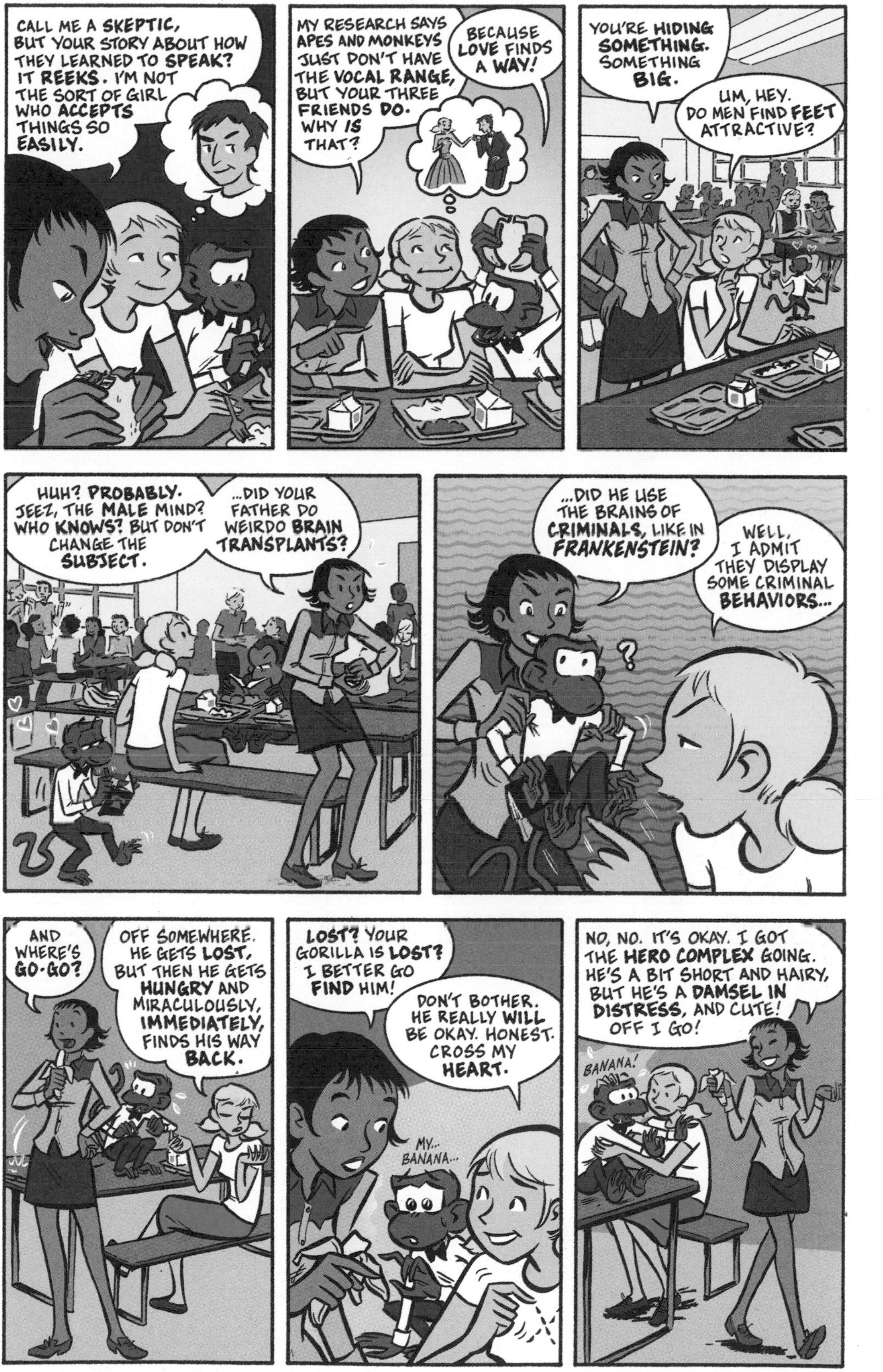
CALL ME A SKEPTIC, BUT YOUR STORY ABOUT HOW THEY LEARNED TO SPEAK? IT REEKS. I'M NOT THE SORT OF GIRL WHO ACCEPTS THINGS SO EASILY.
MY RESEARCH SAYS APES AND MONKEYS JUST DON'T HAVE THE VOCAL RANGE, BUT YOUR THREE FRIENDS DO. WHY IS THAT?
BECAUSE LOVE FINDS A WAY!
YOU'RE HIDING SOMETHING. SOMETHING BIG.
UM, HEY. DO MEN FIND FEET ATTRACTIVE?
HUH? PROBABLY. JEEZ, THE MALE MIND? WHO KNOWS? BUT DON'T CHANGE THE SUBJECT.
...DID YOUR FATHER DO WEIRDO BRAIN TRANSPLANTS?
...DID HE USE THE BRAINS OF CRIMINALS, LIKE IN FRANKENSTEIN?
?
WELL, I ADMIT THEY DISPLAY SOME CRIMINAL BEHAVIORS...
AND WHERE'S GO-GO?
OFF SOMEWHERE. HE GETS LOST, BUT THEN HE GETS HUNGRY AND MIRACULOUSLY, IMMEDIATELY, FINDS HIS WAY BACK.
LOST? YOUR GORILLA IS LOST? I BETTER GO FIND HIM!
DON'T BOTHER. HE REALLY WILL BE OKAY. HONEST. CROSS MY HEART.
MY... BANANA...
NO, NO. IT'S OKAY. I GOT THE HERO COMPLEX GOING. HE'S A BIT SHORT AND HAIRY, BUT HE'S A DAMSEL IN DISTRESS, AND CUTE! OFF I GO!
BANANA!

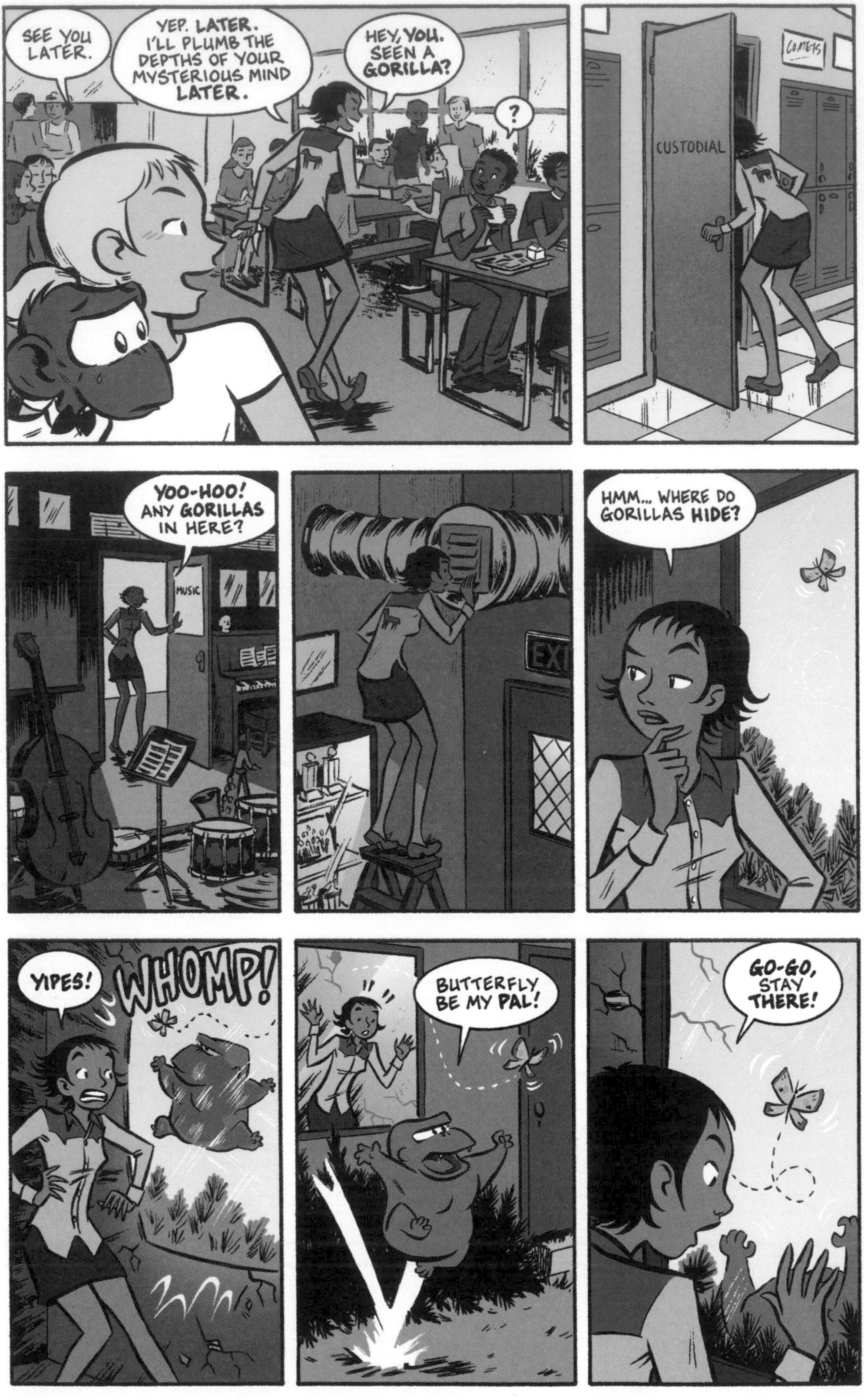
SEE YOU LATER.
YEP. LATER. I'LL PLUMB THE DEPTHS OF YOUR MYSTERIOUS MIND LATER.
HEY, YOU. SEEN A GORILLA?
?
COMETS
CUSTODIAL
YOO-HOO! ANY GORILLAS IN HERE?
MUSIC
HMM... WHERE DO GORILLAS HIDE?
YIPES!
WHOMP!
BUTTERFLY BE MY PAL!
GO-GO, STAY THERE!

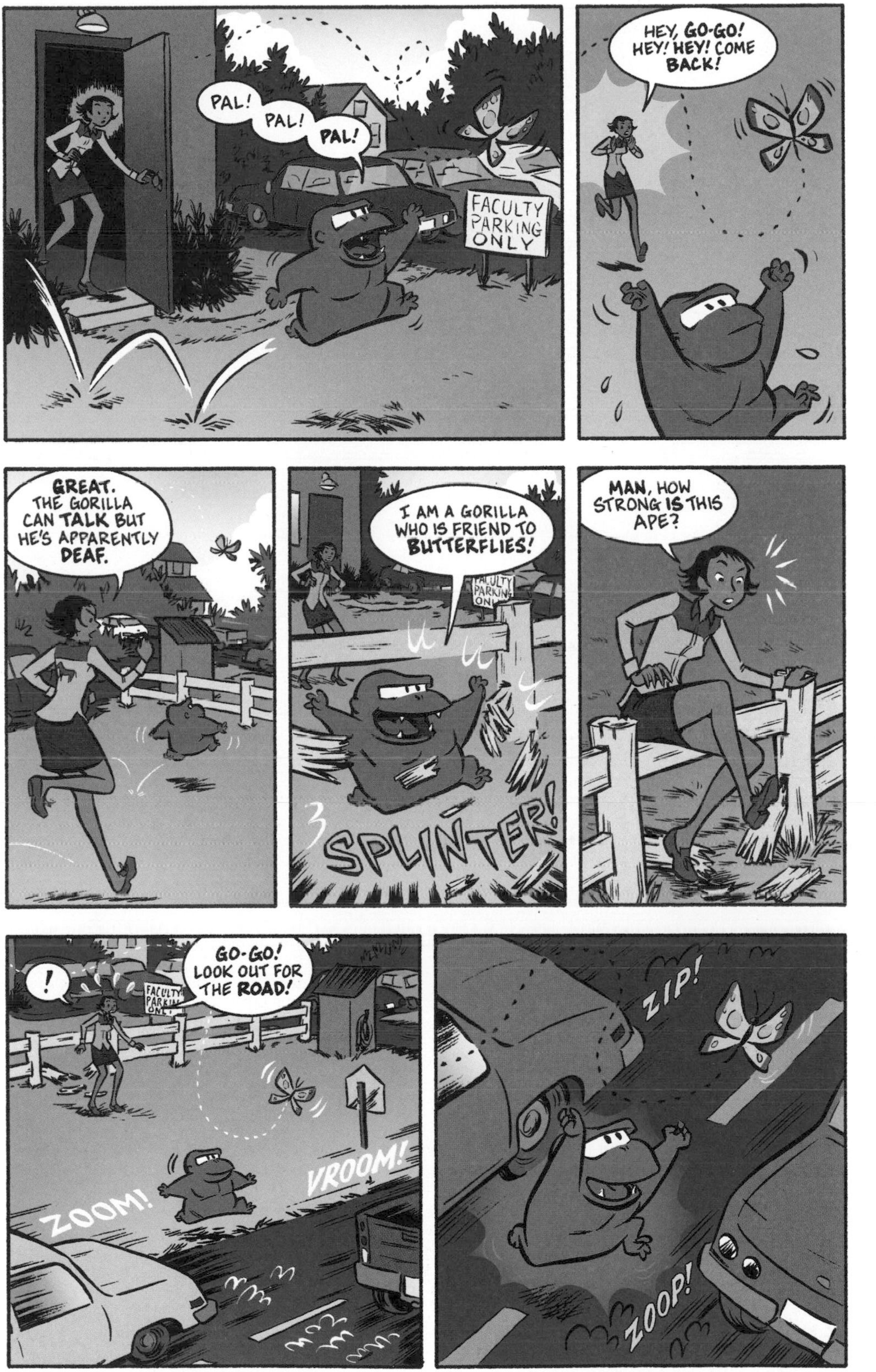
PAL!
PAL!
PAL!
FACULTY PARKING ONLY
HEY, GO-GO! HEY! HEY! COME BACK!
GREAT. THE GORILLA CAN TALK BUT HE'S APPARENTLY DEAF.
I AM A GORILLA WHO IS FRIEND TO BUTTERFLIES!
SPLINTER!
MAN, HOW STRONG IS THIS APE?
!
GO-GO! LOOK OUT FOR THE ROAD!
VROOM!
ZOOM!
ZIP!
ZOOP!

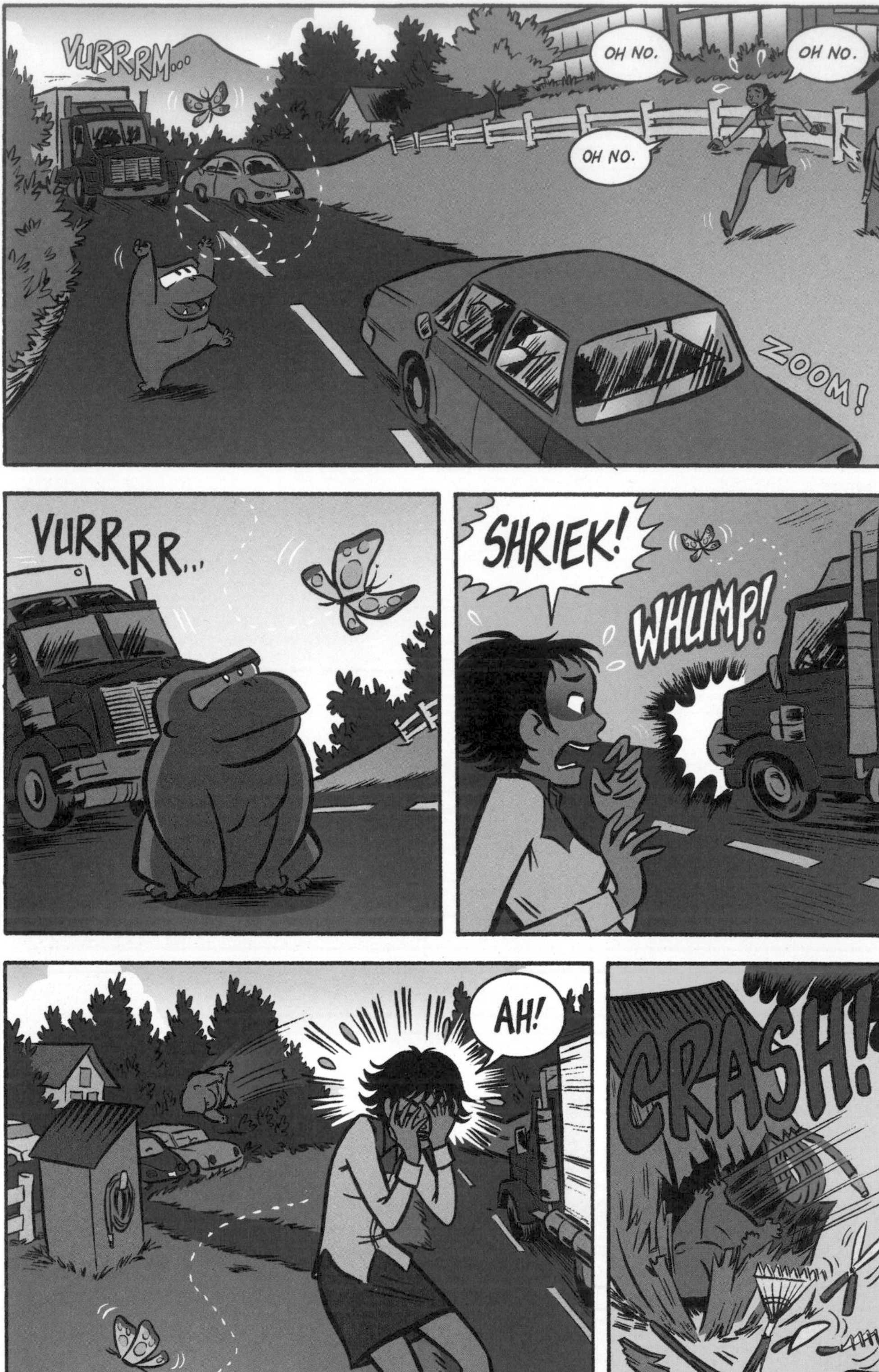
VURRRM...
OH NO.
OH NO.
OH NO.
ZOOM!
VURRRR...
SHRIEK!
WHUMP!
AH!
CRASH!

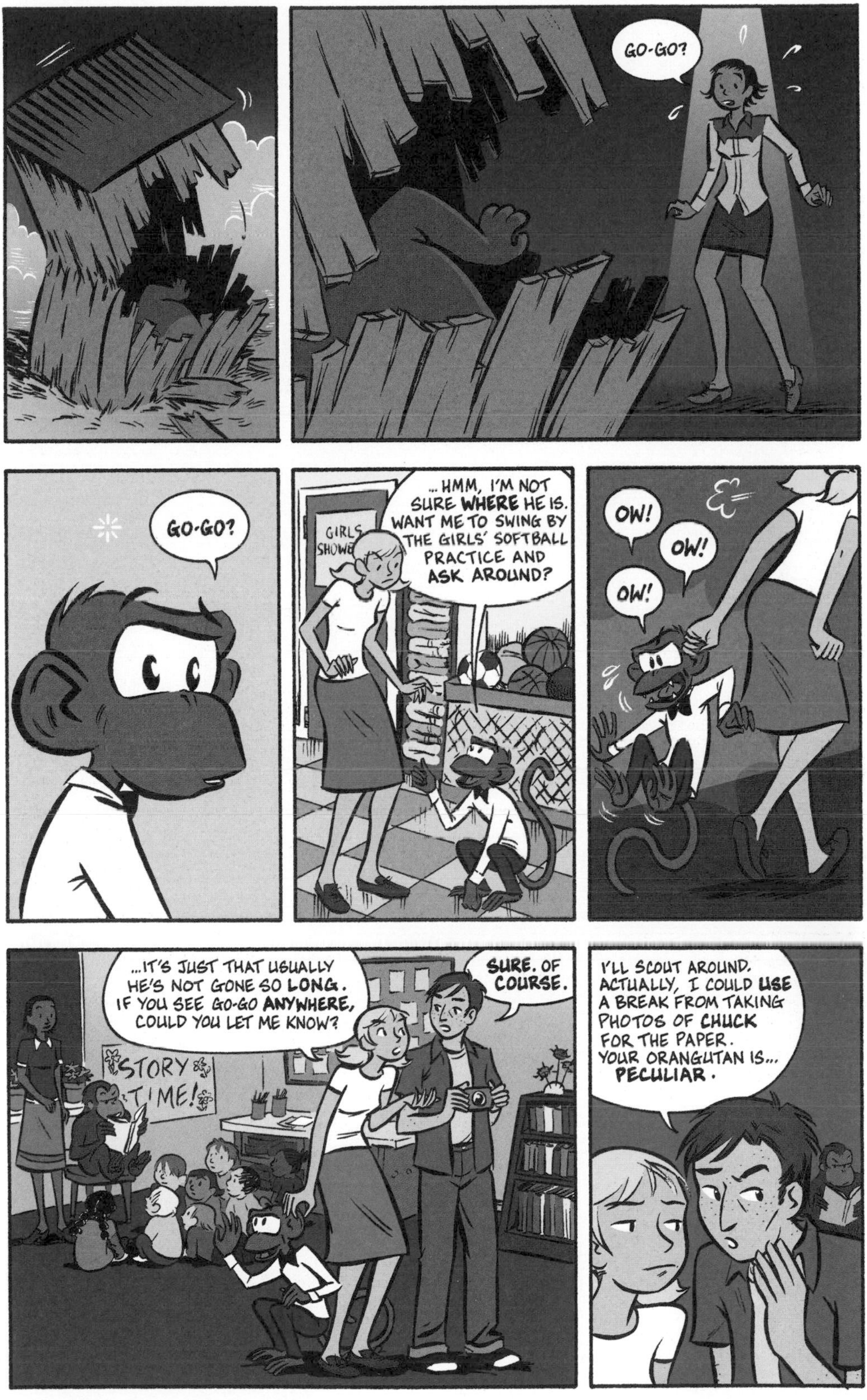
GO-GO?
GO-GO?
GIRLS SHOWE
...HMM, I'M NOT SURE WHERE HE IS. WANT ME TO SWING BY THE GIRLS' SOFTBALL PRACTICE AND ASK AROUND?
OW!
OW!
OW!
...IT'S JUST THAT USUALLY HE'S NOT GONE SO LONG. IF YOU SEE GO-GO ANYWHERE, COULD YOU LET ME KNOW?
SURE. OF COURSE.
STORY TIME!
I'LL SCOUT AROUND. ACTUALLY, I COULD USE A BREAK FROM TAKING PHOTOS OF CHUCK FOR THE PAPER. YOUR ORANGUTAN IS... PECULIAR.

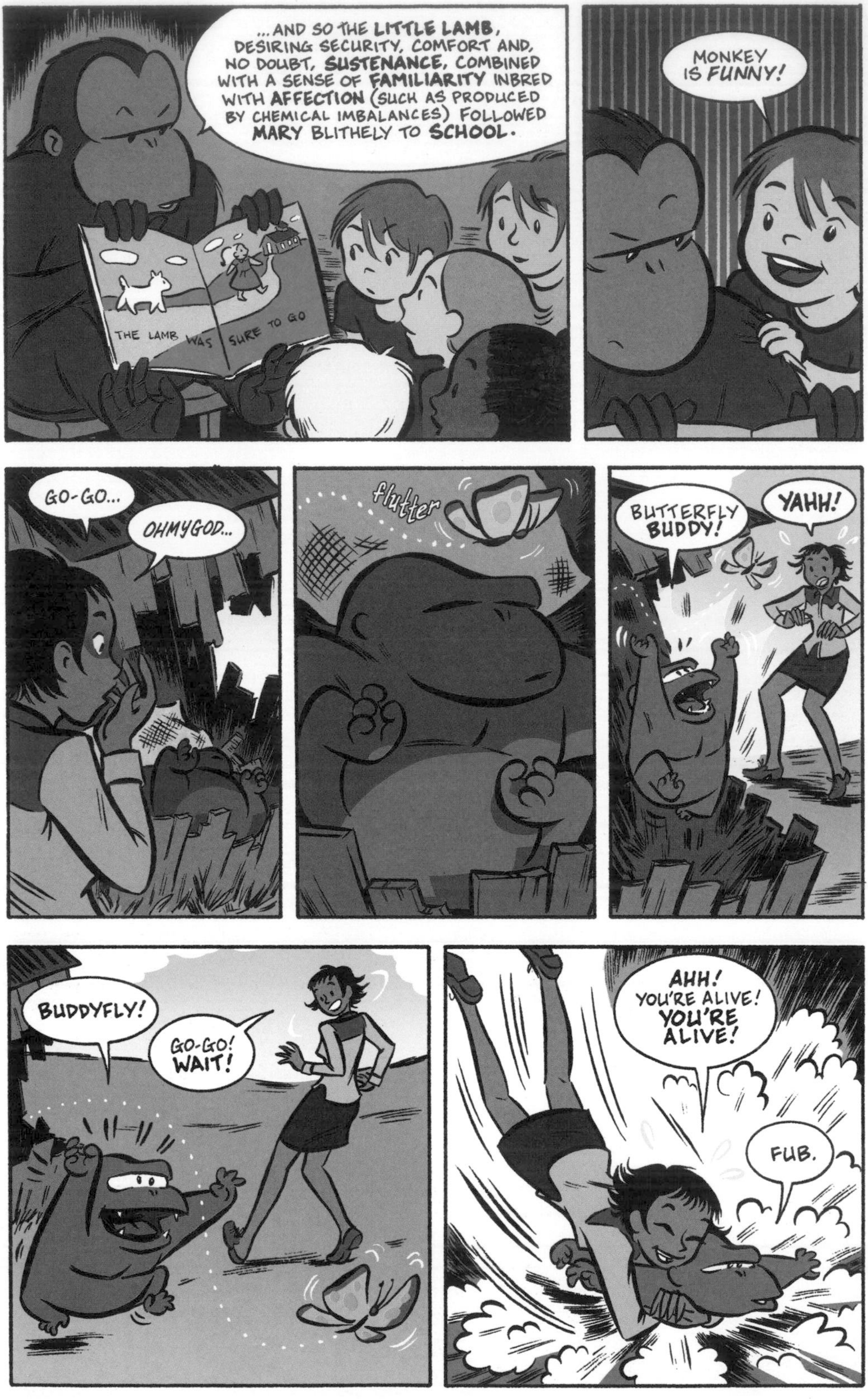
...AND SO THE LITTLE LAMB, DESIRING SECURITY, COMFORT AND, NO DOUBT, SUSTENANCE, COMBINED WITH A SENSE OF FAMILIARITY INBRED WITH AFFECTION (SUCH AS PRODUCED BY CHEMICAL IMBALANCES) FOLLOWED MARY BLITHELY TO SCHOOL.
THE LAMB WAS SURE TO GO
MONKEY IS FUNNY!
GO-GO...
OHMYGOD...
flutter
BUTTERFLY BUDDY!
YAHH!
BUDDYFLY!
GO-GO! WAIT!
AHH! YOU'RE ALIVE! YOU'RE ALIVE!
FUB.

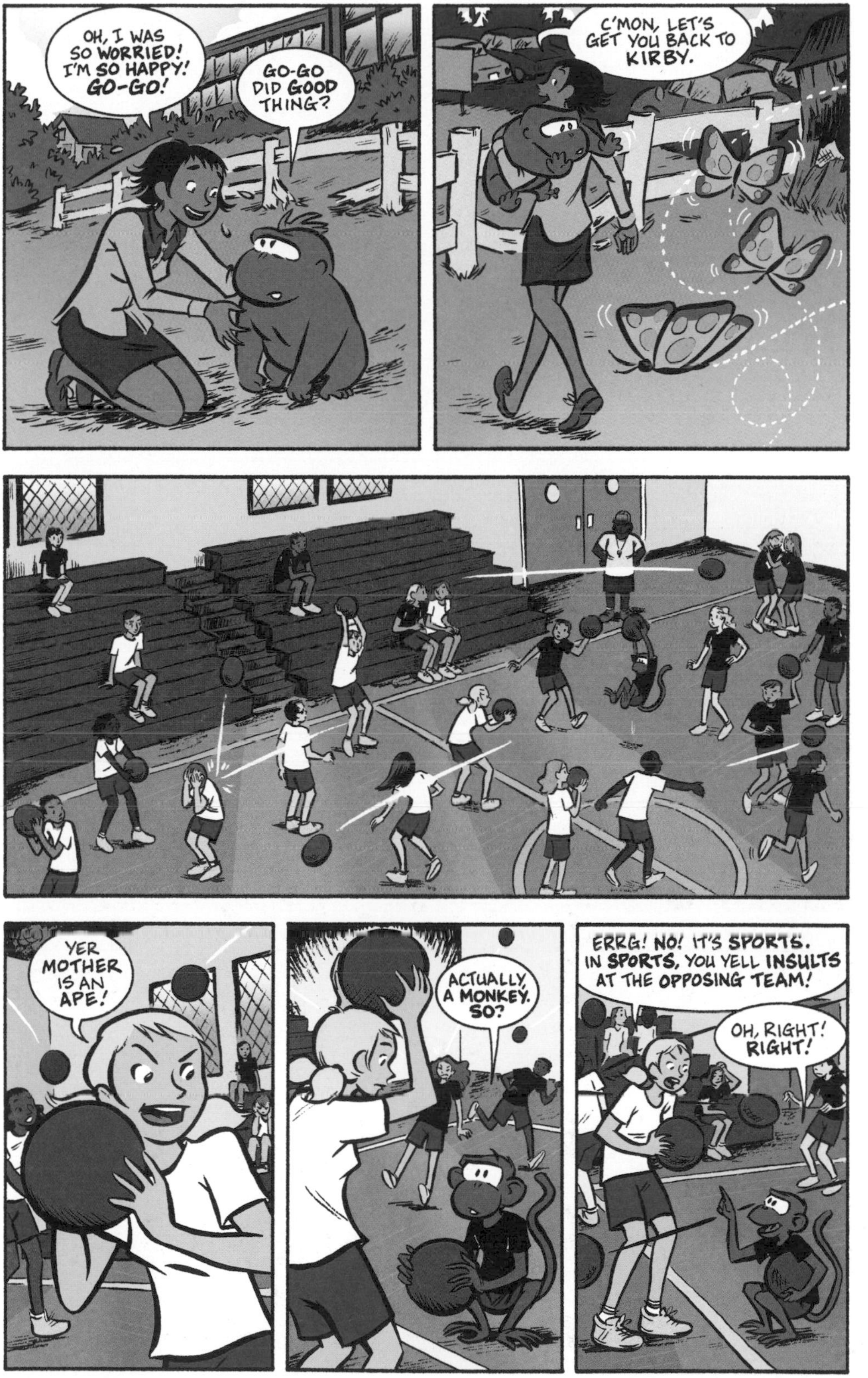
OH, I WAS SO WORRIED! I'M SO HAPPY! GO-GO!
GO-GO DID GOOD THING?
C'MON, LET'S GET YOU BACK TO KIRBY.
YER MOTHER IS AN APE!
ACTUALLY, A MONKEY. SO?
ERRG! NO! IT'S SPORTS. IN SPORTS, YOU YELL INSULTS AT THE OPPOSING TEAM!
OH, RIGHT! RIGHT!

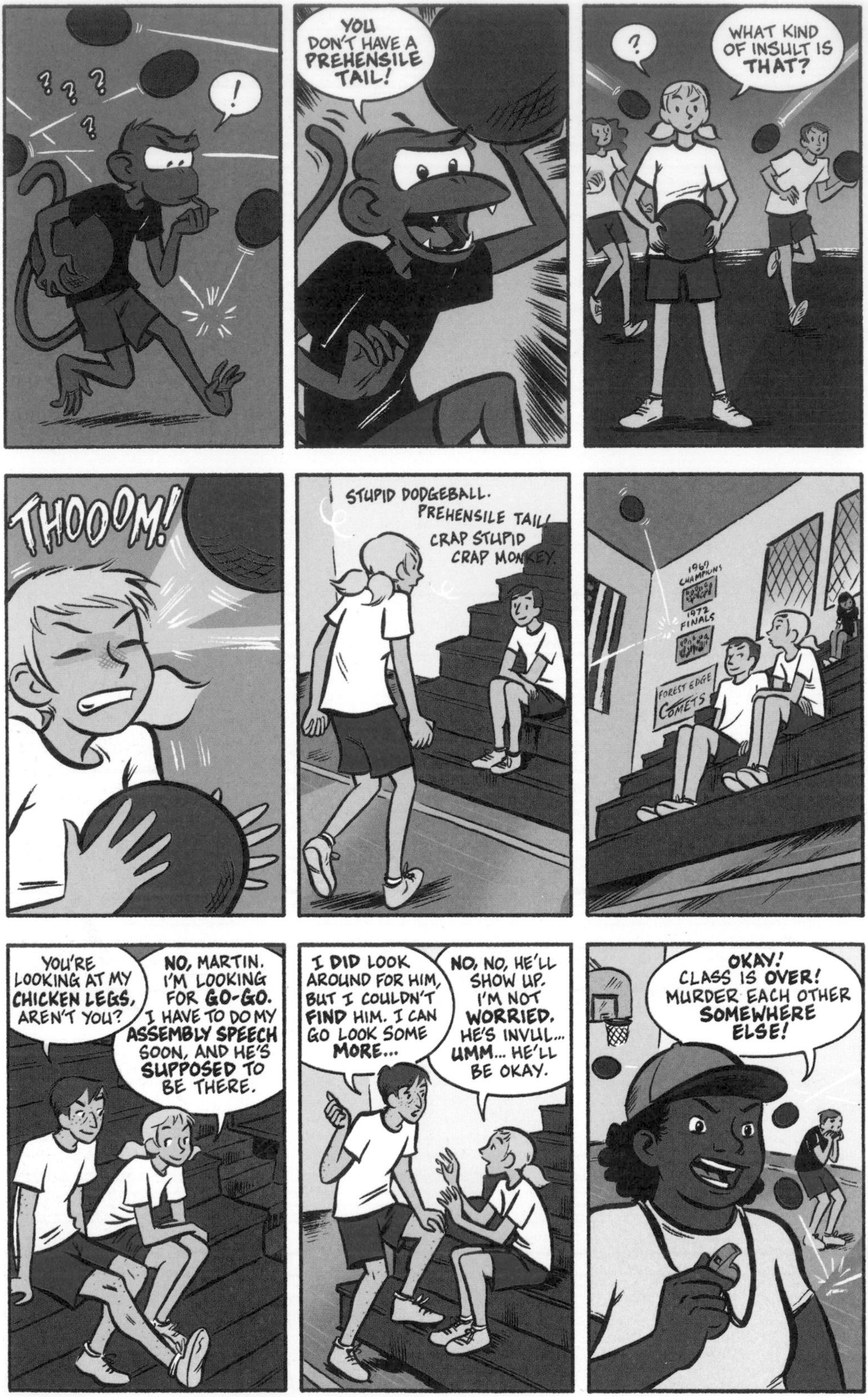
? ? ?
?
!
YOU DON'T HAVE A PREHENSILE TAIL!
?
WHAT KIND OF INSULT IS THAT?
THOOOM!
STUPID DODGEBALL.
PREHENSILE TAIL!
CRAP STUPID CRAP MONKEY.
1969 CHAMPIONS
1972 FINALS
FOREST EDGE COMETS
YOU'RE LOOKING AT MY CHICKEN LEGS, AREN'T YOU?
NO, MARTIN. I'M LOOKING FOR GO-GO. I HAVE TO DO MY ASSEMBLY SPEECH SOON, AND HE'S SUPPOSED TO BE THERE.
I DID LOOK AROUND FOR HIM, BUT I COULDN'T FIND HIM. I CAN GO LOOK SOME MORE...
NO, NO, HE'LL SHOW UP. I'M NOT WORRIED. HE'S INVUL... UMM... HE'LL BE OKAY.
OKAY! CLASS IS OVER! MURDER EACH OTHER SOMEWHERE ELSE!

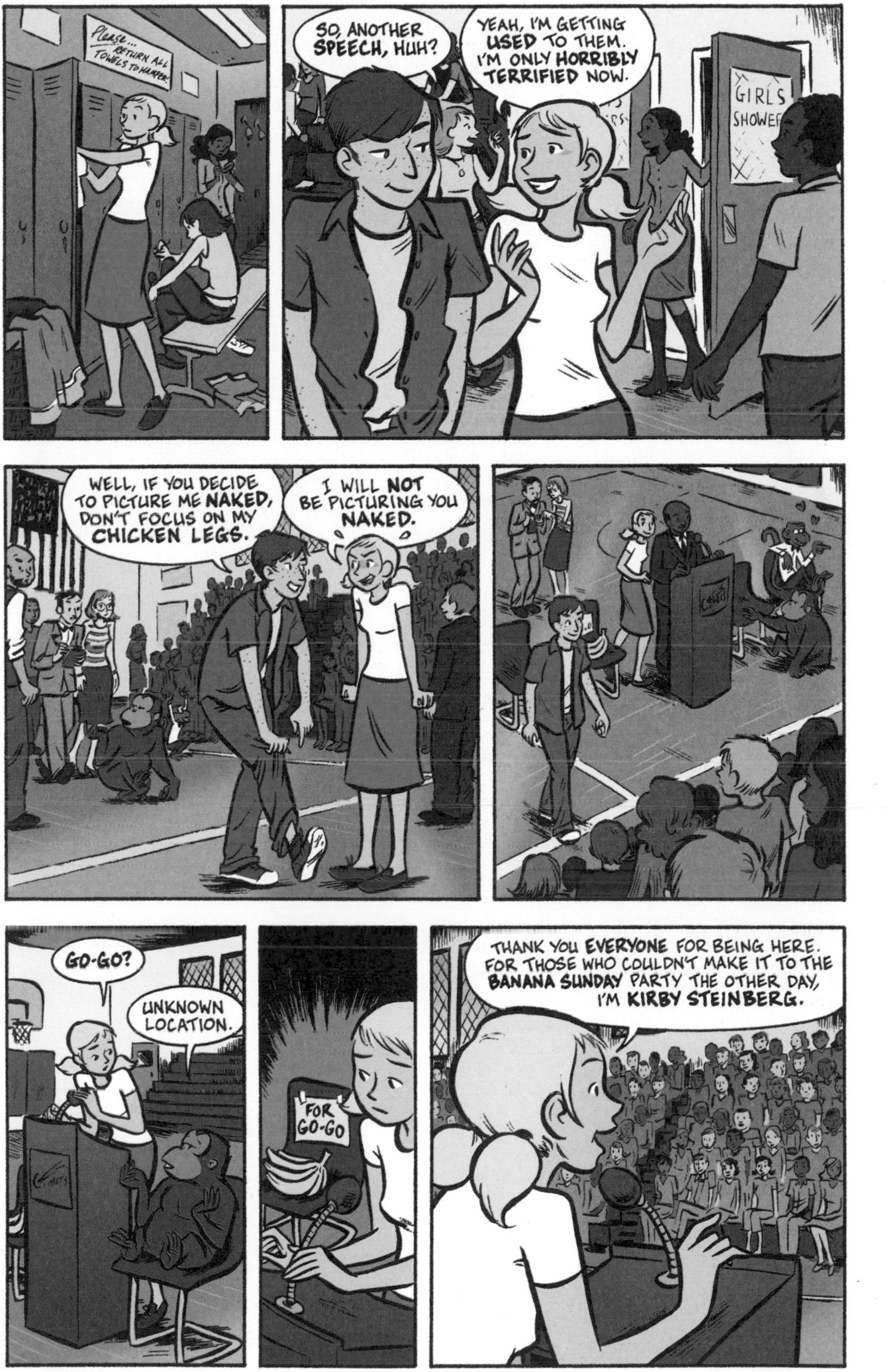
PLEASE... RETURN ALL TOWELS TO HAMPER!
SO, ANOTHER SPEECH, HUH?
YEAH, I'M GETTING USED TO THEM. I'M ONLY HORRIBLY TERRIFIED NOW.
GIRLS SHOWER
WELL, IF YOU DECIDE TO PICTURE ME NAKED, DON'T FOCUS ON MY CHICKEN LEGS.
I WILL NOT BE PICTURING YOU NAKED.
GO-GO?
UNKNOWN LOCATION.
FOR GO-GO
THANK YOU EVERYONE FOR BEING HERE. FOR THOSE WHO COULDN'T MAKE IT TO THE BANANA SUNDAY PARTY THE OTHER DAY, I'M KIRBY STEINBERG.

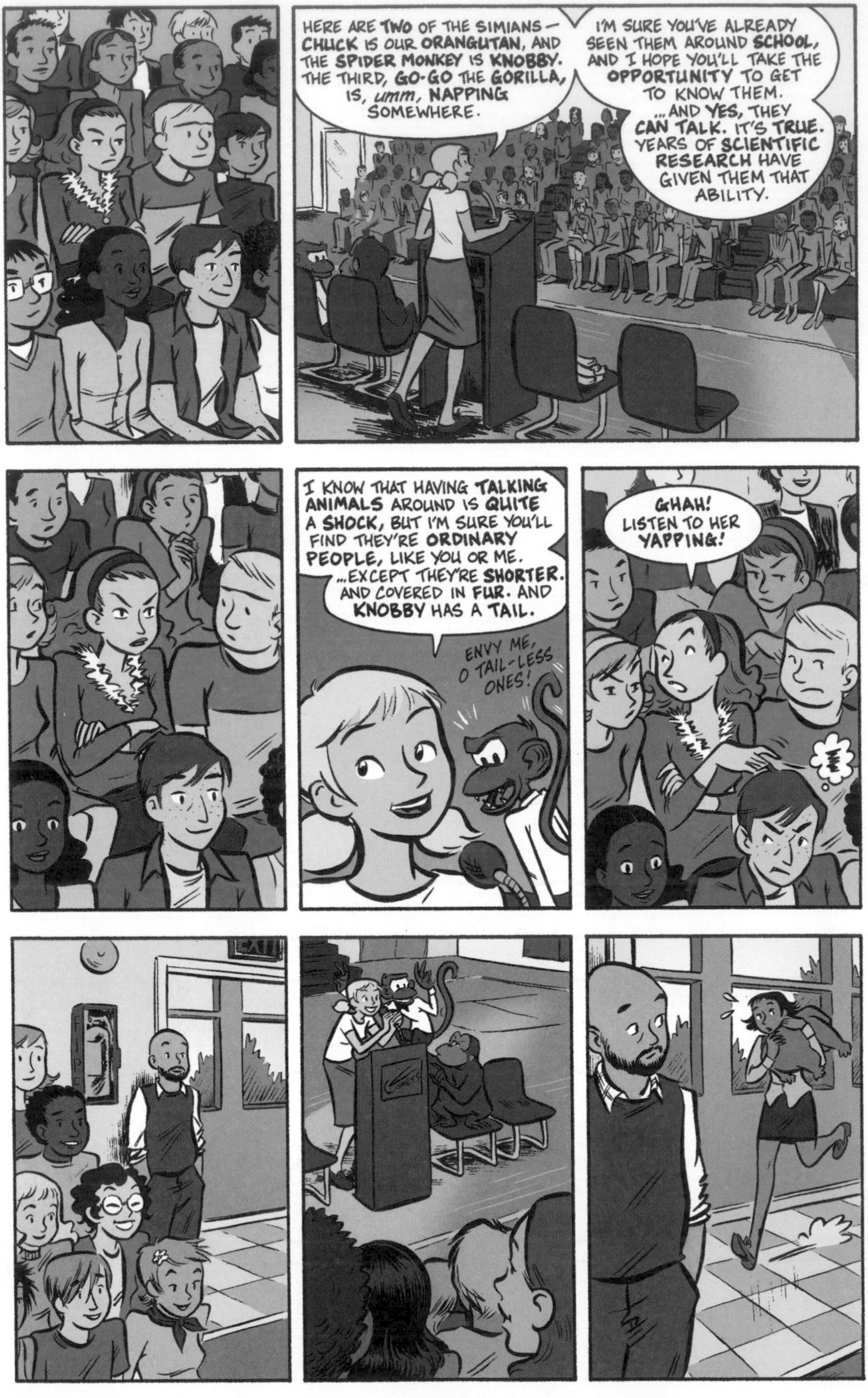
HERE ARE TWO OF THE SIMIANS— CHUCK IS OUR ORANGUTAN, AND THE SPIDER MONKEY IS KNOBBY. THE THIRD, GO-GO THE GORILLA, IS, umm, NAPPING SOMEWHERE.
I'M SURE YOU'VE ALREADY SEEN THEM AROUND SCHOOL, AND I HOPE YOU'LL TAKE THE OPPORTUNITY TO GET TO KNOW THEM. ...AND YES, THEY CAN TALK. IT'S TRUE. YEARS OF SCIENTIFIC RESEARCH HAVE GIVEN THEM THAT ABILITY.
I KNOW THAT HAVING TALKING ANIMALS AROUND IS QUITE A SHOCK, BUT I'M SURE YOU'LL FIND THEY'RE ORDINARY PEOPLE, LIKE YOU OR ME. ...EXCEPT THEY'RE SHORTER. AND COVERED IN FUR. AND KNOBBY HAS A TAIL.
ENVY ME, O TAIL-LESS ONES!
GHAH! LISTEN TO HER YAPPING!

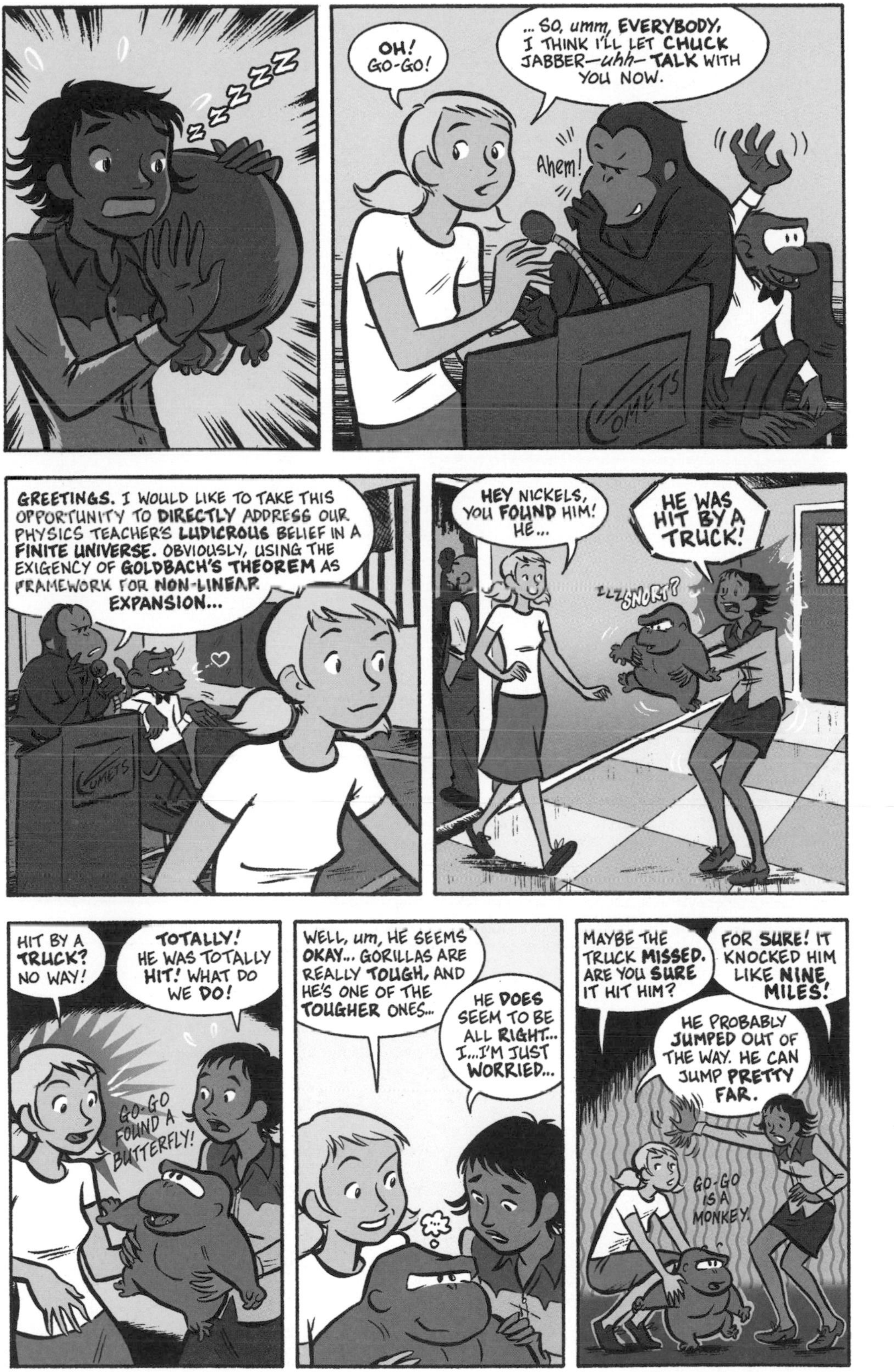
ZZZZZZ
OH! GO-GO!
... SO, umm, EVERYBODY, I THINK I'LL LET CHUCK JABBER—uhh— TALK WITH YOU NOW.
Ahem!
COMETS
GREETINGS. I WOULD LIKE TO TAKE THIS OPPORTUNITY TO DIRECTLY ADDRESS OUR PHYSICS TEACHER'S LUDICROUS BELIEF IN A FINITE UNIVERSE. OBVIOUSLY, USING THE EXIGENCY OF GOLDBACH'S THEOREM AS FRAMEWORK FOR NON-LINEAR EXPANSION...
COMETS
HEY NICKELS, YOU FOUND HIM! HE...
HE WAS HIT BY A TRUCK!
ZZZSNORT?
HIT BY A TRUCK? NO WAY!
TOTALLY! HE WAS TOTALLY HIT! WHAT DO WE DO!
GO-GO FOUND A BUTTERFLY!
WELL, um, HE SEEMS OKAY... GORILLAS ARE REALLY TOUGH, AND HE'S ONE OF THE TOUGHER ONES...
HE DOES SEEM TO BE ALL RIGHT... I...I'M JUST WORRIED...
MAYBE THE TRUCK MISSED. ARE YOU SURE IT HIT HIM?
FOR SURE! IT KNOCKED HIM LIKE NINE MILES!
HE PROBABLY JUMPED OUT OF THE WAY. HE CAN JUMP PRETTY FAR.
GO-GO IS A MONKEY.

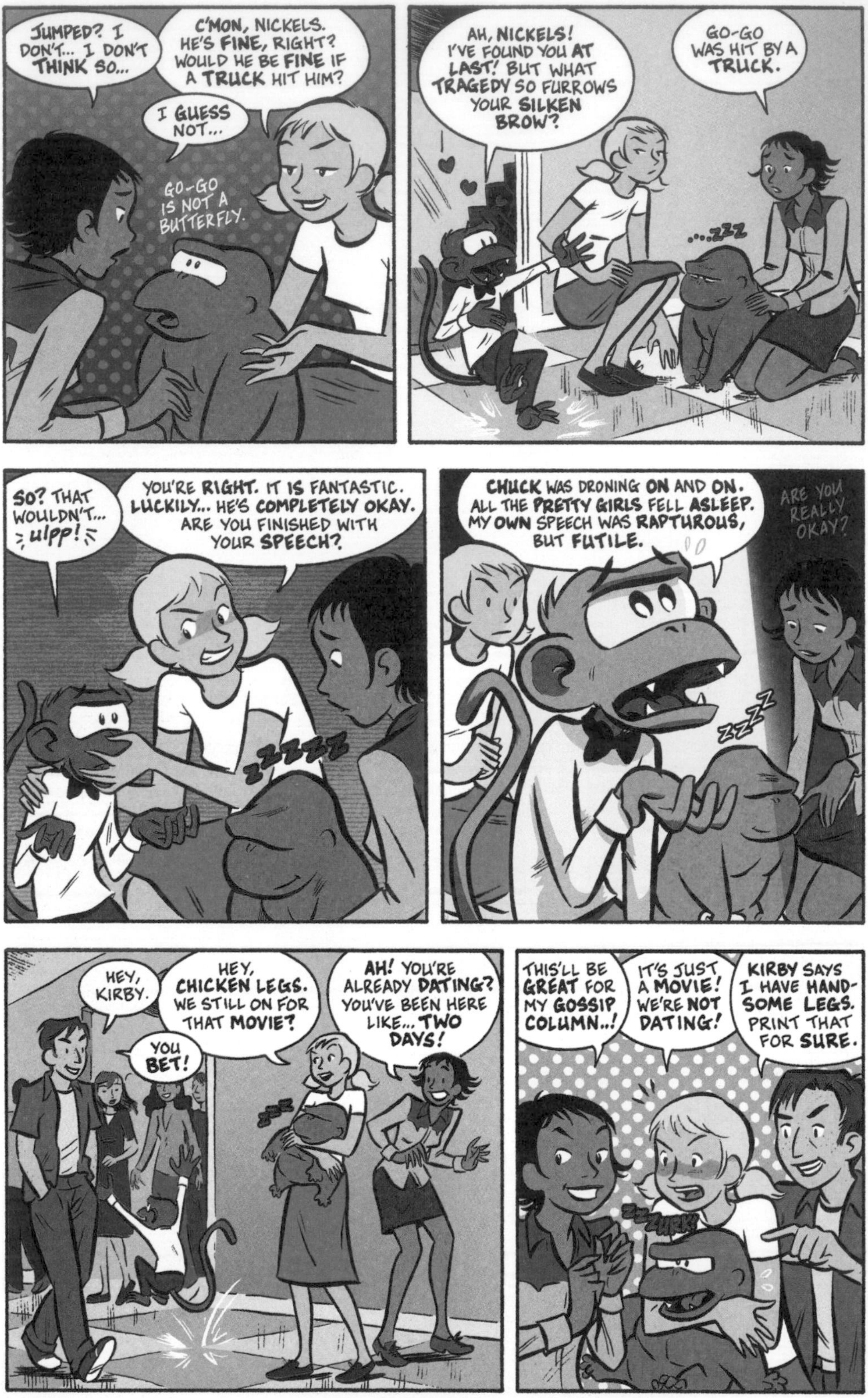
JUMPED? I DON'T... I DON'T THINK SO...
C'MON, NICKELS. HE'S FINE, RIGHT? WOULD HE BE FINE IF A TRUCK HIT HIM?
I GUESS NOT...
GO-GO IS NOT A BUTTERFLY.
AH, NICKELS! I'VE FOUND YOU AT LAST! BUT WHAT TRAGEDY SO FURROWS YOUR SILKEN BROW?
GO-GO WAS HIT BY A TRUCK.
...ZZZ
SO? THAT WOULDN'T... ulpp!
YOU'RE RIGHT. IT IS FANTASTIC. LUCKILY... HE'S COMPLETELY OKAY. ARE YOU FINISHED WITH YOUR SPEECH?
ZZZZZ
CHUCK WAS DRONING ON AND ON. ALL THE PRETTY GIRLS FELL ASLEEP. MY OWN SPEECH WAS RAPTUROUS, BUT FUTILE.
ARE YOU REALLY OKAY?
ZZZZ
HEY, KIRBY.
HEY, CHICKEN LEGS. WE STILL ON FOR THAT MOVIE?
YOU BET!
AH! YOU'RE ALREADY DATING? YOU'VE BEEN HERE LIKE... TWO DAYS!
THIS'LL BE GREAT FOR MY GOSSIP COLUMN..!
IT'S JUST A MOVIE! WE'RE NOT DATING!
KIRBY SAYS I HAVE HAND-SOME LEGS. PRINT THAT FOR SURE.

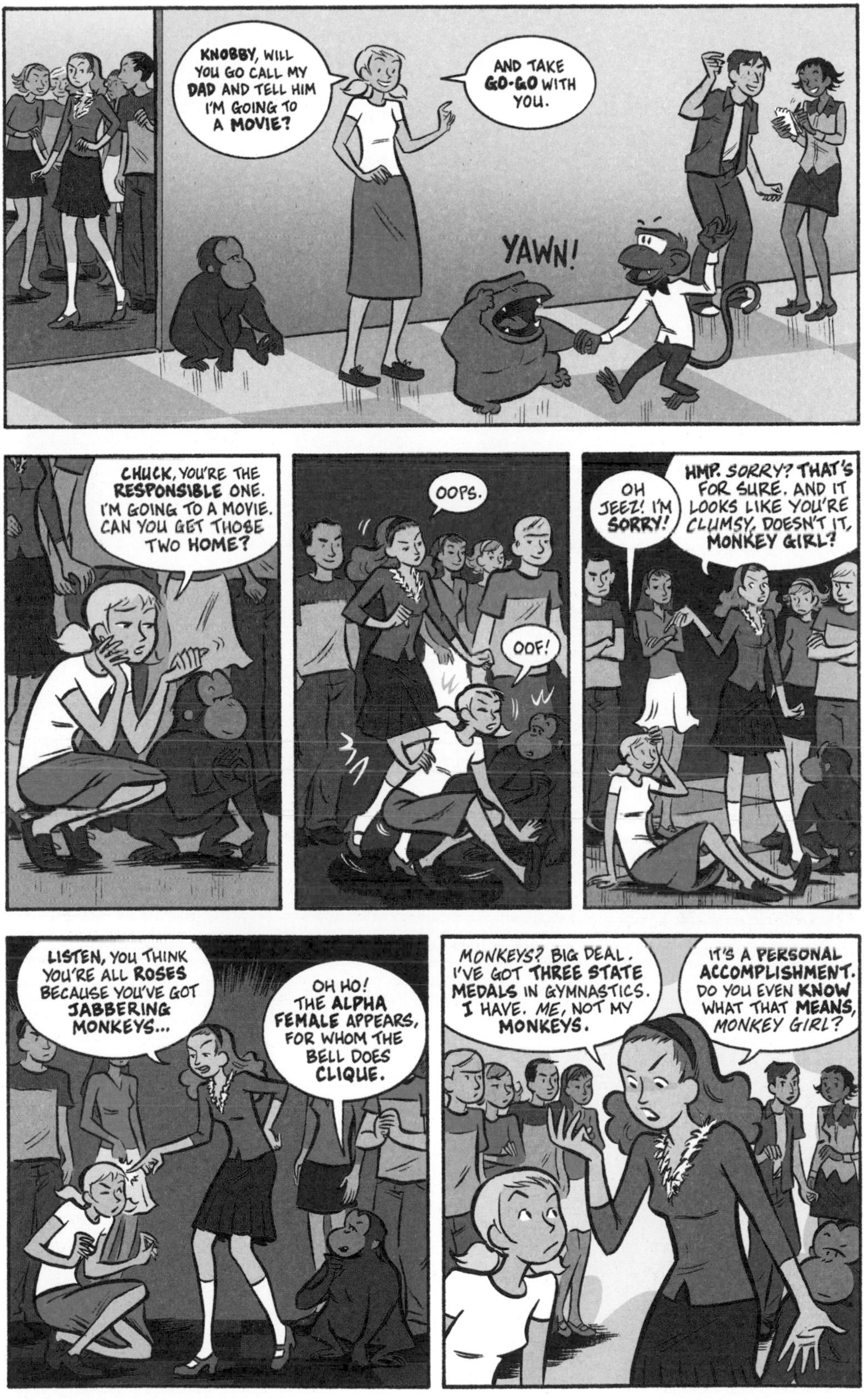
KNOBBY, WILL YOU GO CALL MY DAD AND TELL HIM I'M GOING TO A MOVIE?
AND TAKE GO-GO WITH YOU.
YAWN!
CHUCK, YOU'RE THE RESPONSIBLE ONE. I'M GOING TO A MOVIE. CAN YOU GET THOSE TWO HOME?
OOPS.
OOF!
OH JEEZ! I'M SORRY!
HMP. SORRY? THAT'S FOR SURE. AND IT LOOKS LIKE YOU'RE CLUMSY, DOESN'T IT, MONKEY GIRL?
LISTEN, YOU THINK YOU'RE ALL ROSES BECAUSE YOU'VE GOT JABBERING MONKEYS...
OH HO! THE ALPHA FEMALE APPEARS, FOR WHOM THE BELL DOES CLIQUE.
MONKEYS? BIG DEAL. I'VE GOT THREE STATE MEDALS IN GYMNASTICS. I HAVE. ME, NOT MY MONKEYS.
IT'S A PERSONAL ACCOMPLISHMENT. DO YOU EVEN KNOW WHAT THAT MEANS, MONKEY GIRL?

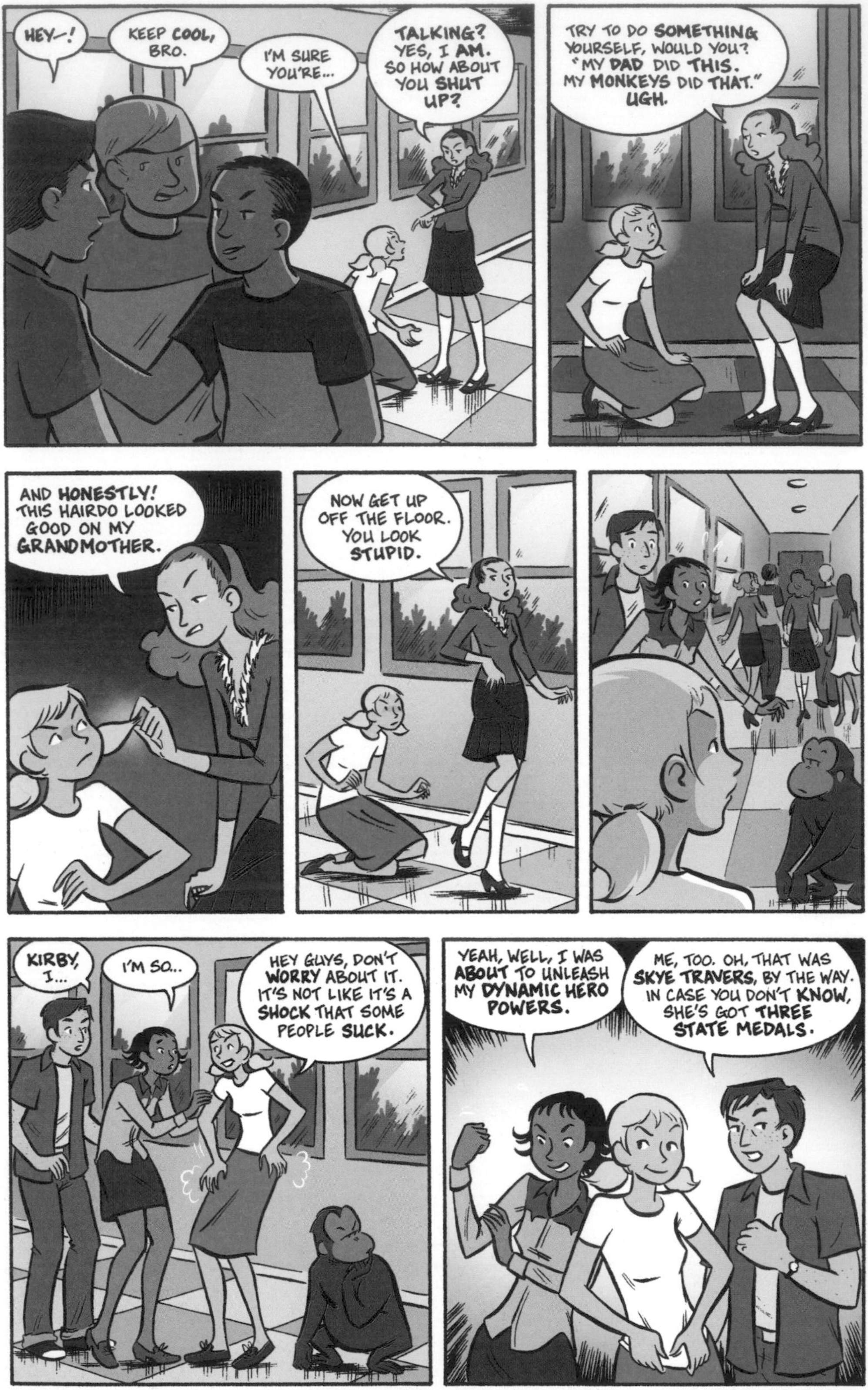
HEY—!
KEEP COOL, BRO.
I'M SURE YOU'RE...
TALKING? YES, I AM. SO HOW ABOUT YOU SHUT UP?
TRY TO DO SOMETHING YOURSELF, WOULD YOU? "MY DAD DID THIS. MY MONKEYS DID THAT." UGH.
AND HONESTLY! THIS HAIRDO LOOKED GOOD ON MY GRANDMOTHER.
NOW GET UP OFF THE FLOOR. YOU LOOK STUPID.
KIRBY, I...
I'M SO...
HEY GUYS, DON'T WORRY ABOUT IT. IT'S NOT LIKE IT'S A SHOCK THAT SOME PEOPLE SUCK.
YEAH, WELL, I WAS ABOUT TO UNLEASH MY DYNAMIC HERO POWERS.
ME, TOO. OH, THAT WAS SKYE TRAVERS, BY THE WAY. IN CASE YOU DON'T KNOW, SHE'S GOT THREE STATE MEDALS.

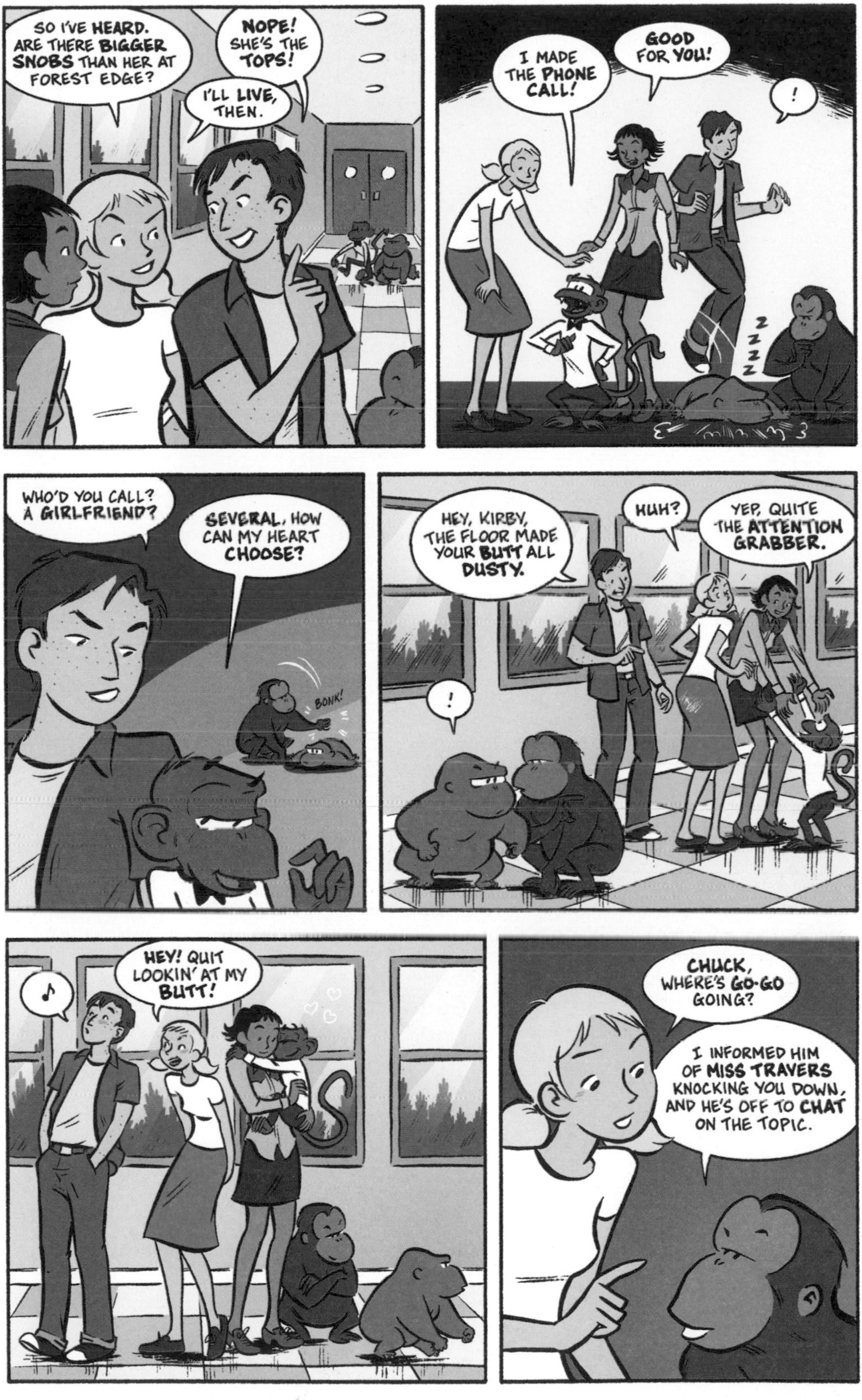
SO I'VE HEARD. ARE THERE BIGGER SNOBS THAN HER AT FOREST EDGE?
NOPE! SHE'S THE TOPS!
I'LL LIVE, THEN.
I MADE THE PHONE CALL!
GOOD FOR YOU!
!
WHO'D YOU CALL? A GIRLFRIEND?
SEVERAL. HOW CAN MY HEART CHOOSE?
BONK!
HEY, KIRBY, THE FLOOR MADE YOUR BUTT ALL DUSTY.
HUH?
YEP, QUITE THE ATTENTION GRABBER.
!
♪
HEY! QUIT LOOKIN' AT MY BUTT!
CHUCK, WHERE'S GO-GO GOING?
I INFORMED HIM OF MISS TRAVERS KNOCKING YOU DOWN, AND HE'S OFF TO CHAT ON THE TOPIC.

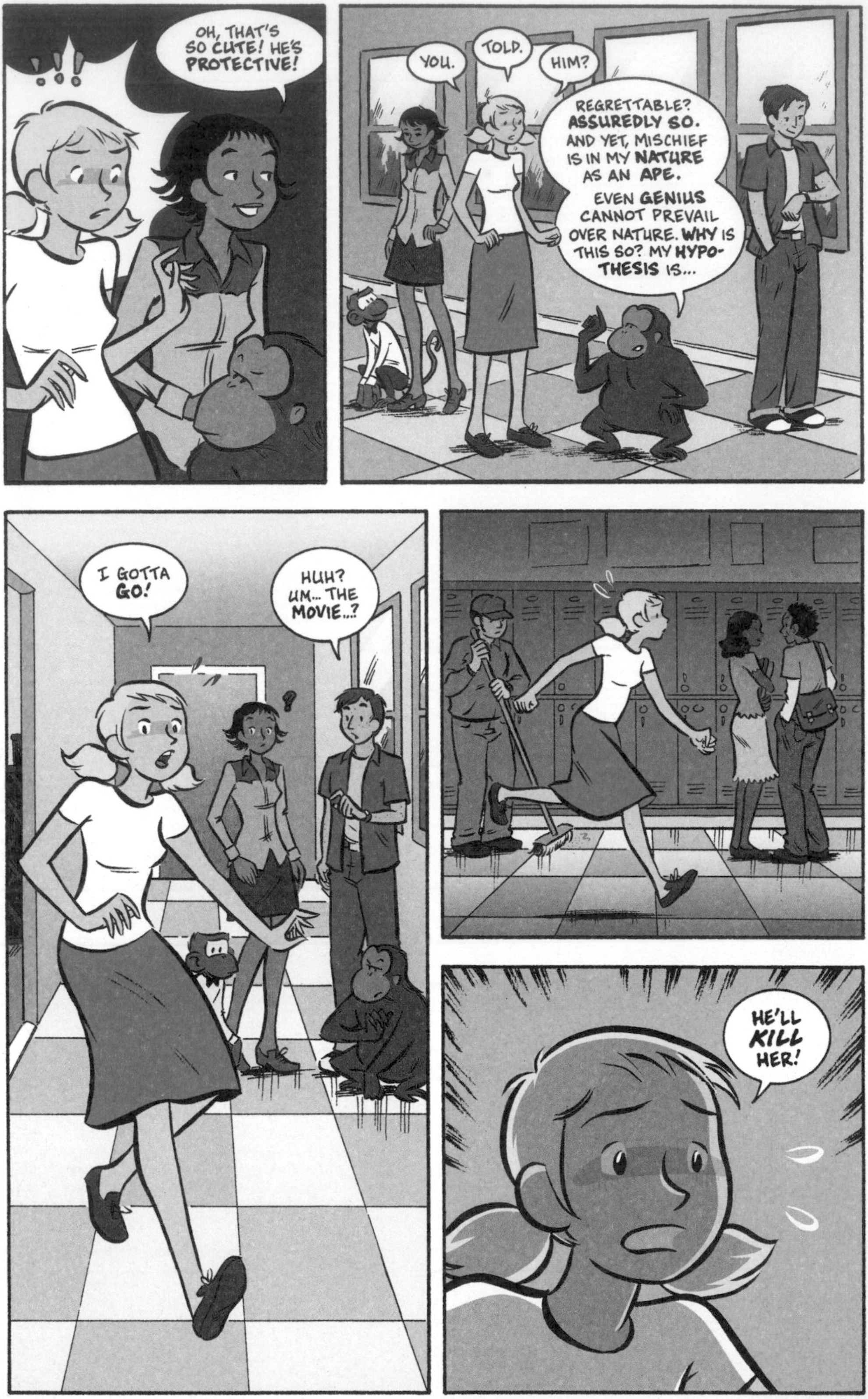
!!
OH, THAT'S SO CUTE! HE'S PROTECTIVE!
YOU.
TOLD.
HIM?
REGRETTABLE? ASSUREDLY SO. AND YET, MISCHIEF IS IN MY NATURE AS AN APE.
EVEN GENIUS CANNOT PREVAIL OVER NATURE. WHY IS THIS SO? MY HYPOTHESIS IS...
I GOTTA GO!
HUH? UM... THE MOVIE...?
?
HE'LL KILL HER!

CHAPTER THREE

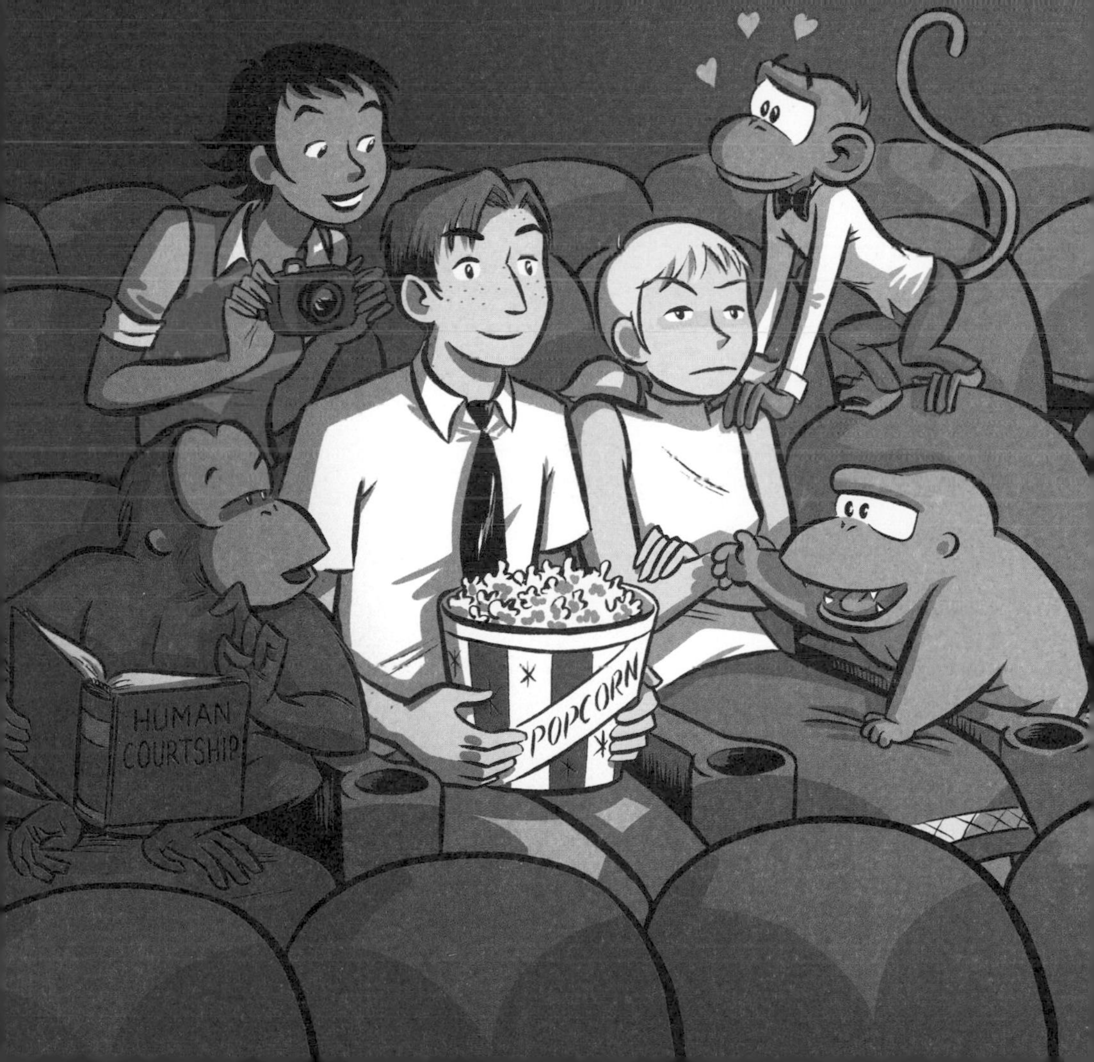
HUMAN COURTSHIP
POPCORN

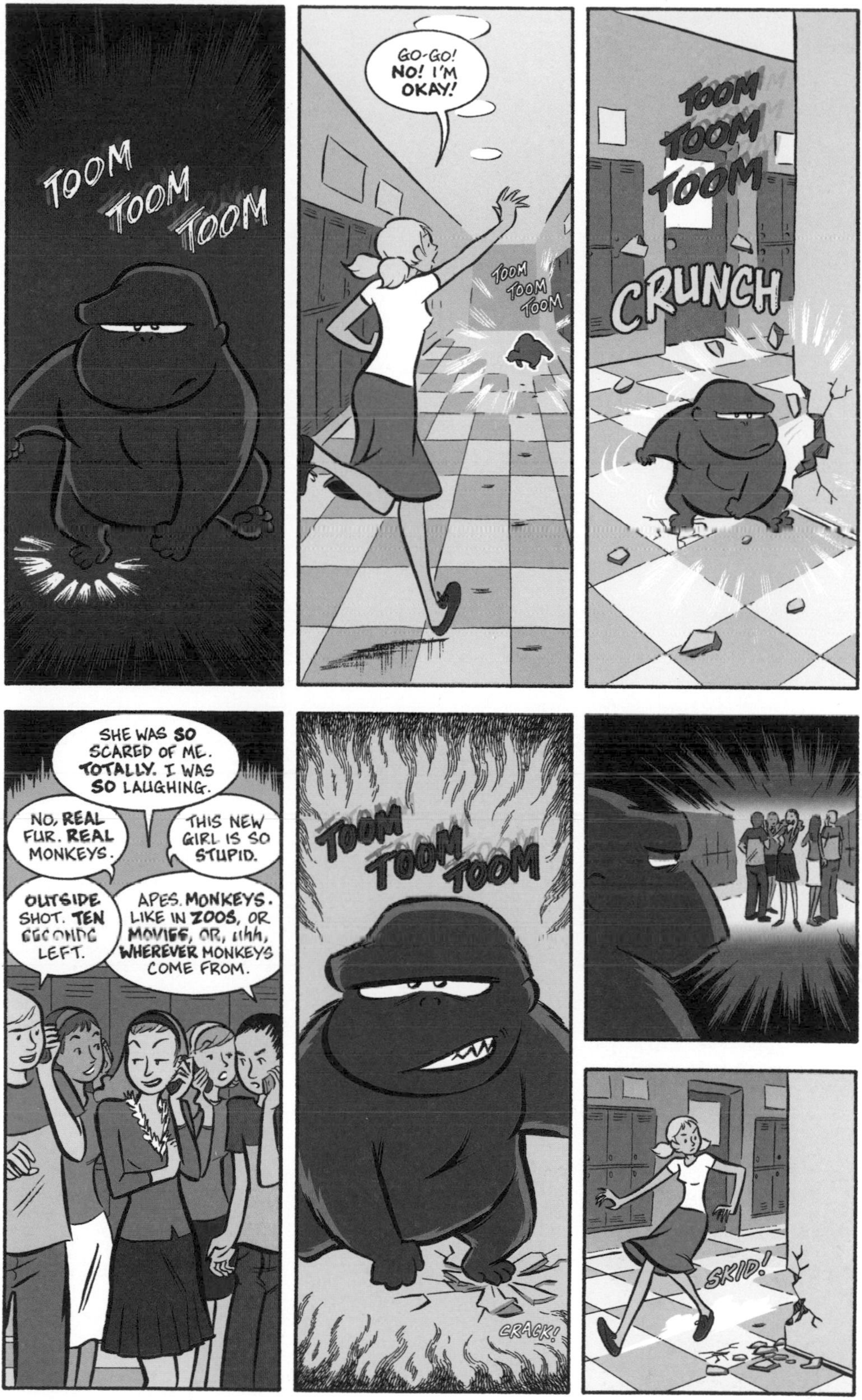
TOOM
TOOM
TOOM
GO-GO! NO! I'M OKAY!
TOOM
TOOM
TOOM
TOOM
TOOM
TOOM
CRUNCH
SHE WAS SO SCARED OF ME. TOTALLY. I WAS SO LAUGHING.
NO, REAL FUR. REAL MONKEYS.
THIS NEW GIRL IS SO STUPID.
OUTSIDE SHOT. TEN SECONDS LEFT.
APES. MONKEYS. LIKE IN ZOOS, OR MOVIES, OR, uhh, WHEREVER MONKEYS COME FROM.
TOOM
TOOM
TOOM
CRACK!
SKID!

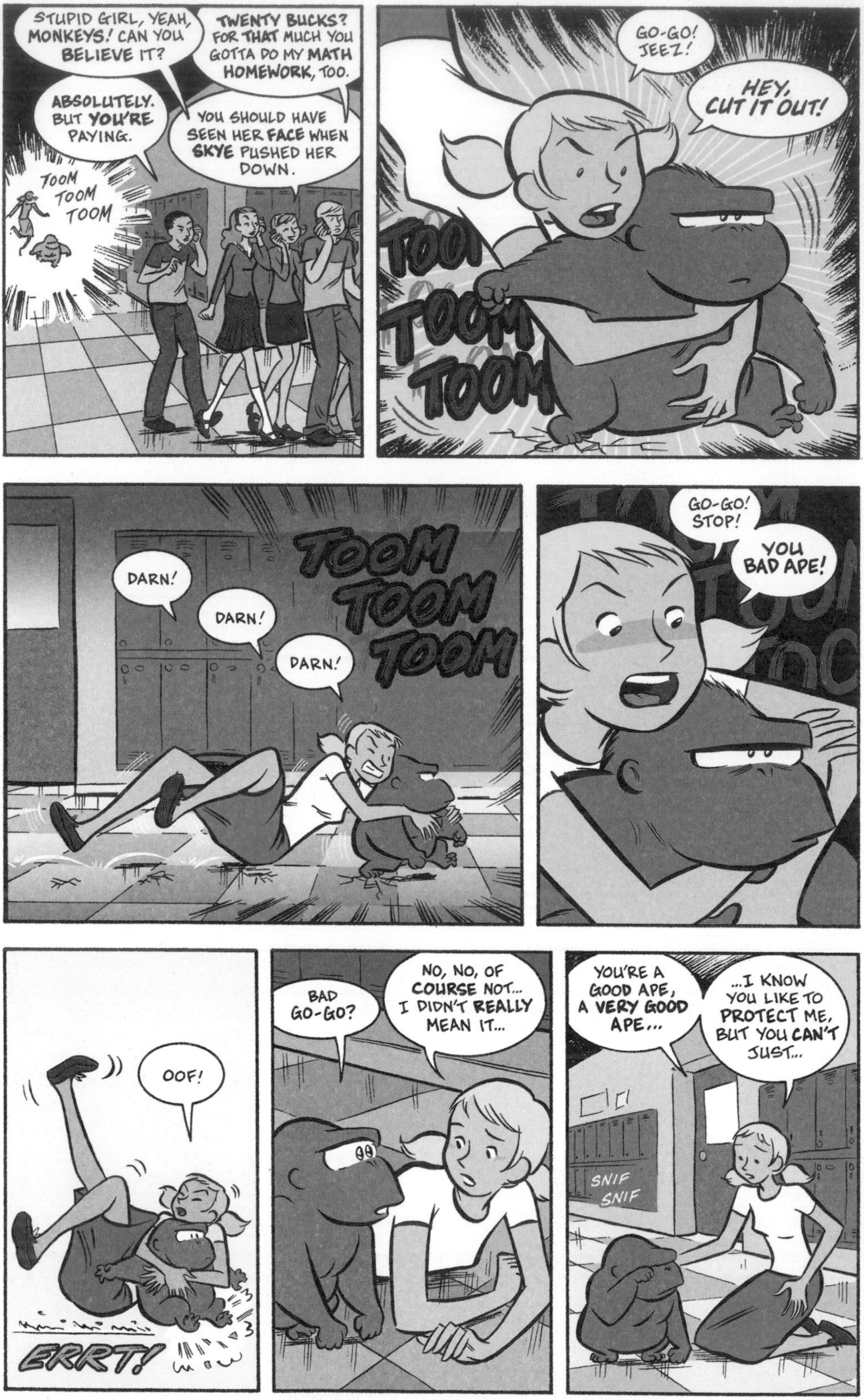
STUPID GIRL, YEAH, MONKEYS! CAN YOU BELIEVE IT?
TWENTY BUCKS? FOR THAT MUCH YOU GOTTA DO MY MATH HOMEWORK, TOO.
ABSOLUTELY. BUT YOU'RE PAYING.
YOU SHOULD HAVE SEEN HER FACE WHEN SKYE PUSHED HER DOWN.
TOOM TOOM TOOM
GO-GO! JEEZ!
HEY, CUT IT OUT!
TOOM TOOM TOOM
TOOM TOOM TOOM
DARN!
DARN!
DARN!
GO-GO! STOP!
YOU BAD APE!
OOF!
ERRT!
BAD GO-GO?
NO, NO, OF COURSE NOT... I DIDN'T REALLY MEAN IT...
YOU'RE A GOOD APE, A VERY GOOD APE...
...I KNOW YOU LIKE TO PROTECT ME, BUT YOU CAN'T JUST...
SNIF SNIF

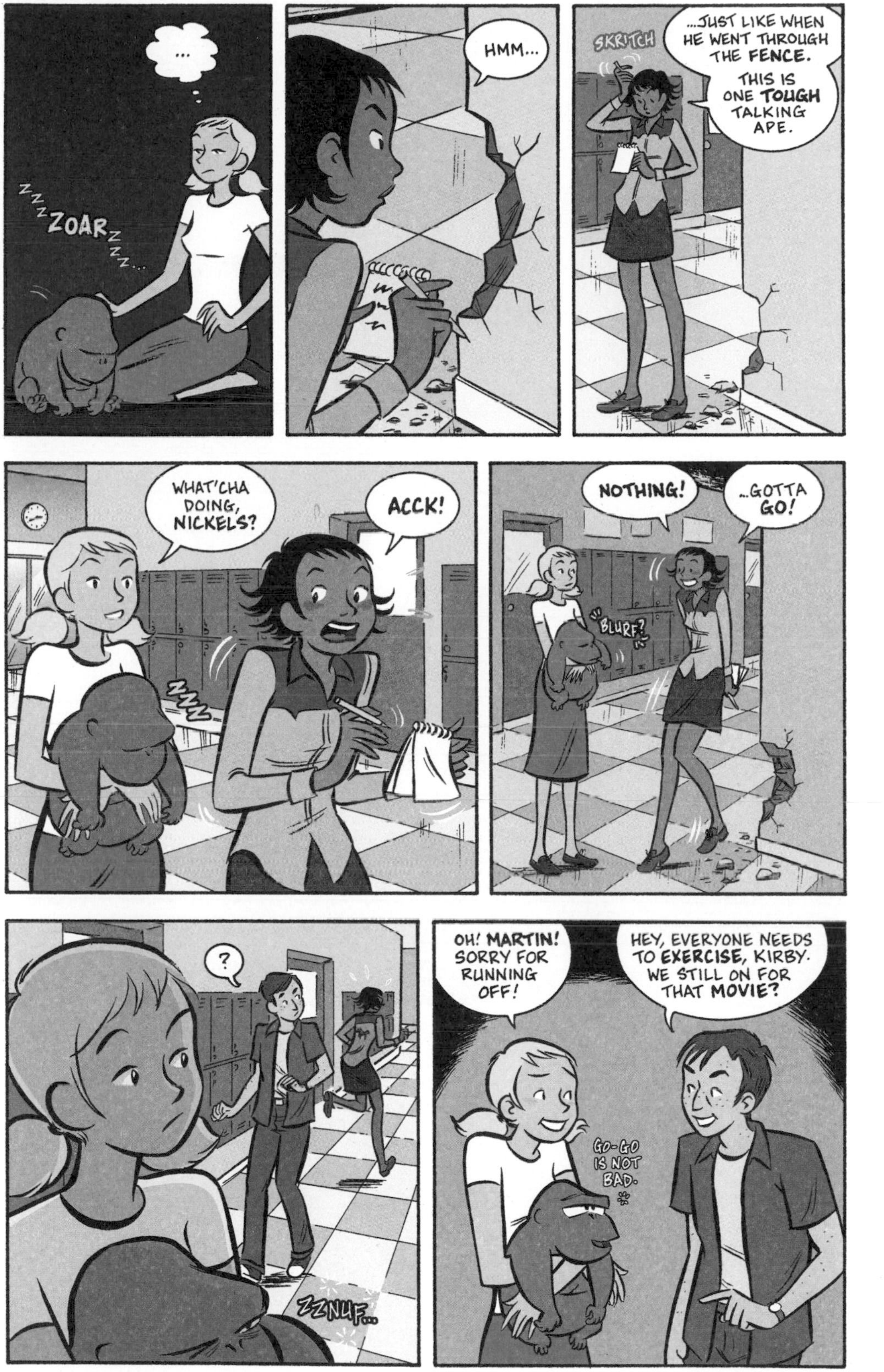
...
ZZZ ZOAR ZZZ...
HMM...
SKRITCH
...JUST LIKE WHEN HE WENT THROUGH THE FENCE.
THIS IS ONE TOUGH TALKING APE.
WHAT'CHA DOING, NICKELS?
ZZZ
ACCK!
NOTHING!
...GOTTA GO!
BLURF?
?
ZZNUF...
OH! MARTIN! SORRY FOR RUNNING OFF!
HEY, EVERYONE NEEDS TO EXERCISE, KIRBY. WE STILL ON FOR THAT MOVIE?
GO-GO IS NOT BAD.

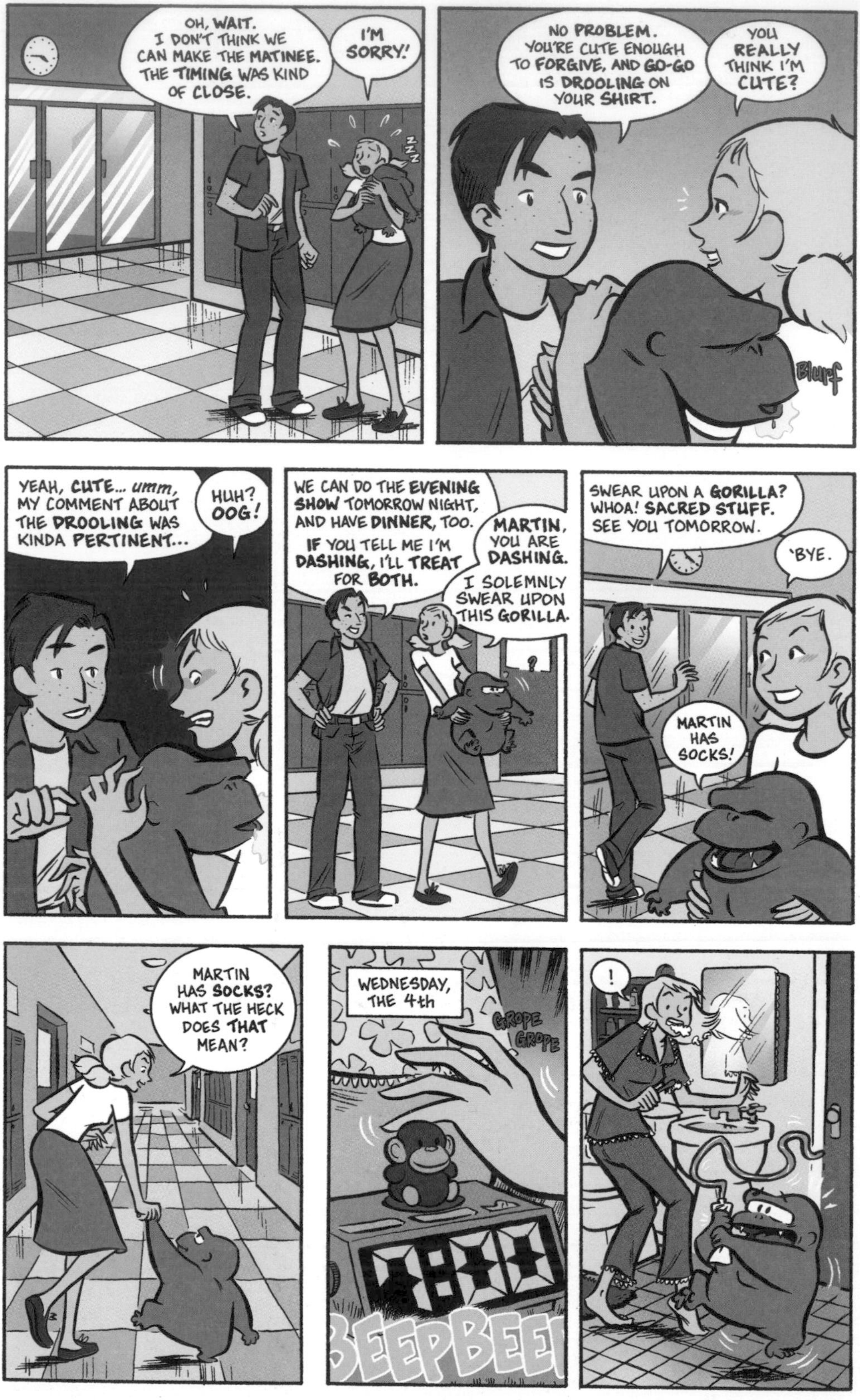
OH, WAIT. I DON'T THINK WE CAN MAKE THE MATINEE. THE TIMING WAS KIND OF CLOSE.
I'M SORRY!
ZZZ
NO PROBLEM. YOU'RE CUTE ENOUGH TO FORGIVE, AND GO-GO IS DROOLING ON YOUR SHIRT.
YOU REALLY THINK I'M CUTE?
Blurf
YEAH, CUTE... umm, MY COMMENT ABOUT THE DROOLING WAS KINDA PERTINENT...
HUH? OOG!
WE CAN DO THE EVENING SHOW TOMORROW NIGHT, AND HAVE DINNER, TOO.
IF YOU TELL ME I'M DASHING, I'LL TREAT FOR BOTH.
MARTIN, YOU ARE DASHING.
I SOLEMNLY SWEAR UPON THIS GORILLA.
SWEAR UPON A GORILLA? WHOA! SACRED STUFF. SEE YOU TOMORROW.
'BYE.
MARTIN HAS SOCKS!
MARTIN HAS SOCKS? WHAT THE HECK DOES THAT MEAN?
WEDNESDAY, THE 4th
GROPE GROPE
BEEPBEEP
!

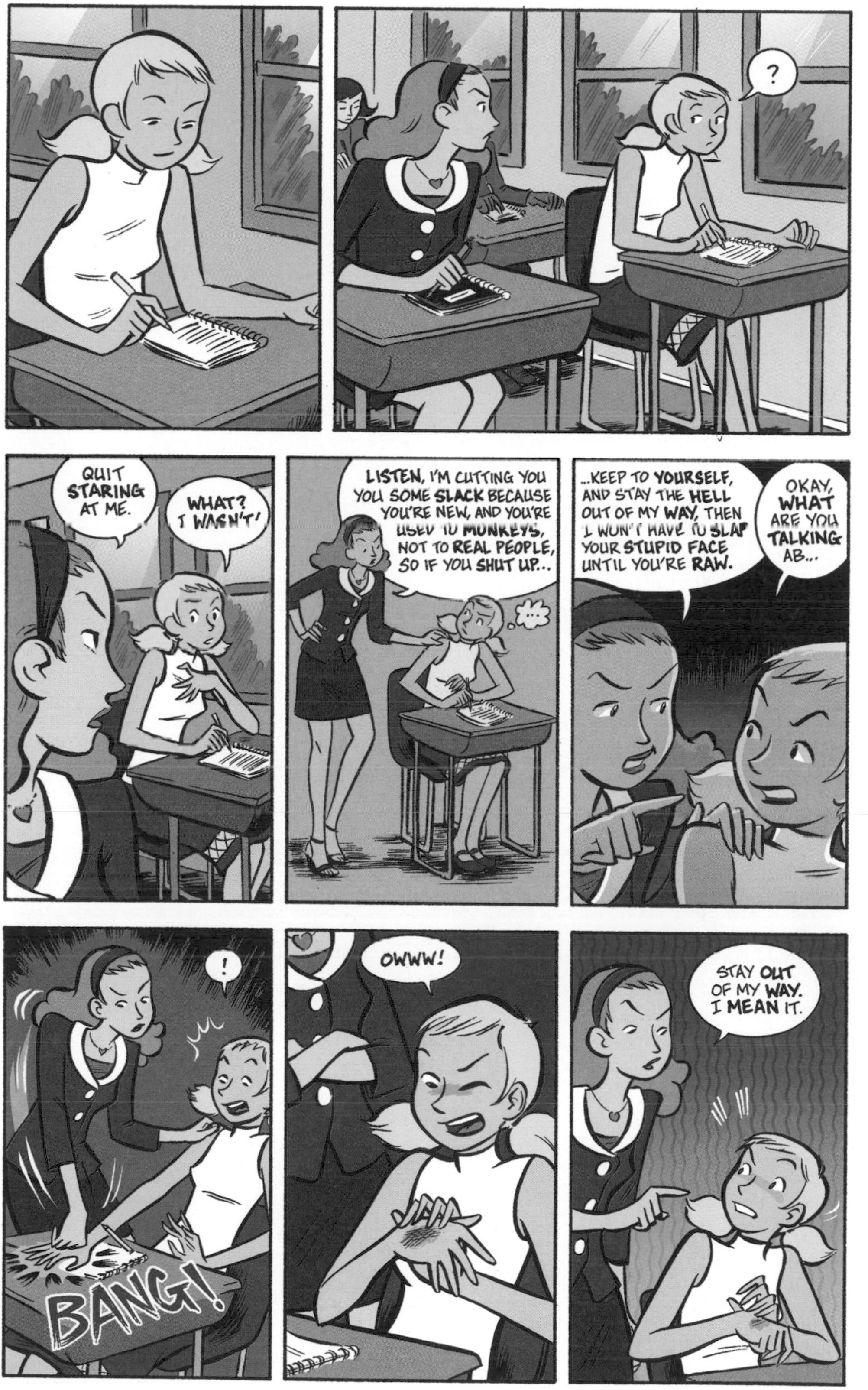
?
QUIT STARING AT ME.
WHAT? I WASN'T!
LISTEN, I'M CUTTING YOU YOU SOME SLACK BECAUSE YOU'RE NEW, AND YOU'RE USED TO MONKEYS, NOT TO REAL PEOPLE, SO IF YOU SHUT UP...
...KEEP TO YOURSELF, AND STAY THE HELL OUT OF MY WAY, THEN I WON'T HAVE TO SLAP YOUR STUPID FACE UNTIL YOU'RE RAW.
OKAY, WHAT ARE YOU TALKING AB...
!
BANG!
OWWW!
STAY OUT OF MY WAY. I MEAN IT.

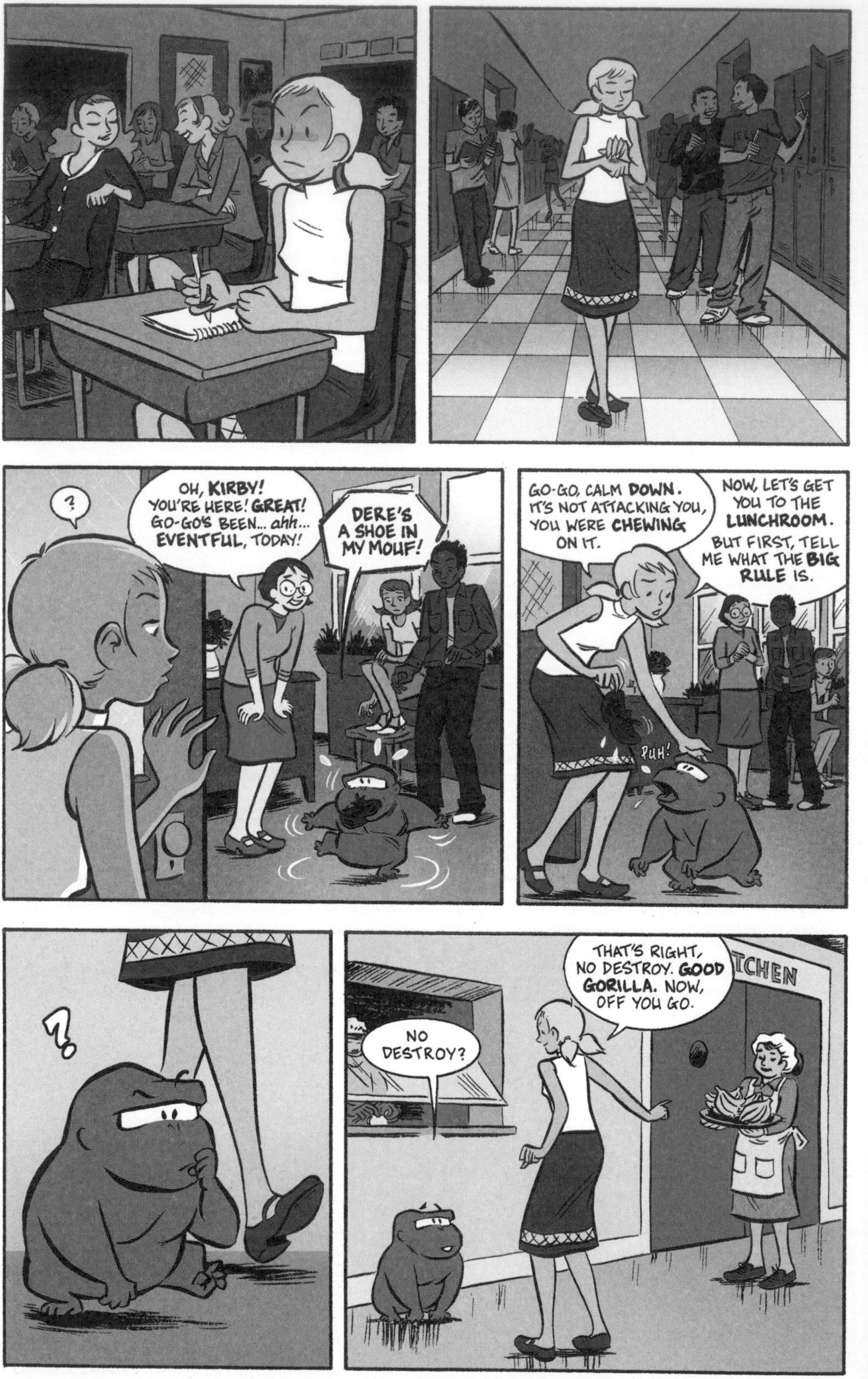
?
OH, KIRBY! YOU'RE HERE! GREAT! GO-GO'S BEEN... ahh... EVENTFUL, TODAY!
DERE'S A SHOE IN MY MOUF!
GO-GO, CALM DOWN. IT'S NOT ATTACKING YOU, YOU WERE CHEWING ON IT.
NOW, LET'S GET YOU TO THE LUNCHROOM. BUT FIRST, TELL ME WHAT THE BIG RULE IS.
PUH!
?
NO DESTROY?
THAT'S RIGHT, NO DESTROY. GOOD GORILLA. NOW, OFF YOU GO.
TCHEN

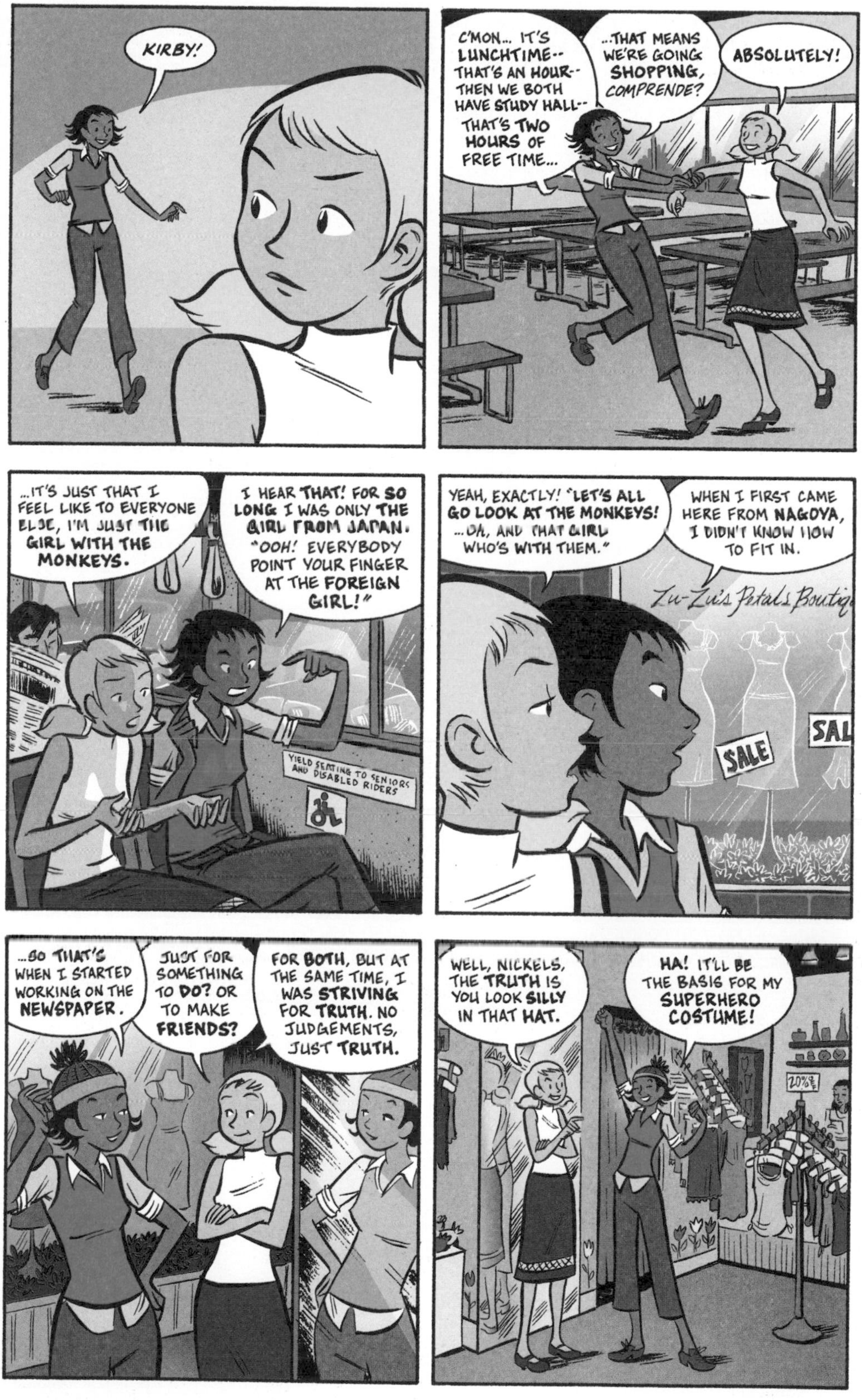
KIRBY!
C'MON... IT'S LUNCHTIME-- THAT'S AN HOUR-- THEN WE BOTH HAVE STUDY HALL-- THAT'S TWO HOURS OF FREE TIME...
...THAT MEANS WE'RE GOING SHOPPING, COMPRENDE?
ABSOLUTELY!
...IT'S JUST THAT I FEEL LIKE TO EVERYONE ELSE, I'M JUST THE GIRL WITH THE MONKEYS.
I HEAR THAT! FOR SO LONG I WAS ONLY THE GIRL FROM JAPAN. "OOH! EVERYBODY POINT YOUR FINGER AT THE FOREIGN GIRL!"
YIELD SEATING TO SENIORS AND DISABLED RIDERS
YEAH, EXACTLY! "LET'S ALL GO LOOK AT THE MONKEYS! ...OH, AND THAT GIRL WHO'S WITH THEM."
WHEN I FIRST CAME HERE FROM NAGOYA, I DIDN'T KNOW HOW TO FIT IN.
Zu-Zu's Petals Boutiq
SALE
SAL
...SO THAT'S WHEN I STARTED WORKING ON THE NEWSPAPER.
JUST FOR SOMETHING TO DO? OR TO MAKE FRIENDS?
FOR BOTH, BUT AT THE SAME TIME, I WAS STRIVING FOR TRUTH. NO JUDGEMENTS, JUST TRUTH.
WELL, NICKELS, THE TRUTH IS YOU LOOK SILLY IN THAT HAT.
HA! IT'LL BE THE BASIS FOR MY SUPERHERO COSTUME!
20%

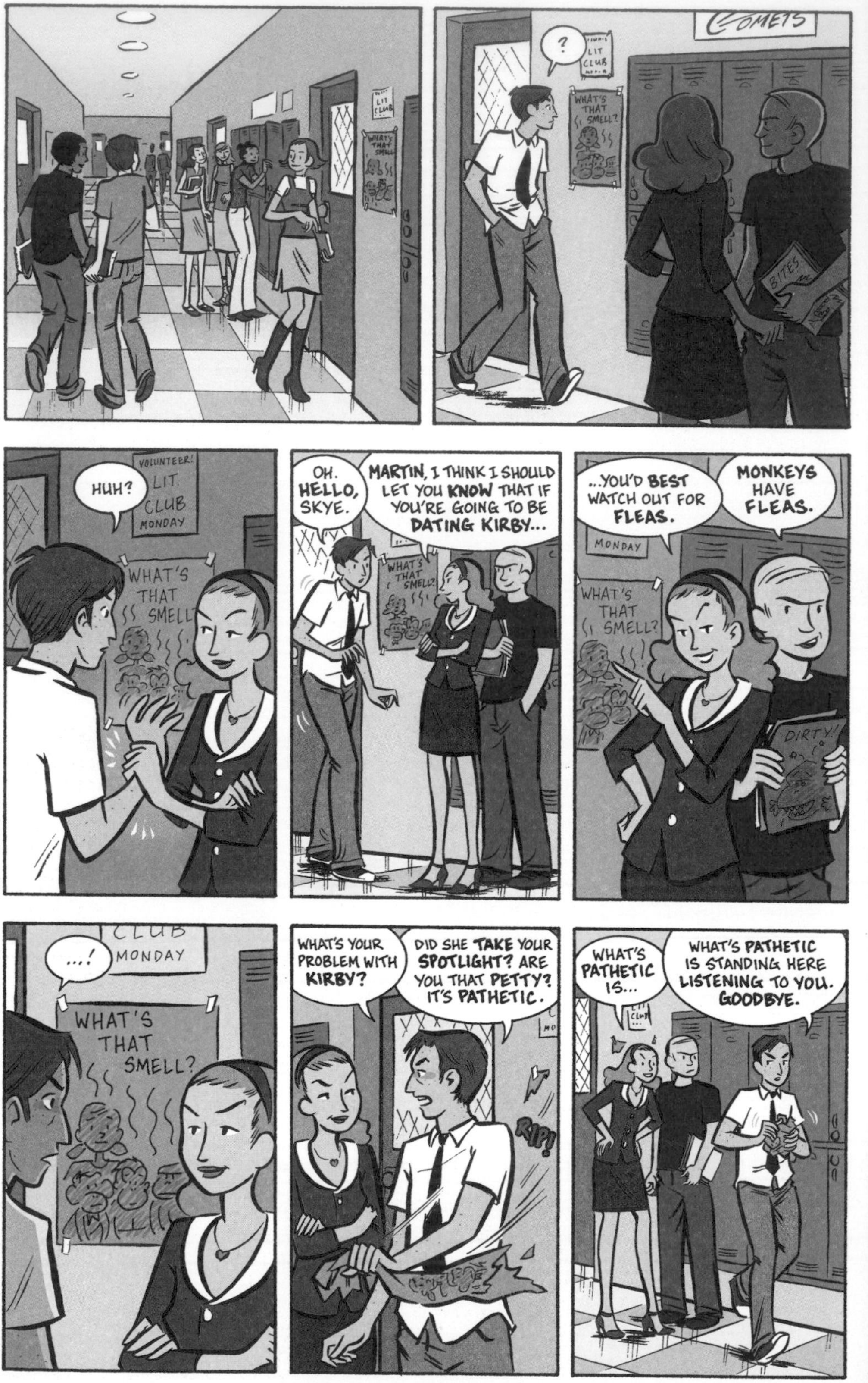
COMETS
?
LIT CLUB
WHAT'S THAT SMELL?
HUH?
VOLUNTEER! LIT CLUB MONDAY
WHAT'S THAT SMELL
OH. HELLO, SKYE.
MARTIN, I THINK I SHOULD LET YOU KNOW THAT IF YOU'RE GOING TO BE DATING KIRBY...
...YOU'D BEST WATCH OUT FOR FLEAS.
MONKEYS HAVE FLEAS.
MONDAY
WHAT'S THAT SMELL?
DIRTY!
...!
CLUB MONDAY
WHAT'S THAT SMELL?
WHAT'S YOUR PROBLEM WITH KIRBY?
DID SHE TAKE YOUR SPOTLIGHT? ARE YOU THAT PETTY? IT'S PATHETIC.
RIP!
WHAT'S PATHETIC IS...
WHAT'S PATHETIC IS STANDING HERE LISTENING TO YOU. GOODBYE.

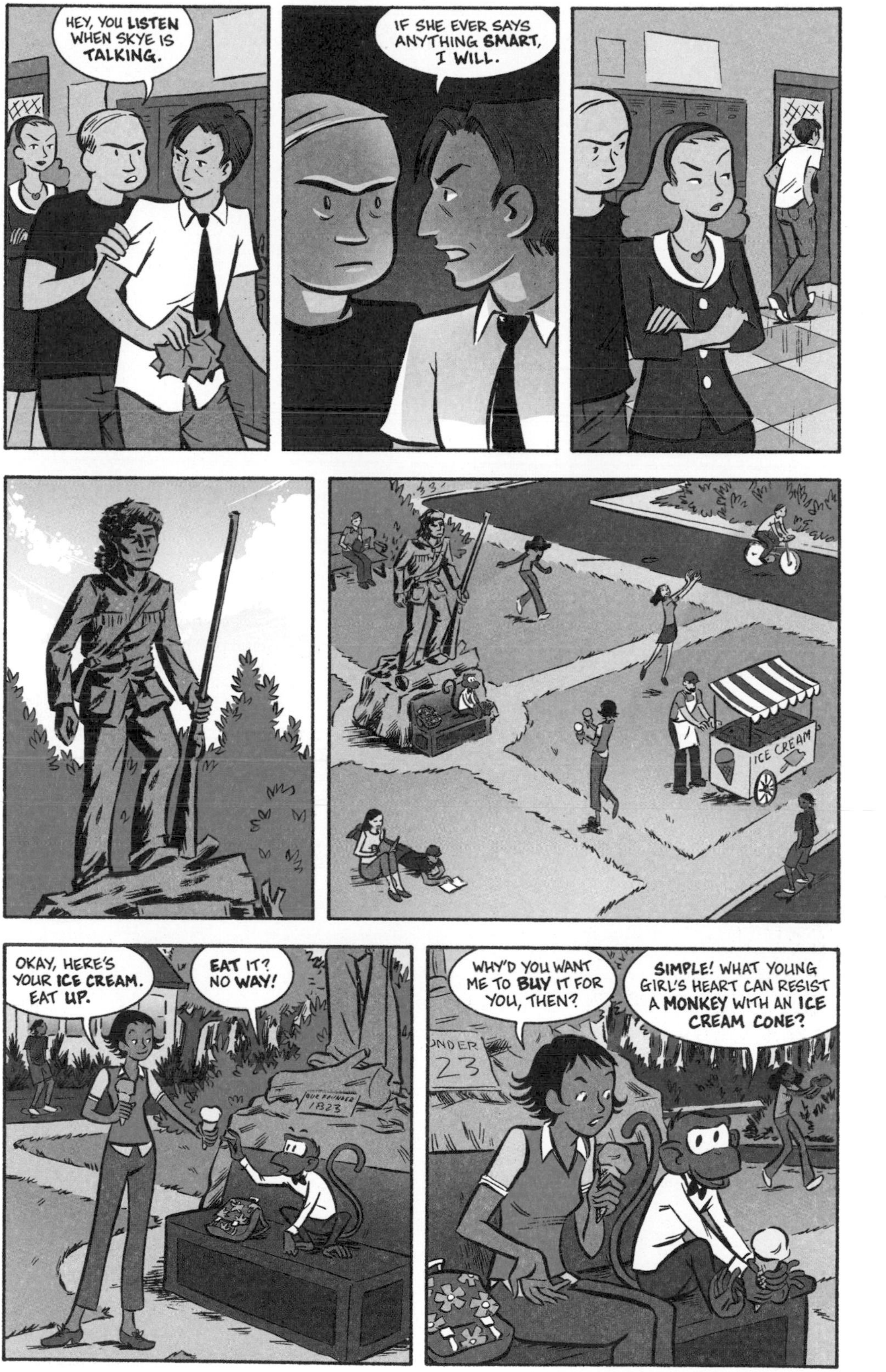
HEY, YOU **LISTEN** WHEN SKYE IS **TALKING**.
IF SHE EVER SAYS ANYTHING **SMART**, I **WILL**.
ICE CREAM
OUR FOUNDER 1823
OKAY, HERE'S YOUR **ICE CREAM**. EAT **UP**.
EAT IT? NO **WAY**!
WHY'D YOU WANT ME TO **BUY** IT FOR YOU, THEN?
SIMPLE! WHAT YOUNG GIRL'S HEART CAN RESIST A **MONKEY** WITH AN **ICE CREAM CONE**?

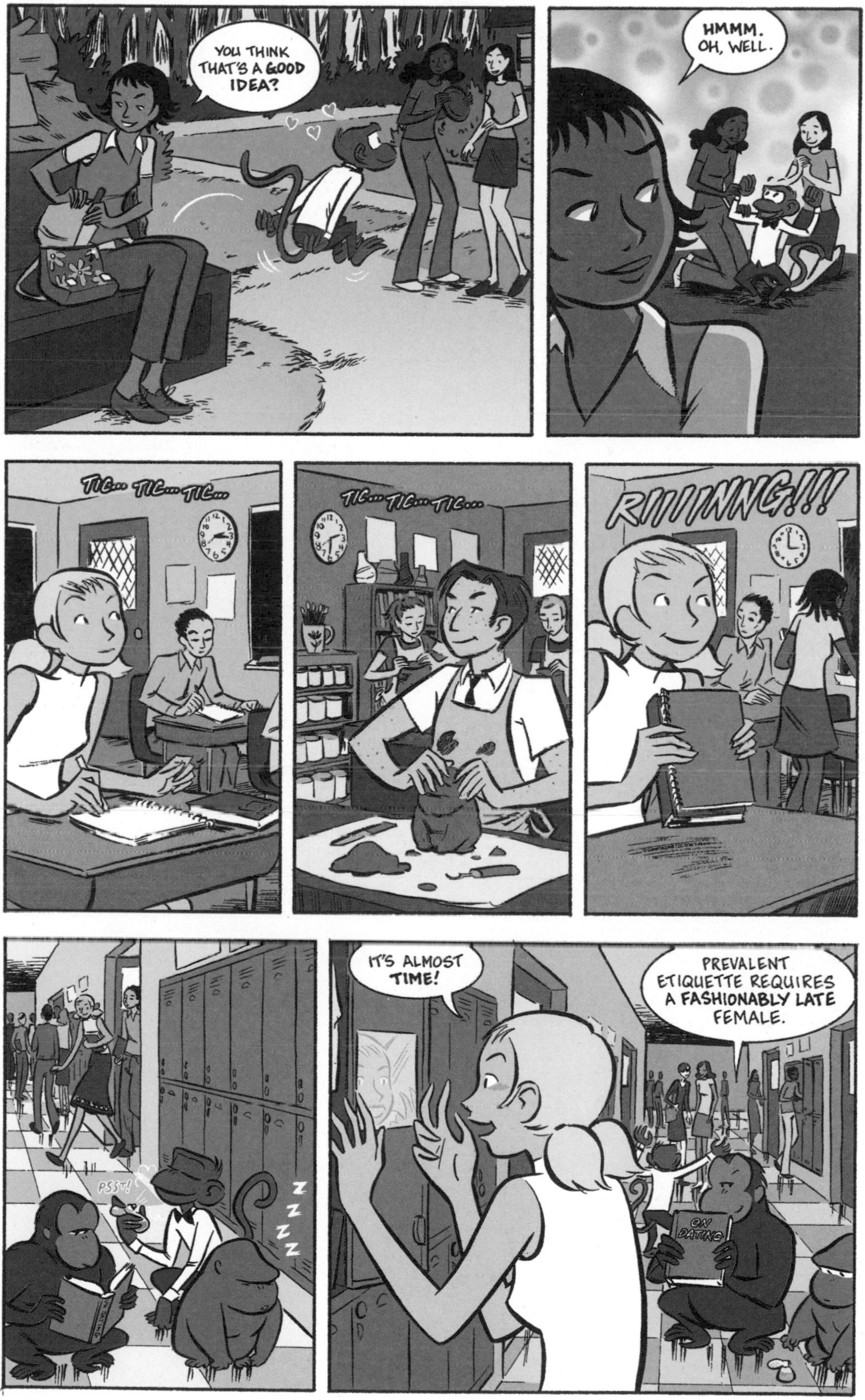
YOU THINK THAT'S A GOOD IDEA?
HMMM. OH, WELL.
TIC... TIC... TIC...
TIC... TIC... TIC...
RIIIINNG!!!
PSST!
Z Z Z Z
IT'S ALMOST TIME!
PREVALENT ETIQUETTE REQUIRES A FASHIONABLY LATE FEMALE.
ON DATING

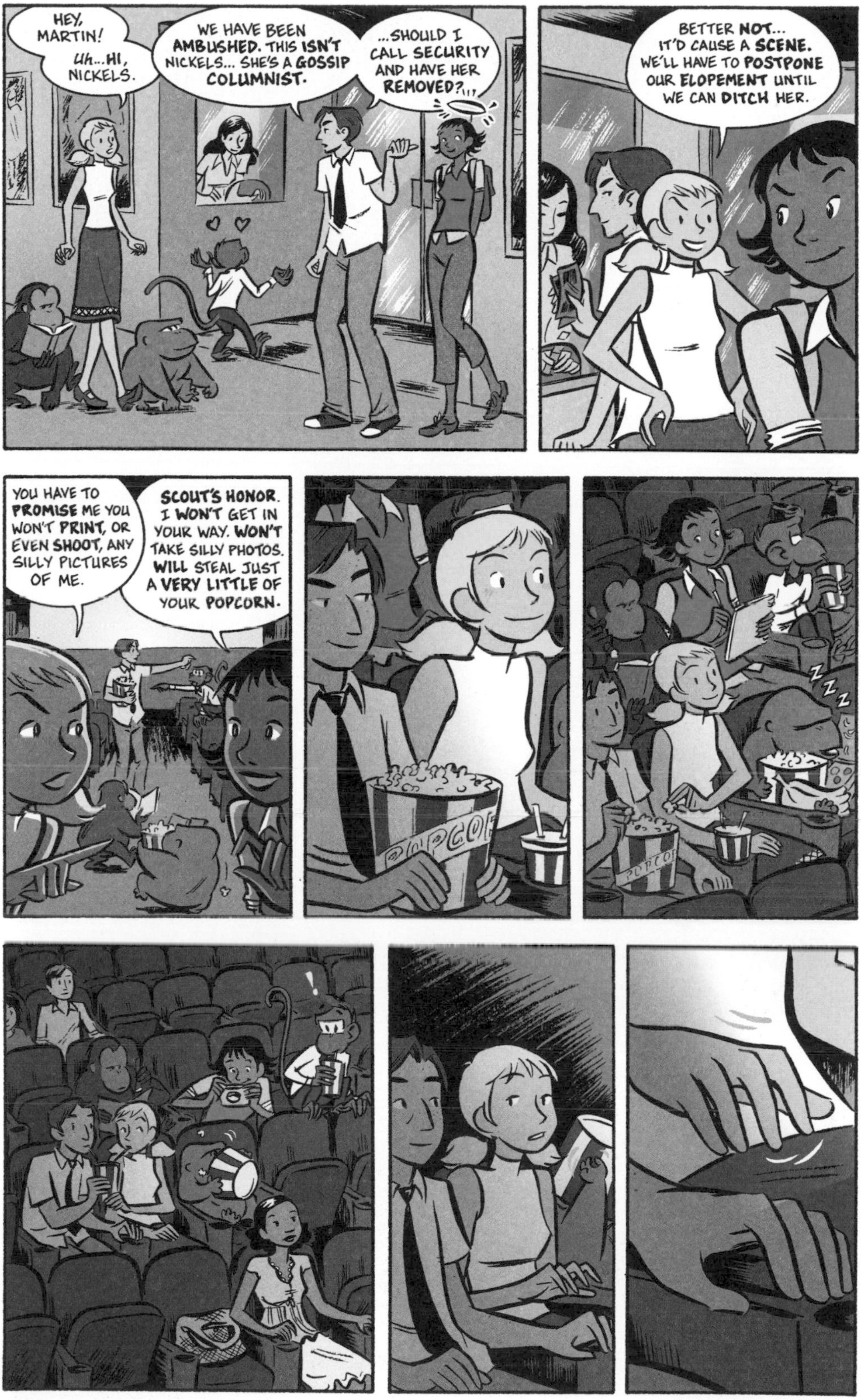
HEY, MARTIN!
Uh...HI, NICKELS.
WE HAVE BEEN AMBUSHED. THIS ISN'T NICKELS... SHE'S A GOSSIP COLUMNIST.
...SHOULD I CALL SECURITY AND HAVE HER REMOVED?
BETTER NOT... IT'D CAUSE A SCENE. WE'LL HAVE TO POSTPONE OUR ELOPEMENT UNTIL WE CAN DITCH HER.
YOU HAVE TO PROMISE ME YOU WON'T PRINT, OR EVEN SHOOT, ANY SILLY PICTURES OF ME.
SCOUT'S HONOR. I WON'T GET IN YOUR WAY. WON'T TAKE SILLY PHOTOS. WILL STEAL JUST A VERY LITTLE OF YOUR POPCORN.
ZZZ

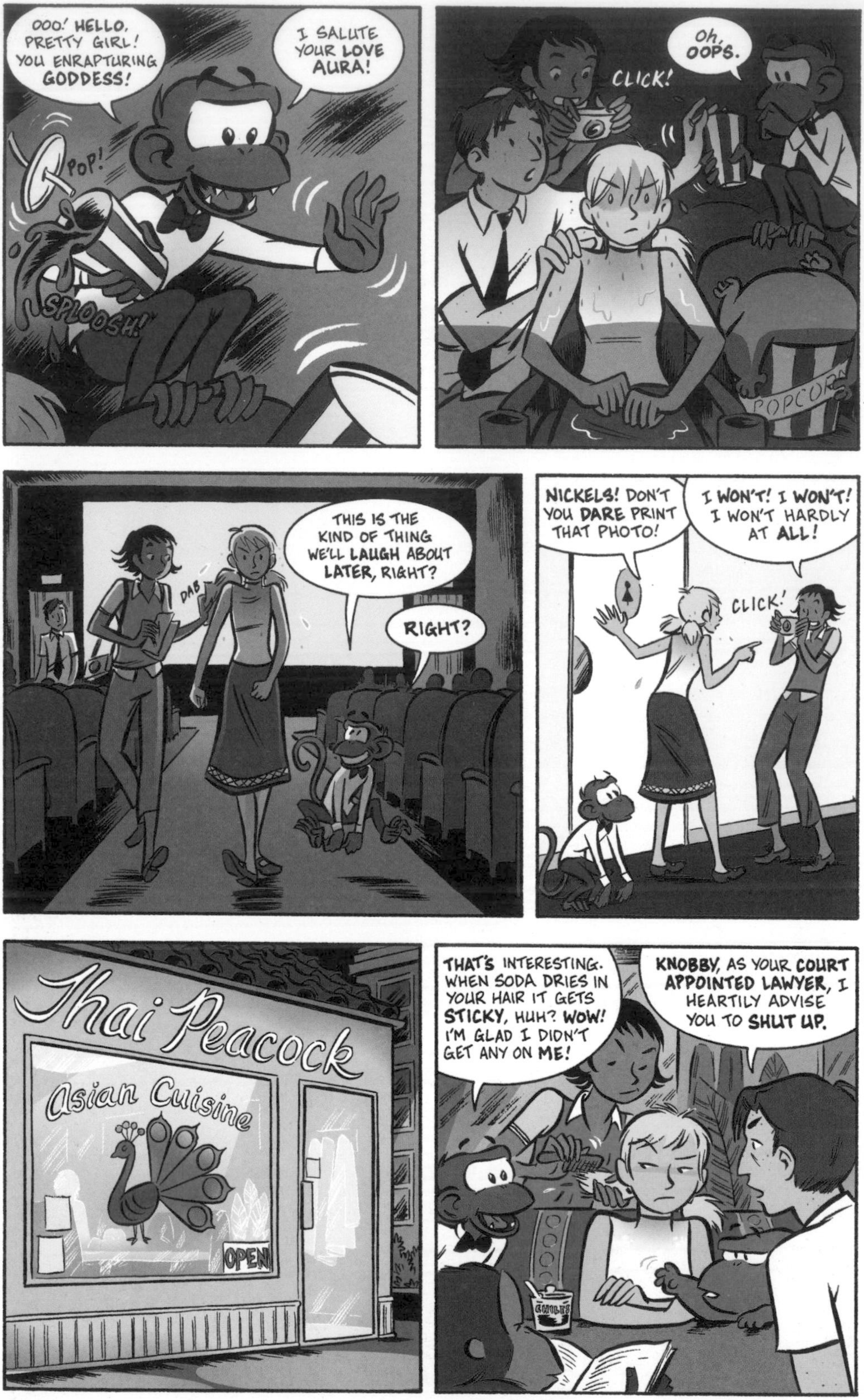
OOO! HELLO, PRETTY GIRL! YOU ENRAPTURING GODDESS!
I SALUTE YOUR LOVE AURA!
POP!
SPLOOSH!
Oh, OOPS.
CLICK!
POPCORN
THIS IS THE KIND OF THING WE'LL LAUGH ABOUT LATER, RIGHT?
RIGHT?
DAB
NICKELS! DON'T YOU DARE PRINT THAT PHOTO!
I WON'T! I WON'T! I WON'T HARDLY AT ALL!
CLICK!
Thai Peacock
Asian Cuisine
OPEN
THAT'S INTERESTING. WHEN SODA DRIES IN YOUR HAIR IT GETS STICKY, HUH? WOW! I'M GLAD I DIDN'T GET ANY ON ME!
KNOBBY, AS YOUR COURT APPOINTED LAWYER, I HEARTILY ADVISE YOU TO SHUT UP.

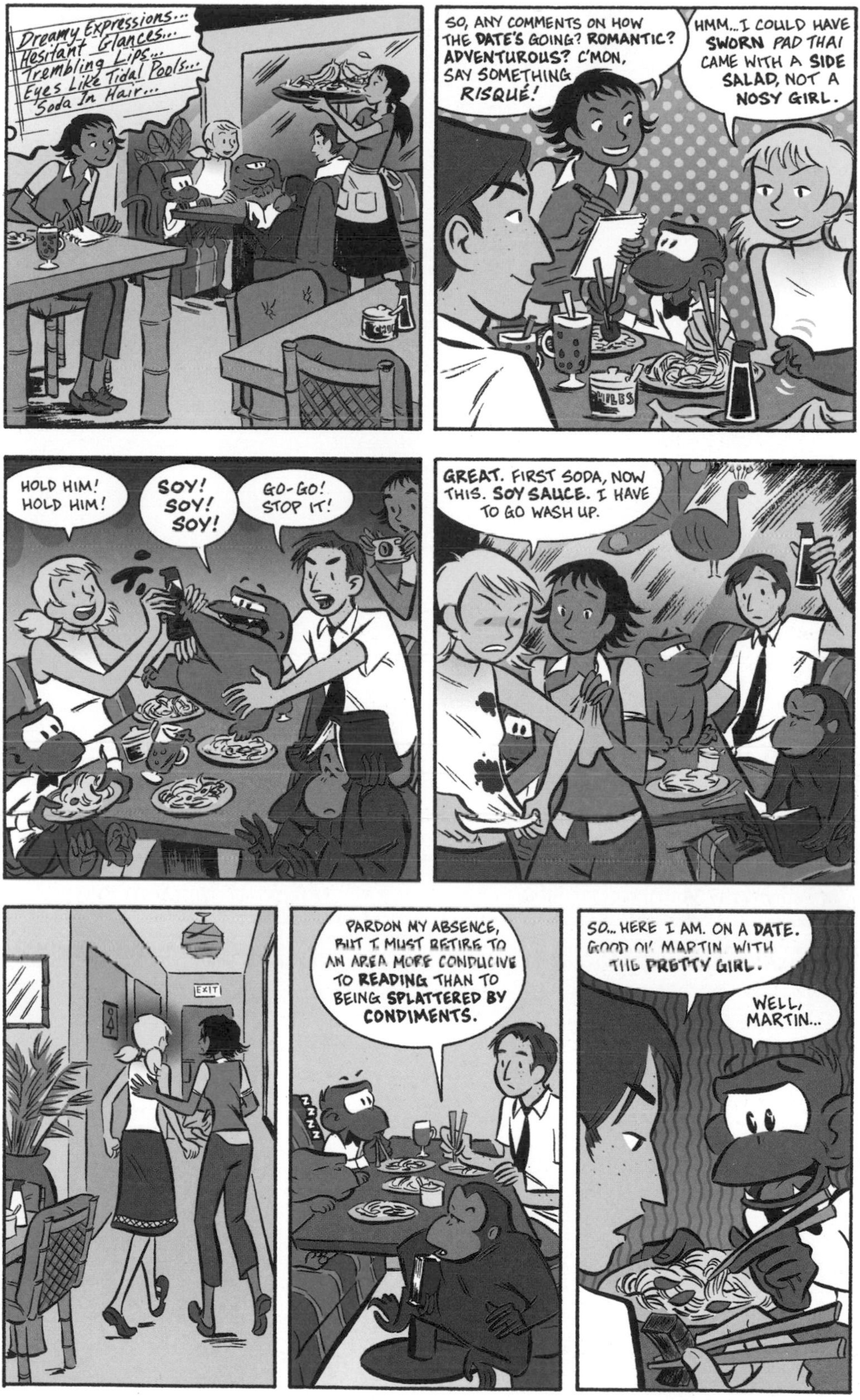

Dreamy Expressions... Hesitant Glances... Trembling Lips... Eyes Like Tidal Pools... Soda In Hair...
SO, ANY COMMENTS ON HOW THE DATE'S GOING? ROMANTIC? ADVENTUROUS? C'MON, SAY SOMETHING RISQUÉ!
HMM... I COULD HAVE SWORN PAD THAI CAME WITH A SIDE SALAD, NOT A NOSY GIRL.
HOLD HIM! HOLD HIM!
SOY! SOY! SOY!
GO-GO! STOP IT!
GREAT. FIRST SODA, NOW THIS. SOY SAUCE. I HAVE TO GO WASH UP.
EXIT
PARDON MY ABSENCE, BUT I MUST RETIRE TO AN AREA MORE CONDUCIVE TO READING THAN TO BEING SPLATTERED BY CONDIMENTS.
SO... HERE I AM. ON A DATE. GOOD OL' MARTIN. WITH THE PRETTY GIRL.
WELL, MARTIN...

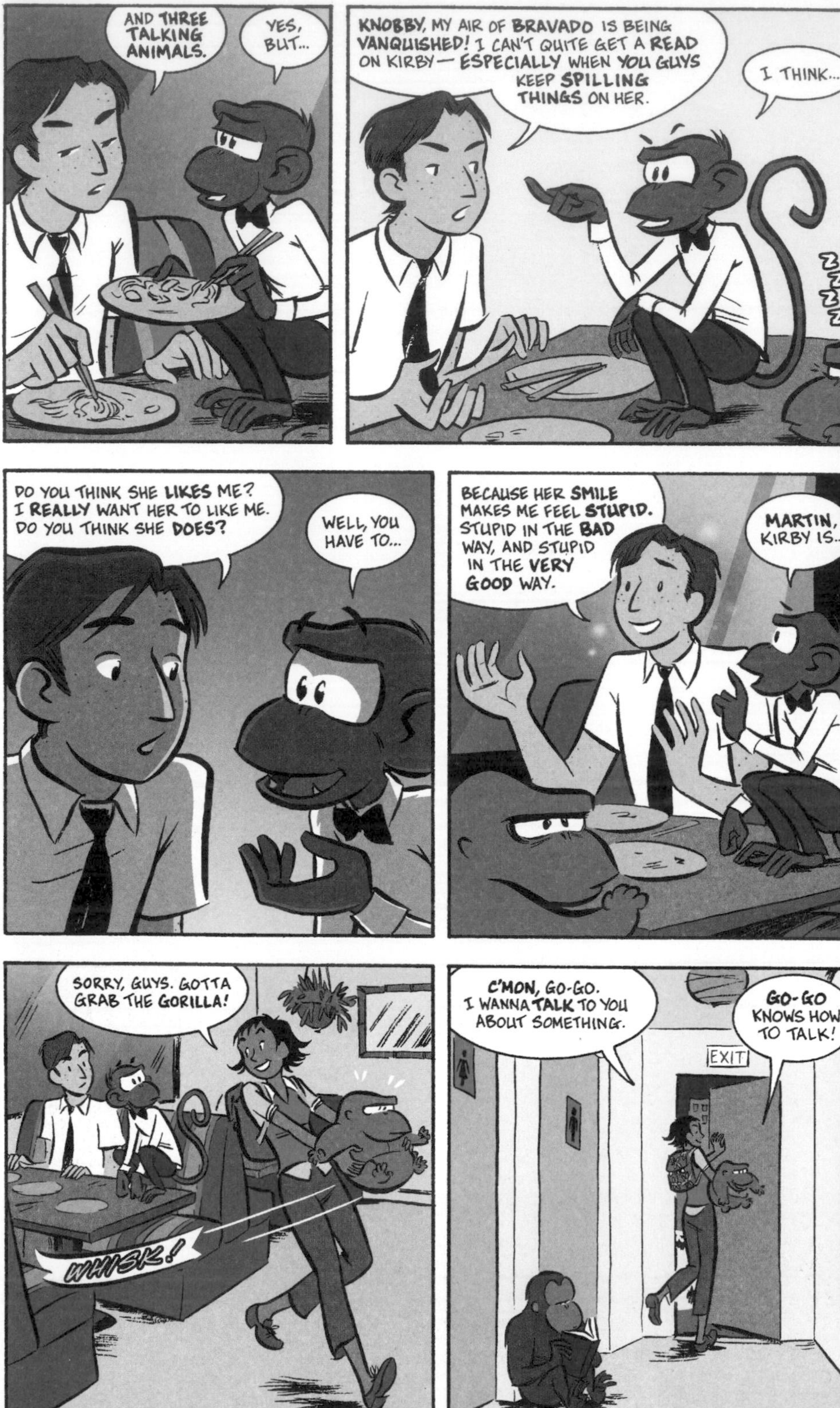

AND THREE TALKING ANIMALS.
YES, BUT...
KNOBBY, MY AIR OF BRAVADO IS BEING VANQUISHED! I CAN'T QUITE GET A READ ON KIRBY — ESPECIALLY WHEN YOU GUYS KEEP SPILLING THINGS ON HER.
I THINK...
ZZZZ
DO YOU THINK SHE LIKES ME? I REALLY WANT HER TO LIKE ME. DO YOU THINK SHE DOES?
WELL, YOU HAVE TO...
BECAUSE HER SMILE MAKES ME FEEL STUPID. STUPID IN THE BAD WAY, AND STUPID IN THE VERY GOOD WAY.
MARTIN, KIRBY IS...
SORRY, GUYS. GOTTA GRAB THE GORILLA!
WHISK!
C'MON, GO-GO. I WANNA TALK TO YOU ABOUT SOMETHING.
EXIT
GO-GO KNOWS HOW TO TALK!

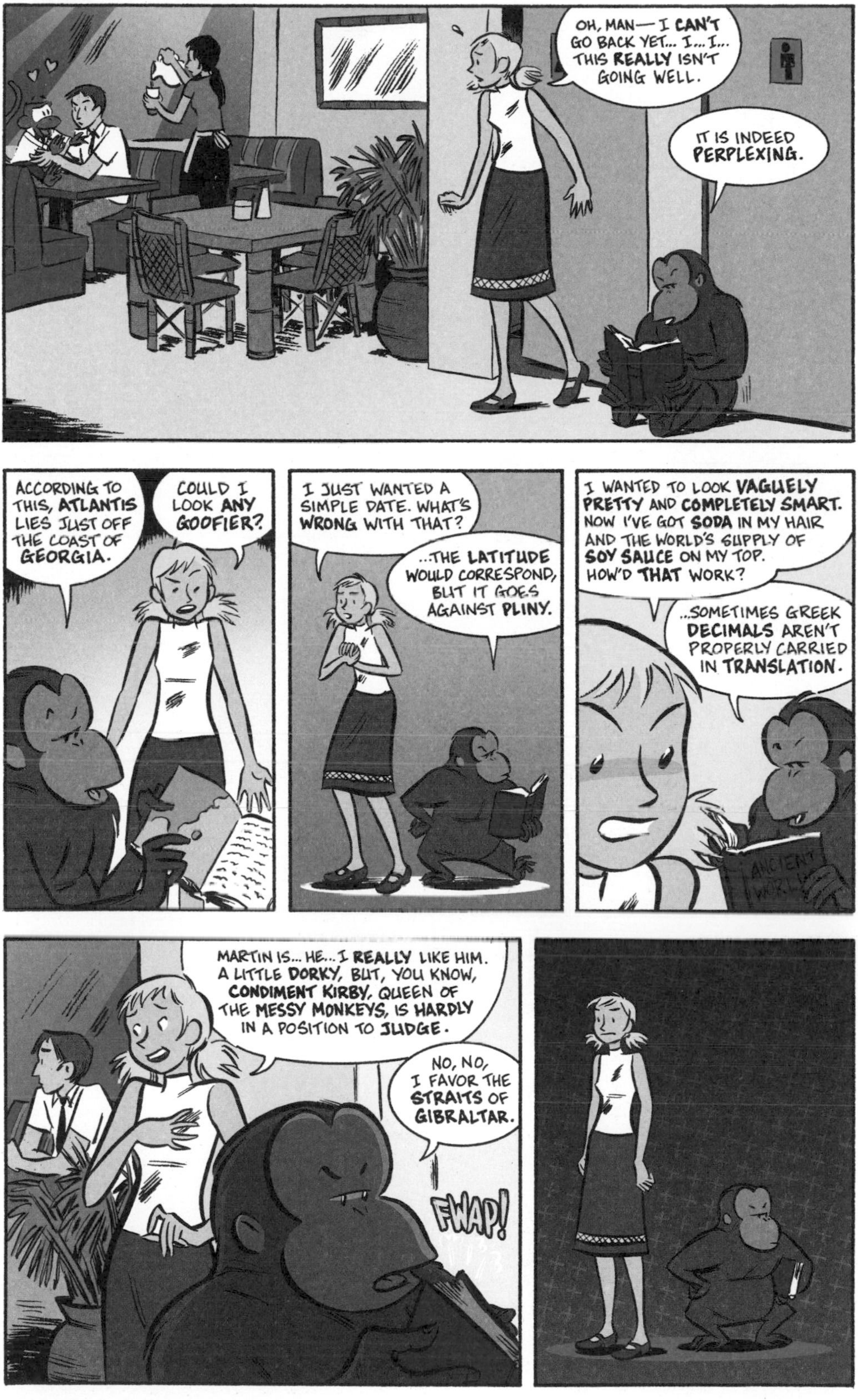
OH, MAN— I CAN'T GO BACK YET... I... I... THIS REALLY ISN'T GOING WELL.
IT IS INDEED PERPLEXING.
ACCORDING TO THIS, ATLANTIS LIES JUST OFF THE COAST OF GEORGIA.
COULD I LOOK ANY GOOFIER?
I JUST WANTED A SIMPLE DATE. WHAT'S WRONG WITH THAT?
...THE LATITUDE WOULD CORRESPOND, BUT IT GOES AGAINST PLINY.
I WANTED TO LOOK VAGUELY PRETTY AND COMPLETELY SMART. NOW I'VE GOT SODA IN MY HAIR AND THE WORLD'S SUPPLY OF SOY SAUCE ON MY TOP. HOW'D THAT WORK?
...SOMETIMES GREEK DECIMALS AREN'T PROPERLY CARRIED IN TRANSLATION.
ANCIENT WORLD
MARTIN IS... HE... I REALLY LIKE HIM. A LITTLE DORKY, BUT, YOU KNOW, CONDIMENT KIRBY, QUEEN OF THE MESSY MONKEYS, IS HARDLY IN A POSITION TO JUDGE.
NO, NO, I FAVOR THE STRAITS OF GIBRALTAR.
FWAP!

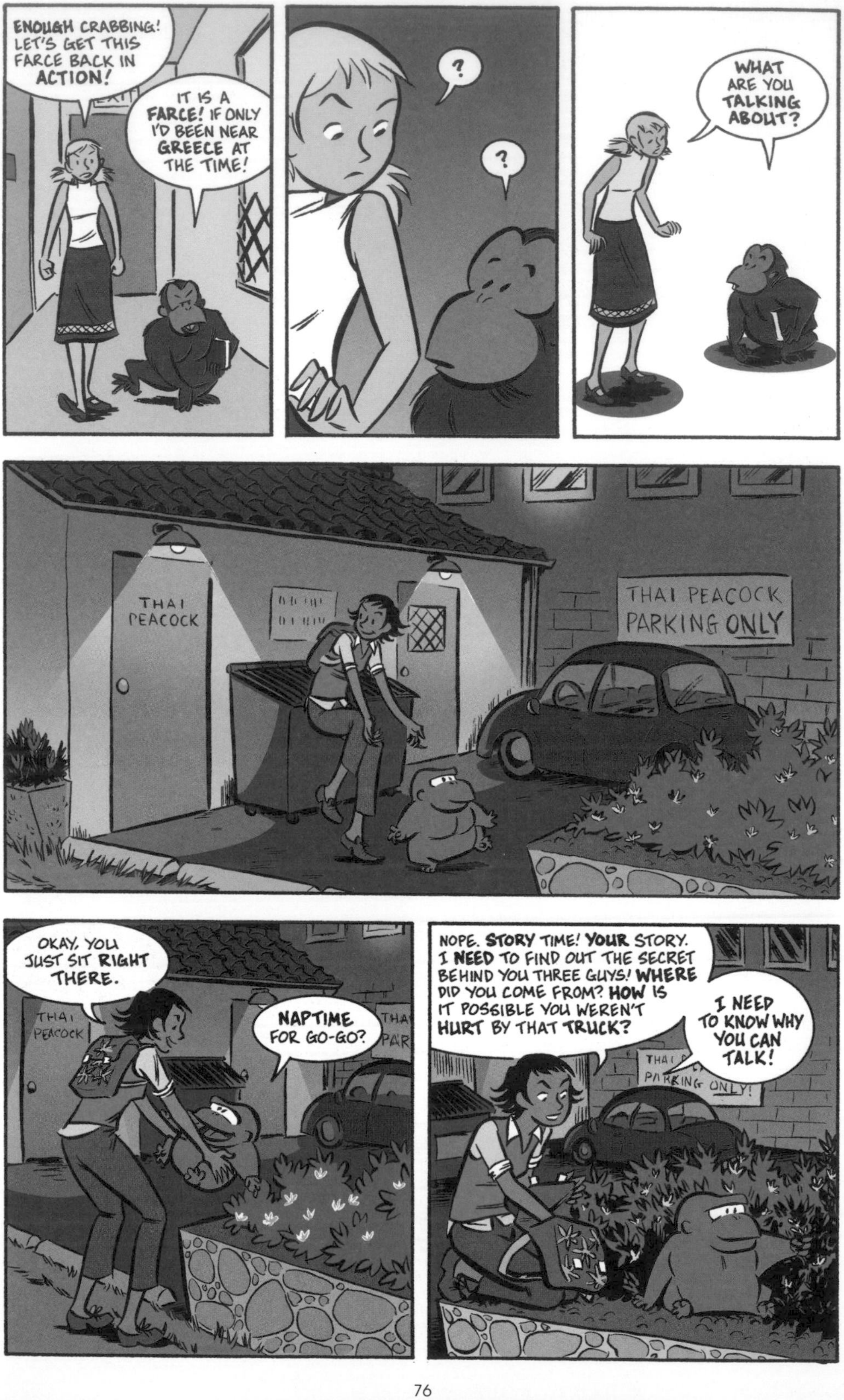
ENOUGH CRABBING! LET'S GET THIS FARCE BACK IN ACTION!
IT IS A FARCE! IF ONLY I'D BEEN NEAR GREECE AT THE TIME!
?
?
WHAT ARE YOU TALKING ABOUT?
THAI PEACOCK
THAI PEACOCK PARKING ONLY
OKAY, YOU JUST SIT RIGHT THERE.
NAPTIME FOR GO-GO?
NOPE. STORY TIME! YOUR STORY. I NEED TO FIND OUT THE SECRET BEHIND YOU THREE GUYS! WHERE DID YOU COME FROM? HOW IS IT POSSIBLE YOU WEREN'T HURT BY THAT TRUCK?
I NEED TO KNOW WHY YOU CAN TALK!

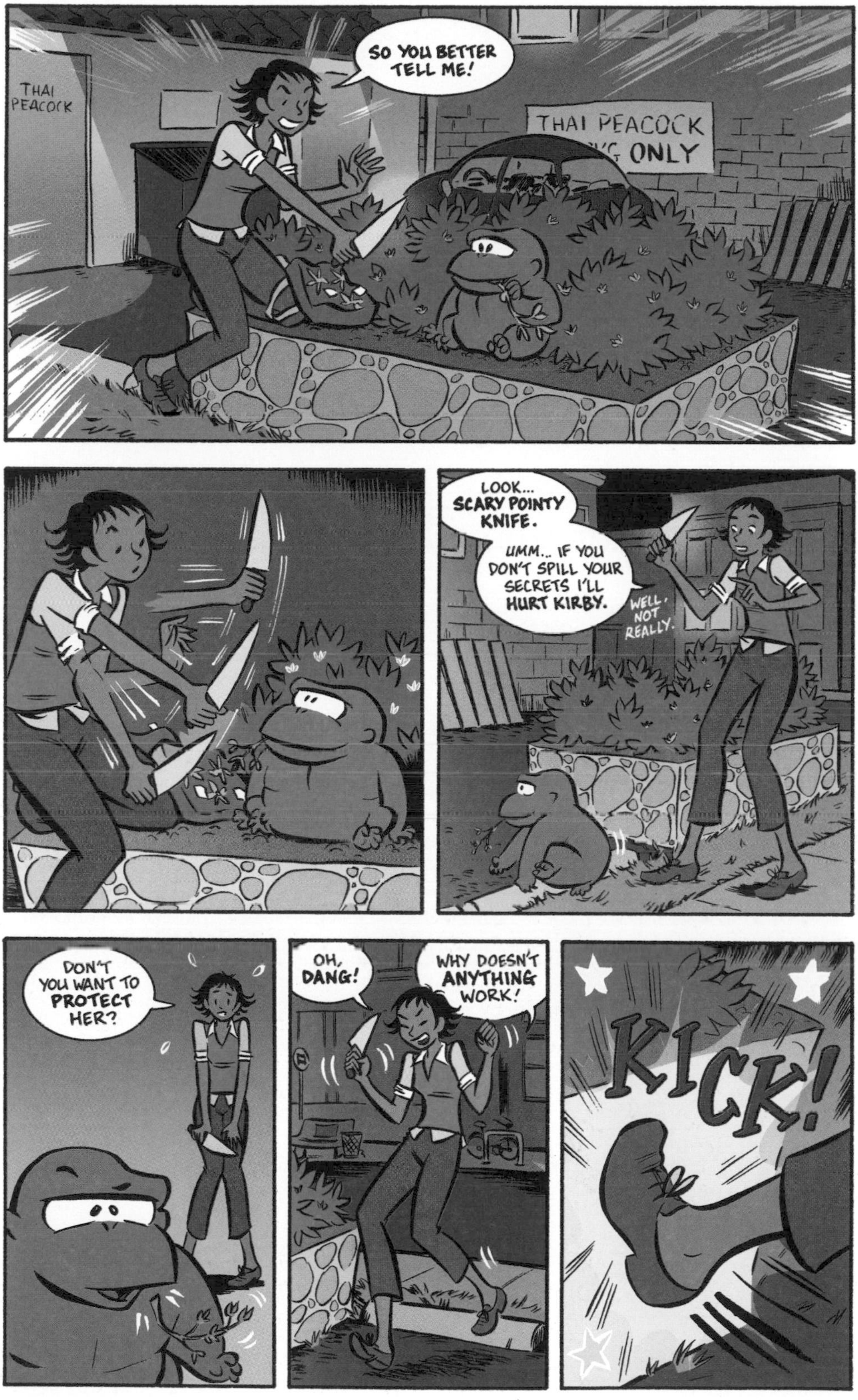

SO YOU BETTER TELL ME!
THAI PEACOCK
THAI PEACOCK ONLY
LOOK... SCARY POINTY KNIFE.
UMM... IF YOU DON'T SPILL YOUR SECRETS I'LL HURT KIRBY.
WELL, NOT REALLY.
DON'T YOU WANT TO PROTECT HER?
OH, DANG!
WHY DOESN'T ANYTHING WORK!
KICK!

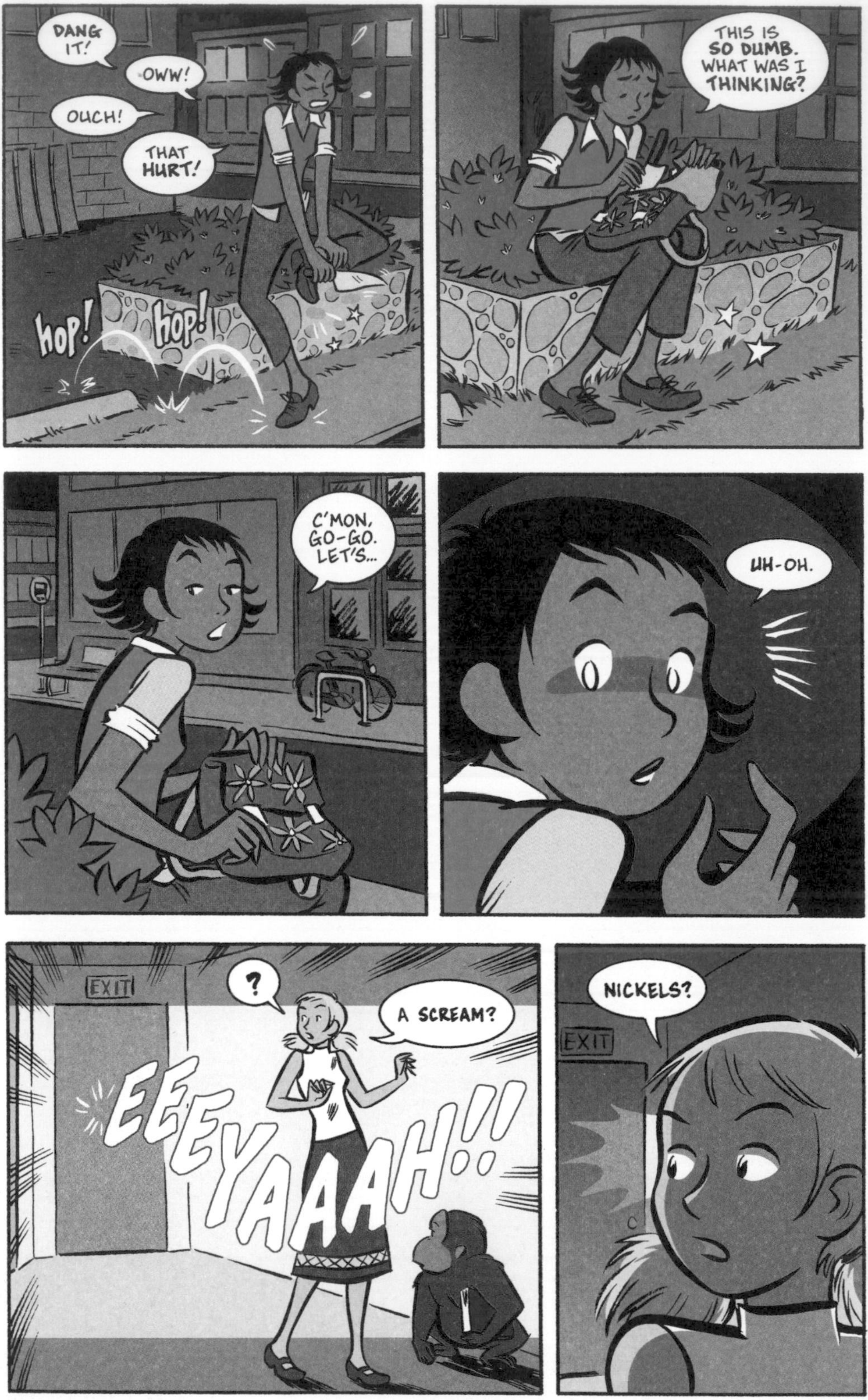
DANG IT!
OWW!
OUCH!
THAT HURT!
hop! hop!
THIS IS SO DUMB. WHAT WAS I THINKING?
C'MON, GO-GO. LET'S...
UH-OH.
EXIT
?
A SCREAM?
EEEYAAAH!!
NICKELS?
EXIT

CHAPTER FOUR

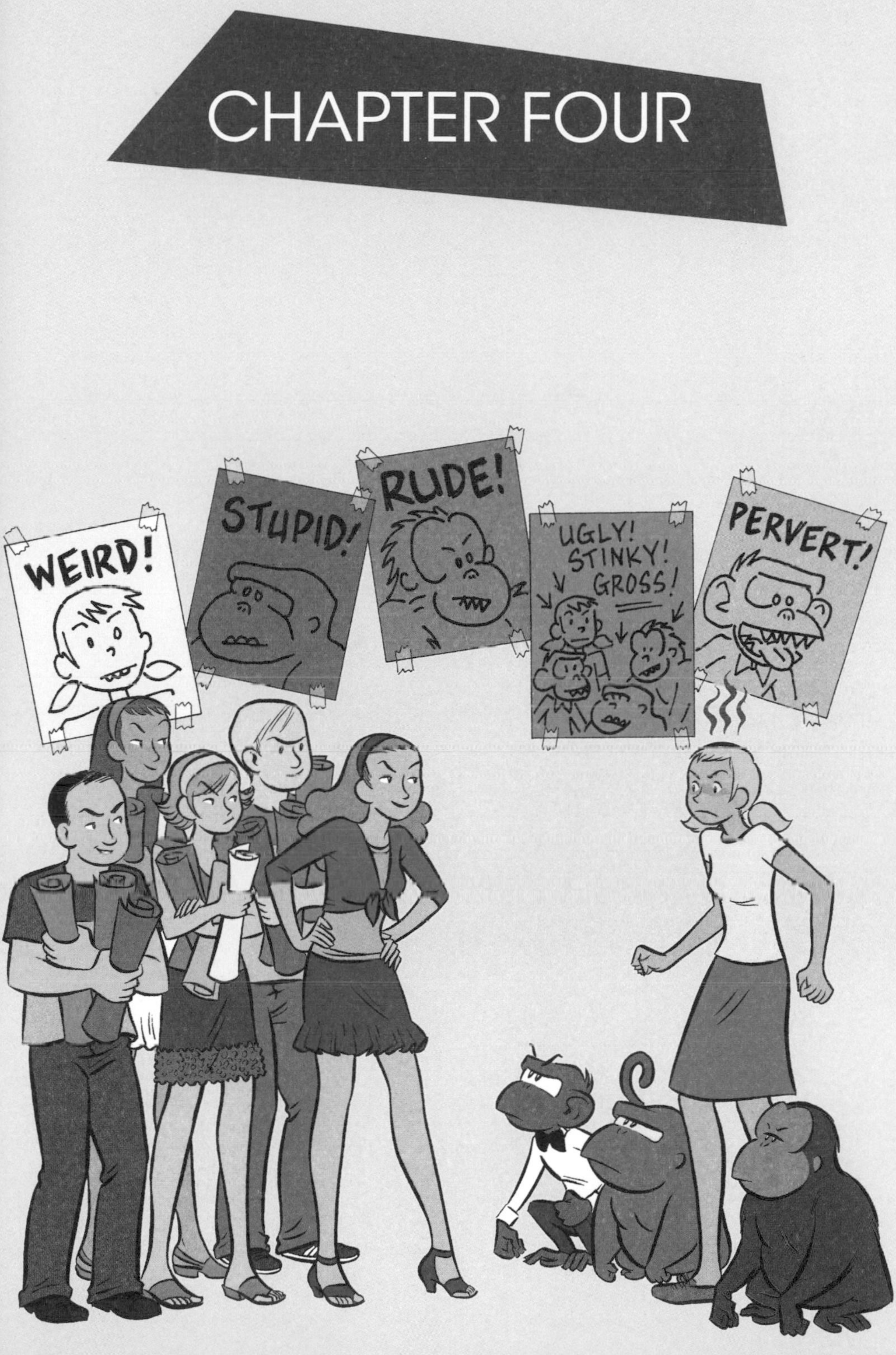

WEIRD!
STUPID!
RUDE!
UGLY!
STINKY!
GROSS!
PERVERT!

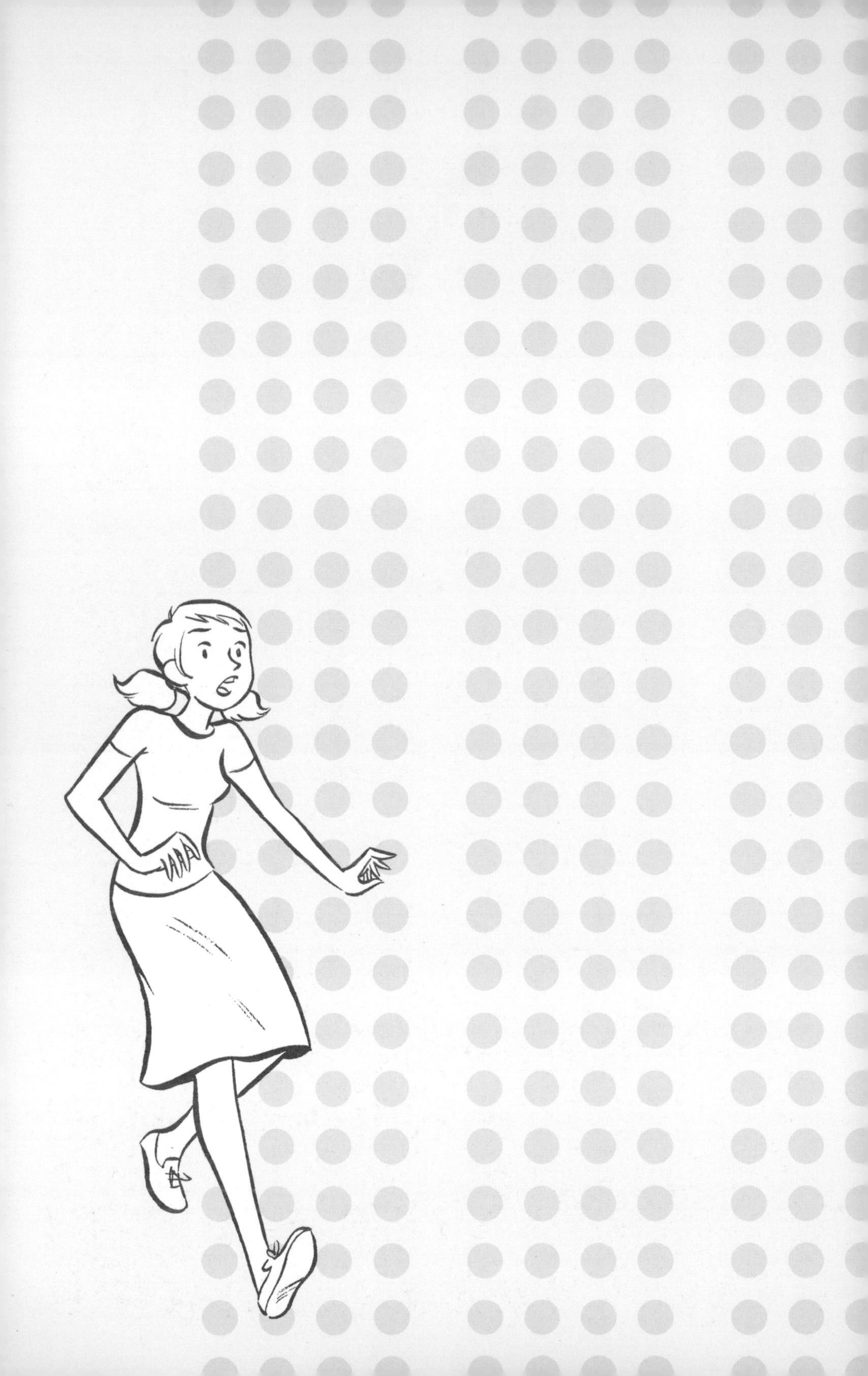

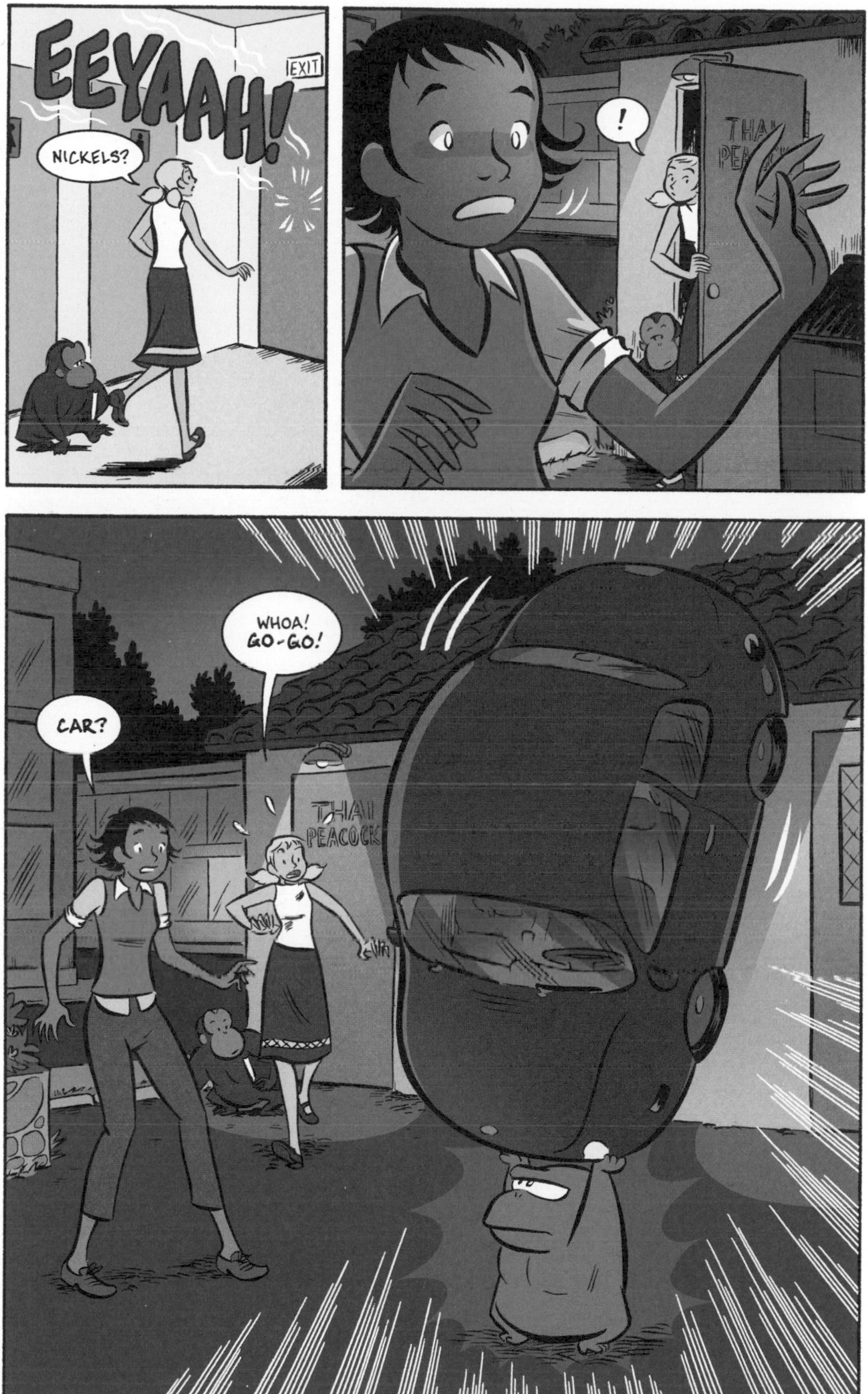
EEYAAH!
EXIT
NICKELS?
!
THAI PEACOCK
CAR?
WHOA! GO-GO!
THAI PEACOCK

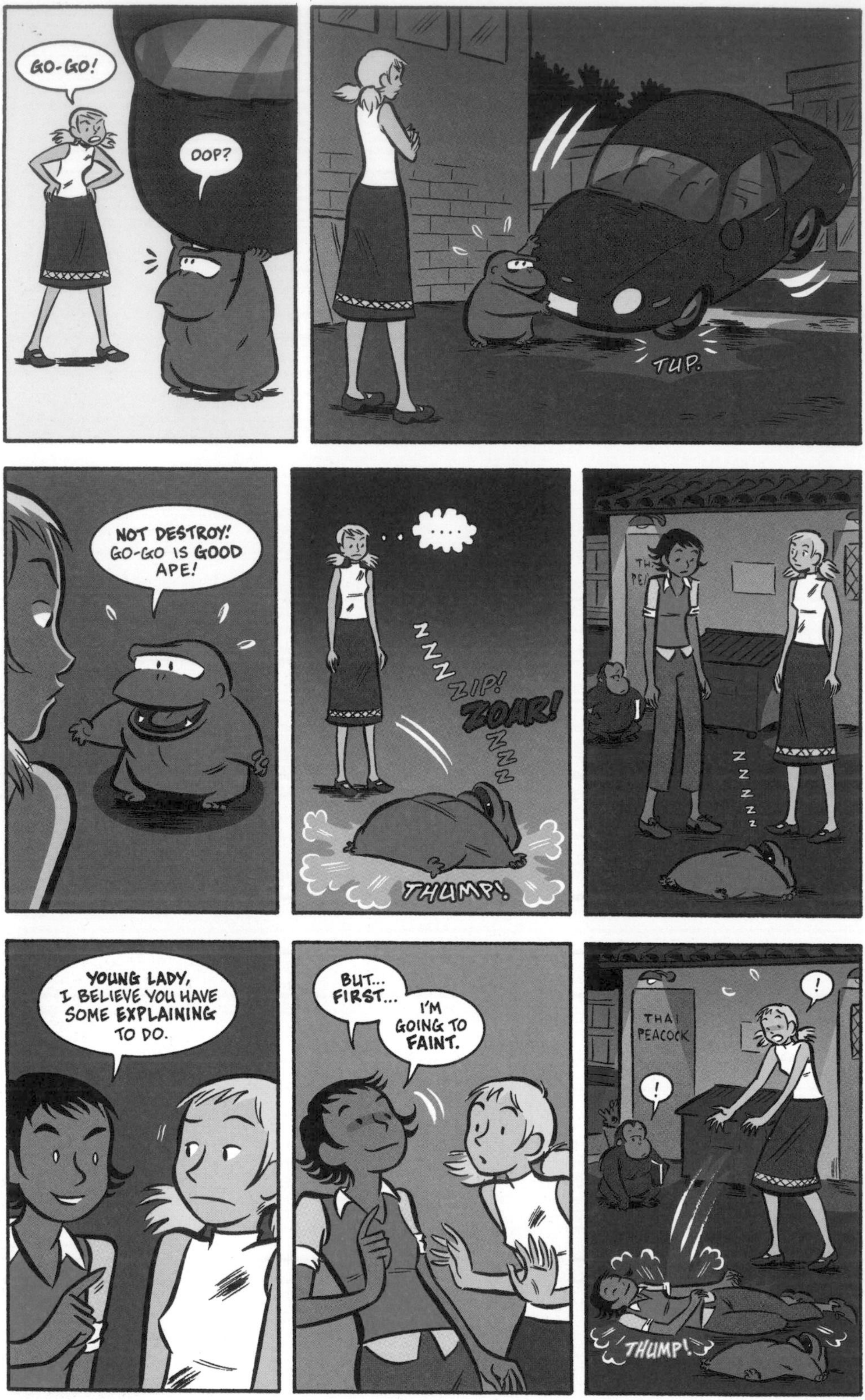
GO-GO!
OOP?
TUP.
NOT DESTROY! GO-GO IS GOOD APE!
. . . . .
ZZZ
ZIP!
ZOAR!
ZZZ
THUMP!
ZZZZZ
YOUNG LADY, I BELIEVE YOU HAVE SOME EXPLAINING TO DO.
BUT... FIRST...
I'M GOING TO FAINT.
THAI PEACOCK
!
!
THUMP!

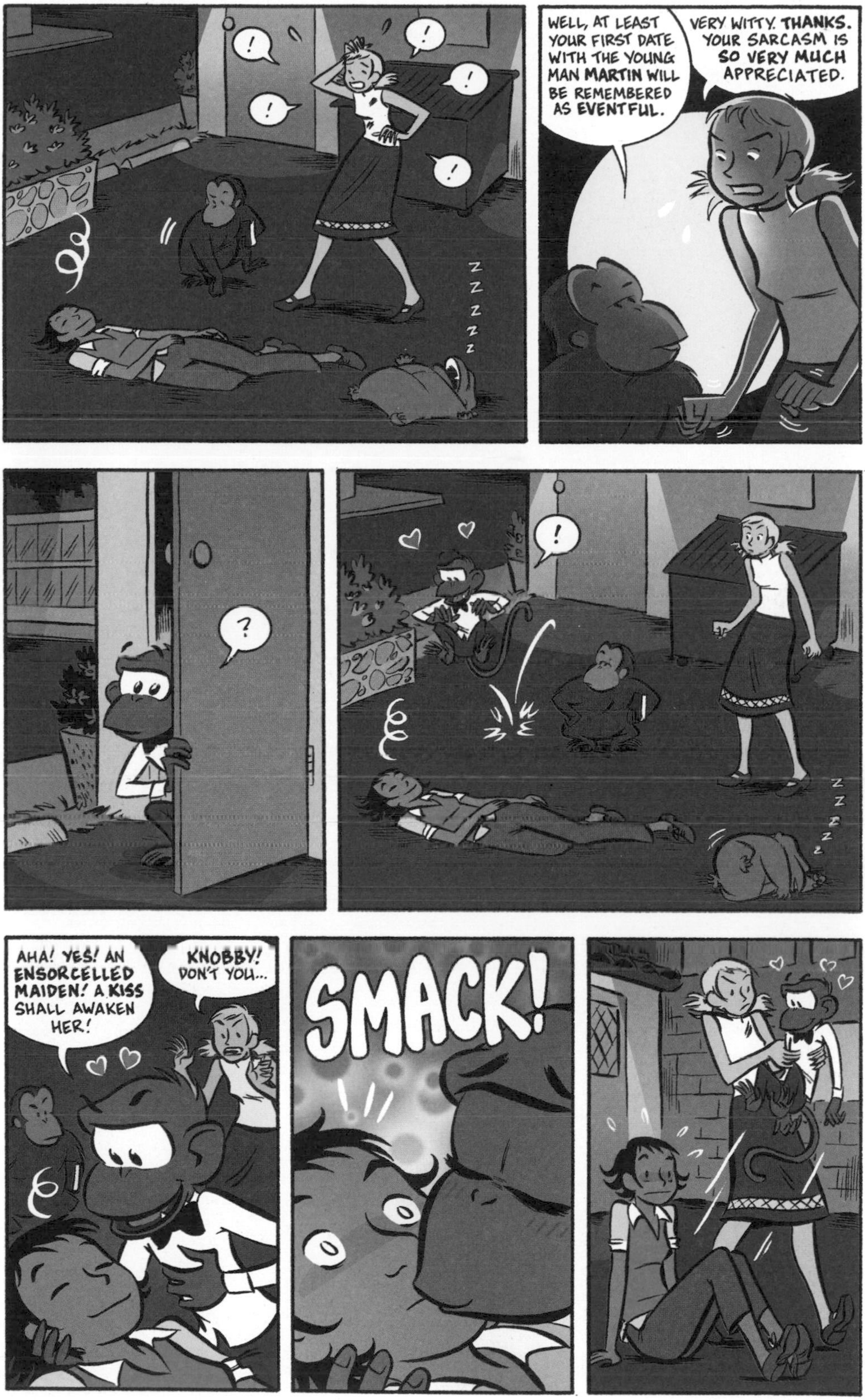
!
!
!
!
!
WELL, AT LEAST YOUR FIRST DATE WITH THE YOUNG MAN MARTIN WILL BE REMEMBERED AS EVENTFUL.
VERY WITTY. THANKS. YOUR SARCASM IS SO VERY MUCH APPRECIATED.
?
!
AHA! YES! AN ENSORCELLED MAIDEN! A KISS SHALL AWAKEN HER!
KNOBBY! DON'T YOU...
SMACK!

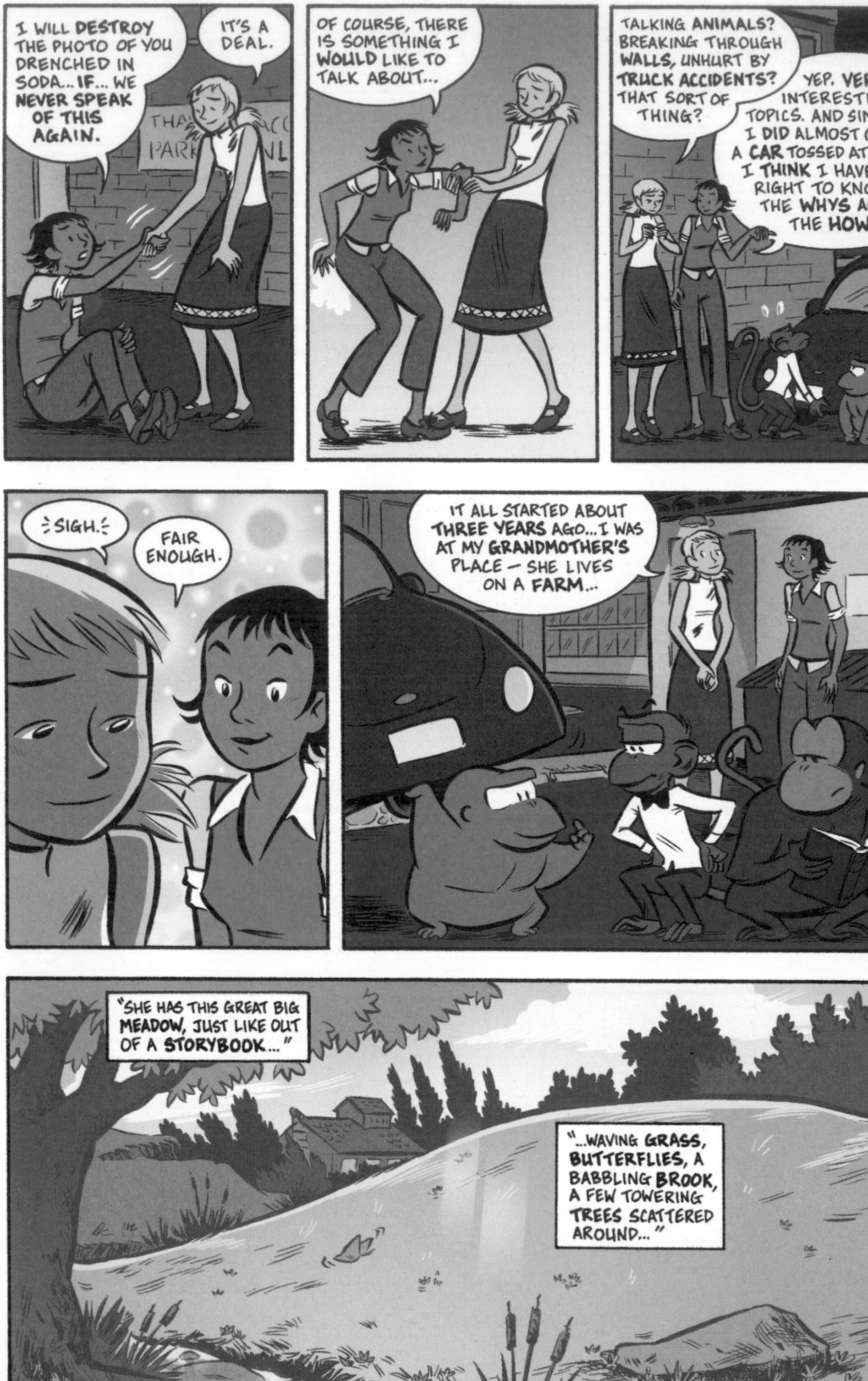
I WILL DESTROY THE PHOTO OF YOU DRENCHED IN SODA... IF... WE NEVER SPEAK OF THIS AGAIN.
IT'S A DEAL.
OF COURSE, THERE IS SOMETHING I WOULD LIKE TO TALK ABOUT...
TALKING ANIMALS? BREAKING THROUGH WALLS, UNHURT BY TRUCK ACCIDENTS? THAT SORT OF THING?
YEP. VERY INTERESTING TOPICS. AND SINCE I DID ALMOST GET A CAR TOSSED AT ME, I THINK I HAVE A RIGHT TO KNOW THE WHYS AND THE HOWS.
?
SIGH.
FAIR ENOUGH.
IT ALL STARTED ABOUT THREE YEARS AGO... I WAS AT MY GRANDMOTHER'S PLACE — SHE LIVES ON A FARM...
"SHE HAS THIS GREAT BIG MEADOW, JUST LIKE OUT OF A STORYBOOK..."
"...WAVING GRASS, BUTTERFLIES, A BABBLING BROOK, A FEW TOWERING TREES SCATTERED AROUND..."

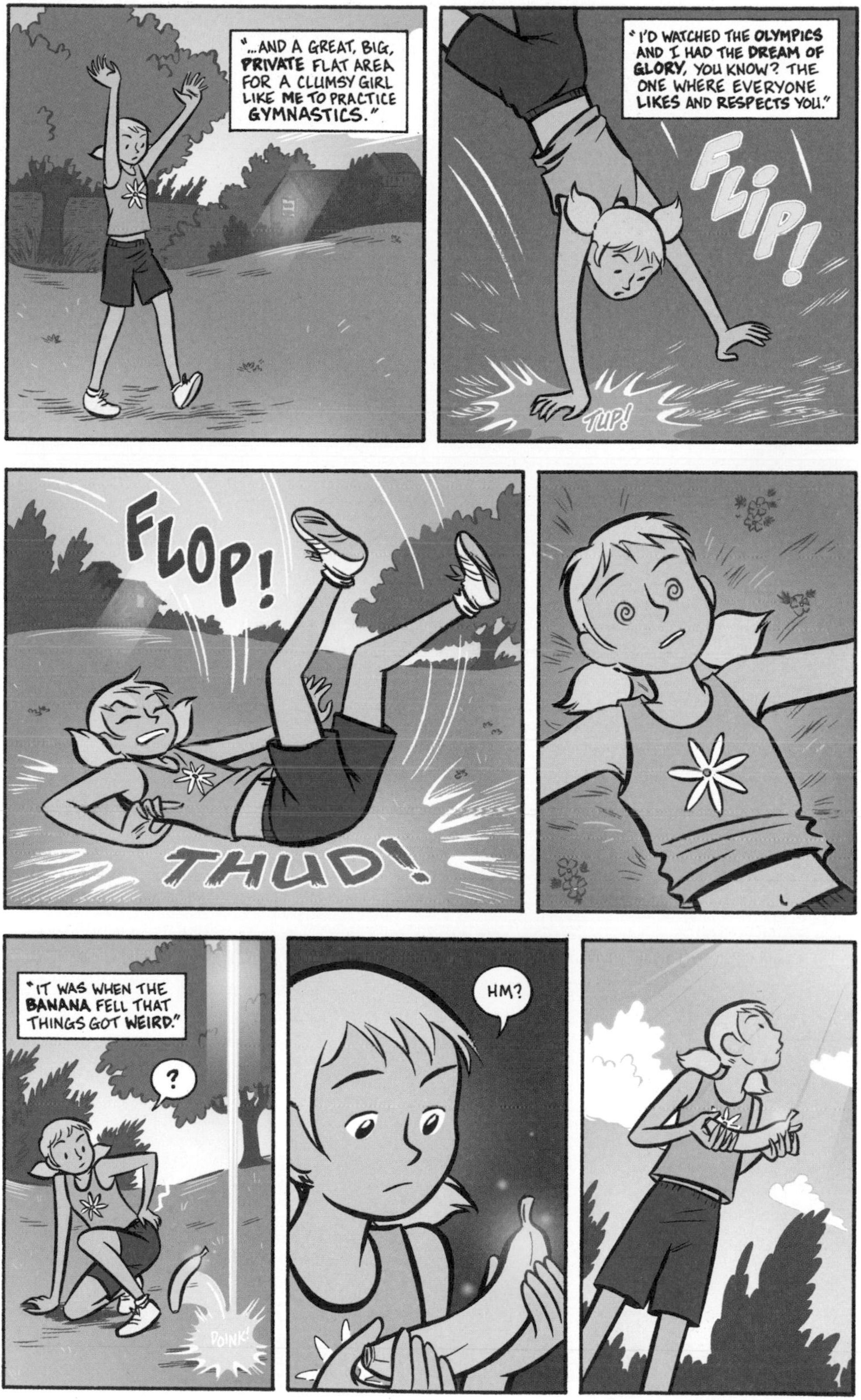
"...AND A GREAT, BIG, PRIVATE FLAT AREA FOR A CLUMSY GIRL LIKE ME TO PRACTICE GYMNASTICS."
"I'D WATCHED THE OLYMPICS AND I HAD THE DREAM OF GLORY, YOU KNOW? THE ONE WHERE EVERYONE LIKES AND RESPECTS YOU."
FLIP!
TUP!
FLOP!
THUD!
"IT WAS WHEN THE BANANA FELL THAT THINGS GOT WEIRD."
?
POINK!
HM?

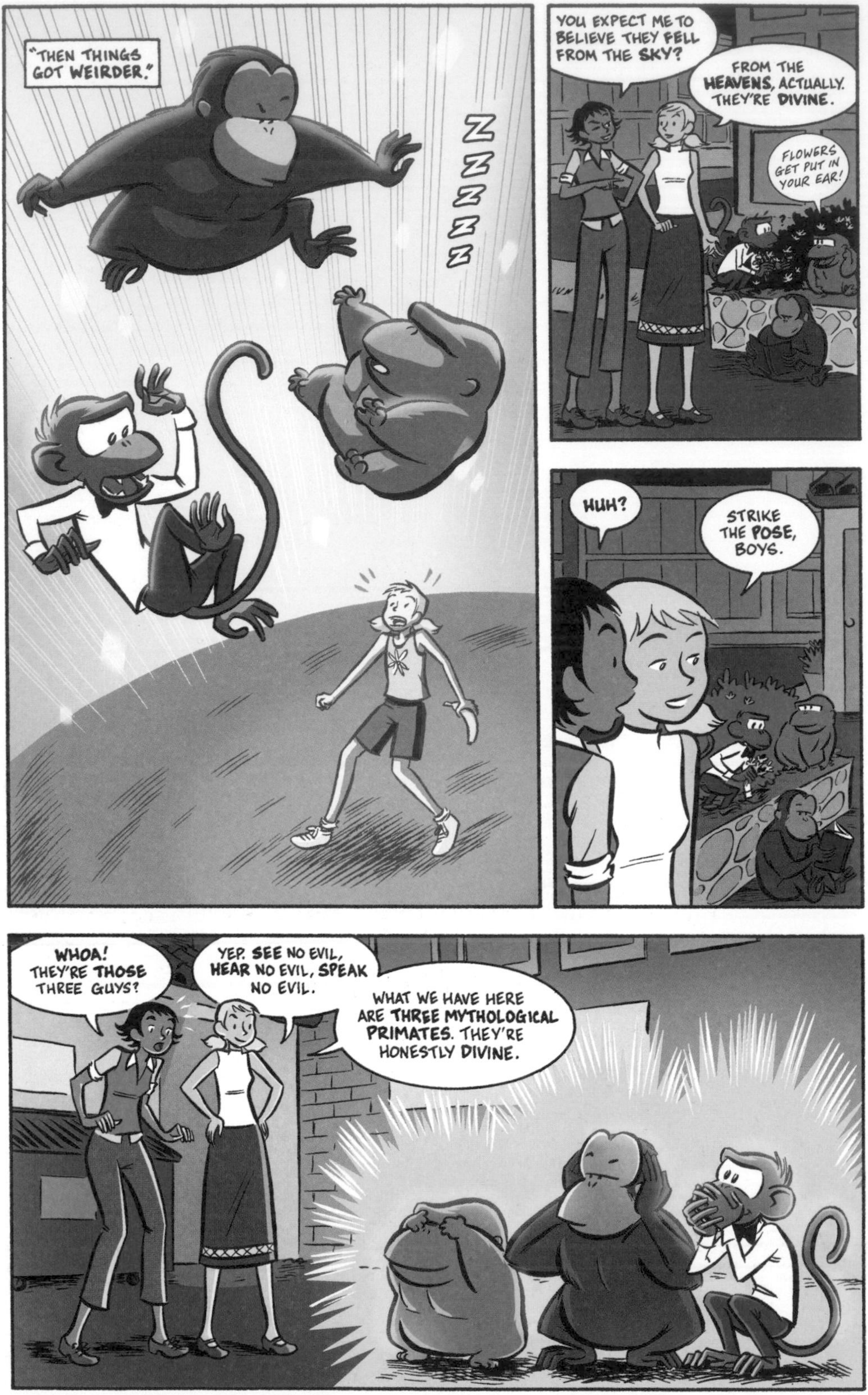
"THEN THINGS GOT WEIRDER."
ZZZZZZ
YOU EXPECT ME TO BELIEVE THEY FELL FROM THE SKY?
FROM THE HEAVENS, ACTUALLY. THEY'RE DIVINE.
FLOWERS GET PUT IN YOUR EAR!
HUH?
STRIKE THE POSE, BOYS.
WHOA! THEY'RE THOSE THREE GUYS?
YEP. SEE NO EVIL, HEAR NO EVIL, SPEAK NO EVIL.
WHAT WE HAVE HERE ARE THREE MYTHOLOGICAL PRIMATES. THEY'RE HONESTLY DIVINE.

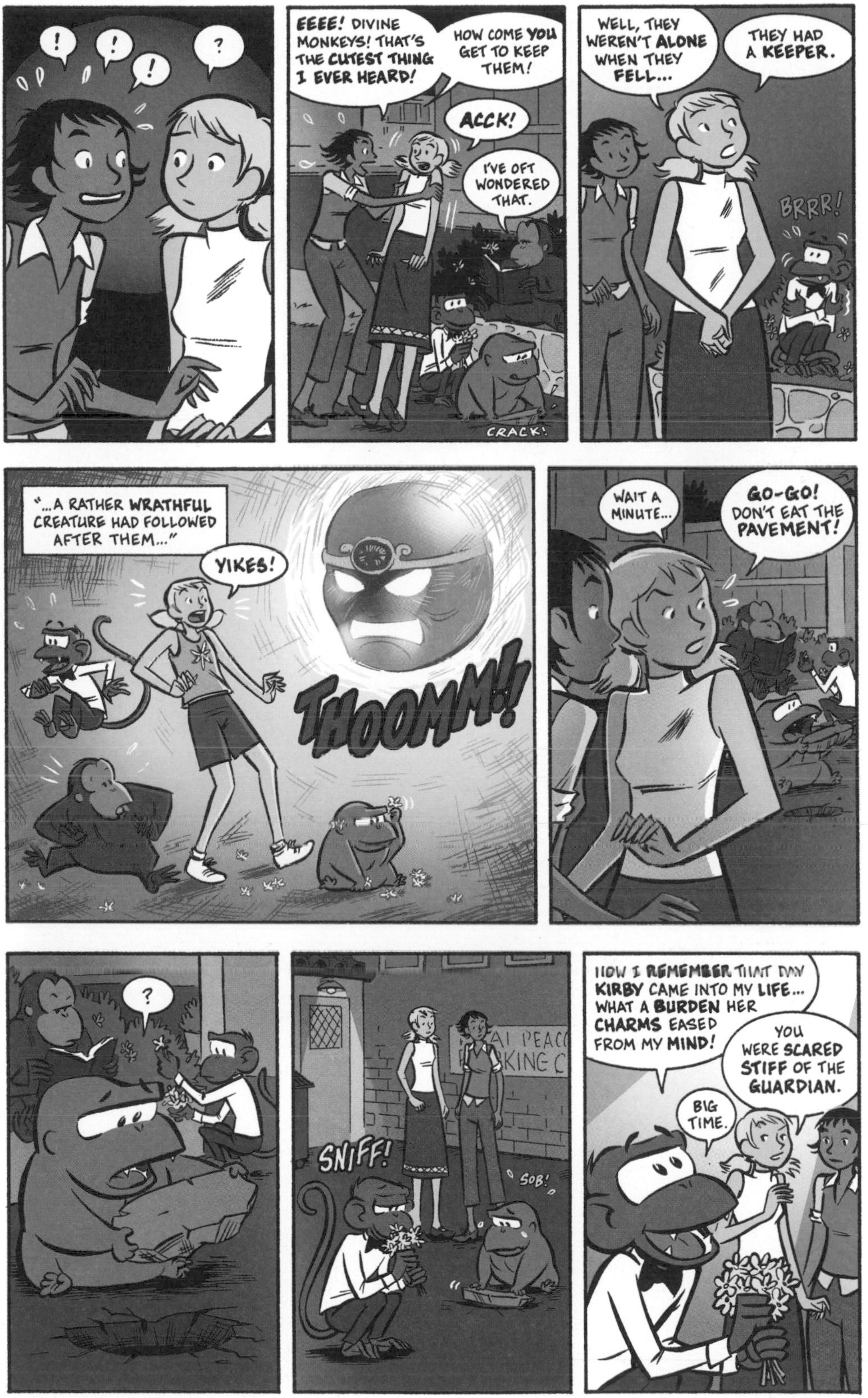
!
!
!
?
EEEE! DIVINE MONKEYS! THAT'S THE CUTEST THING I EVER HEARD!
HOW COME YOU GET TO KEEP THEM!
ACCK!
I'VE OFT WONDERED THAT.
CRACK!
WELL, THEY WEREN'T ALONE WHEN THEY FELL...
THEY HAD A KEEPER.
BRRR!
"...A RATHER WRATHFUL CREATURE HAD FOLLOWED AFTER THEM..."
YIKES!
THOOMM!
WAIT A MINUTE...
GO-GO! DON'T EAT THE PAVEMENT!
?
SNIFF!
SOB!
HOW I REMEMBER THAT DAY KIRBY CAME INTO MY LIFE... WHAT A BURDEN HER CHARMS EASED FROM MY MIND!
YOU WERE SCARED STIFF OF THE GUARDIAN.
BIG TIME.

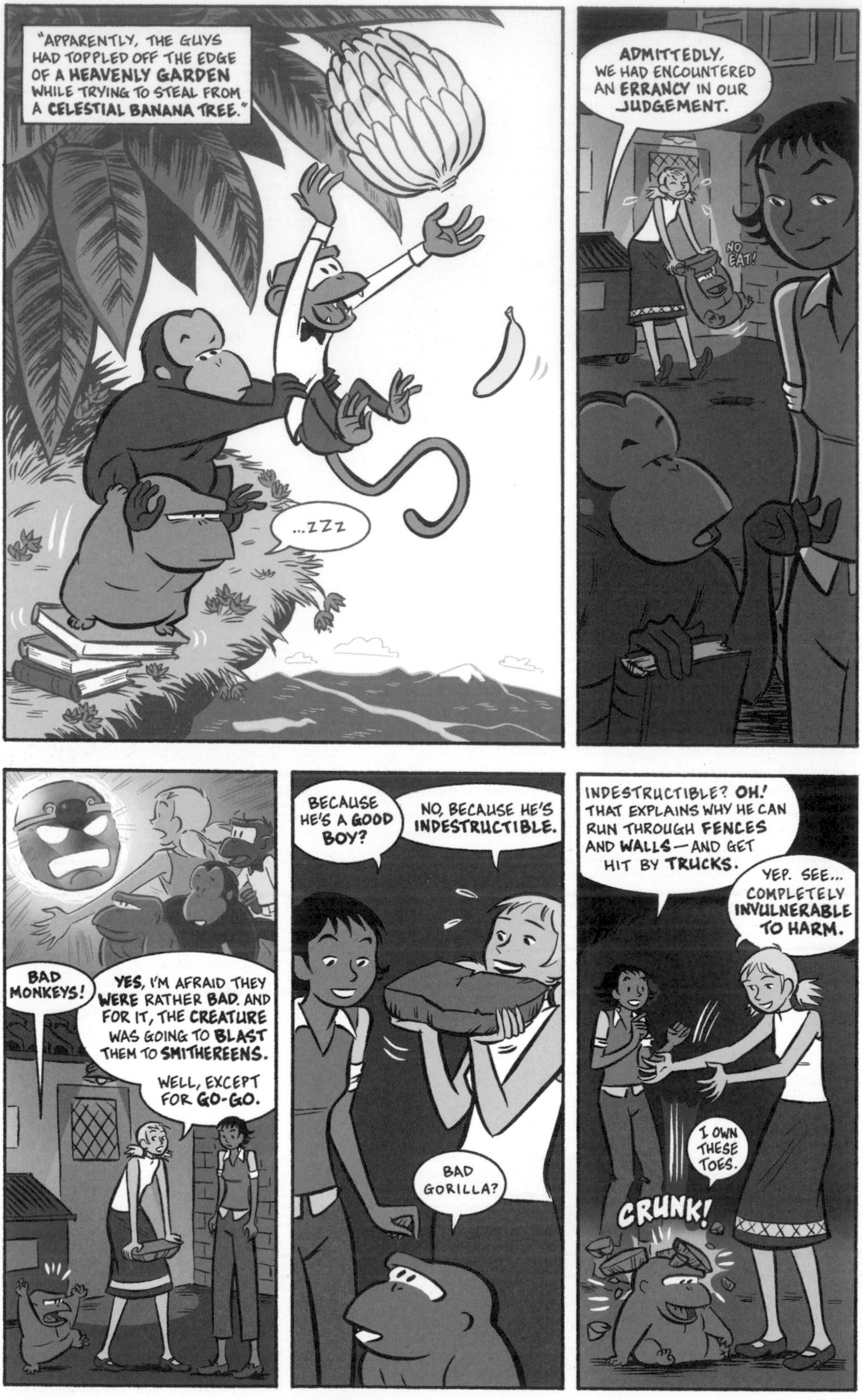
"APPARENTLY, THE GUYS HAD TOPPLED OFF THE EDGE OF A HEAVENLY GARDEN WHILE TRYING TO STEAL FROM A CELESTIAL BANANA TREE."
...ZZz
ADMITTEDLY, WE HAD ENCOUNTERED AN ERRANCY IN OUR JUDGEMENT.
NO EAT!
BAD MONKEYS!
YES, I'M AFRAID THEY WERE RATHER BAD. AND FOR IT, THE CREATURE WAS GOING TO BLAST THEM TO SMITHEREENS.
WELL, EXCEPT FOR GO-GO.
BECAUSE HE'S A GOOD BOY?
NO, BECAUSE HE'S INDESTRUCTIBLE.
BAD GORILLA?
INDESTRUCTIBLE? OH! THAT EXPLAINS WHY HE CAN RUN THROUGH FENCES AND WALLS—AND GET HIT BY TRUCKS.
YEP. SEE... COMPLETELY INVULNERABLE TO HARM.
I OWN THESE TOES.
CRUNK!

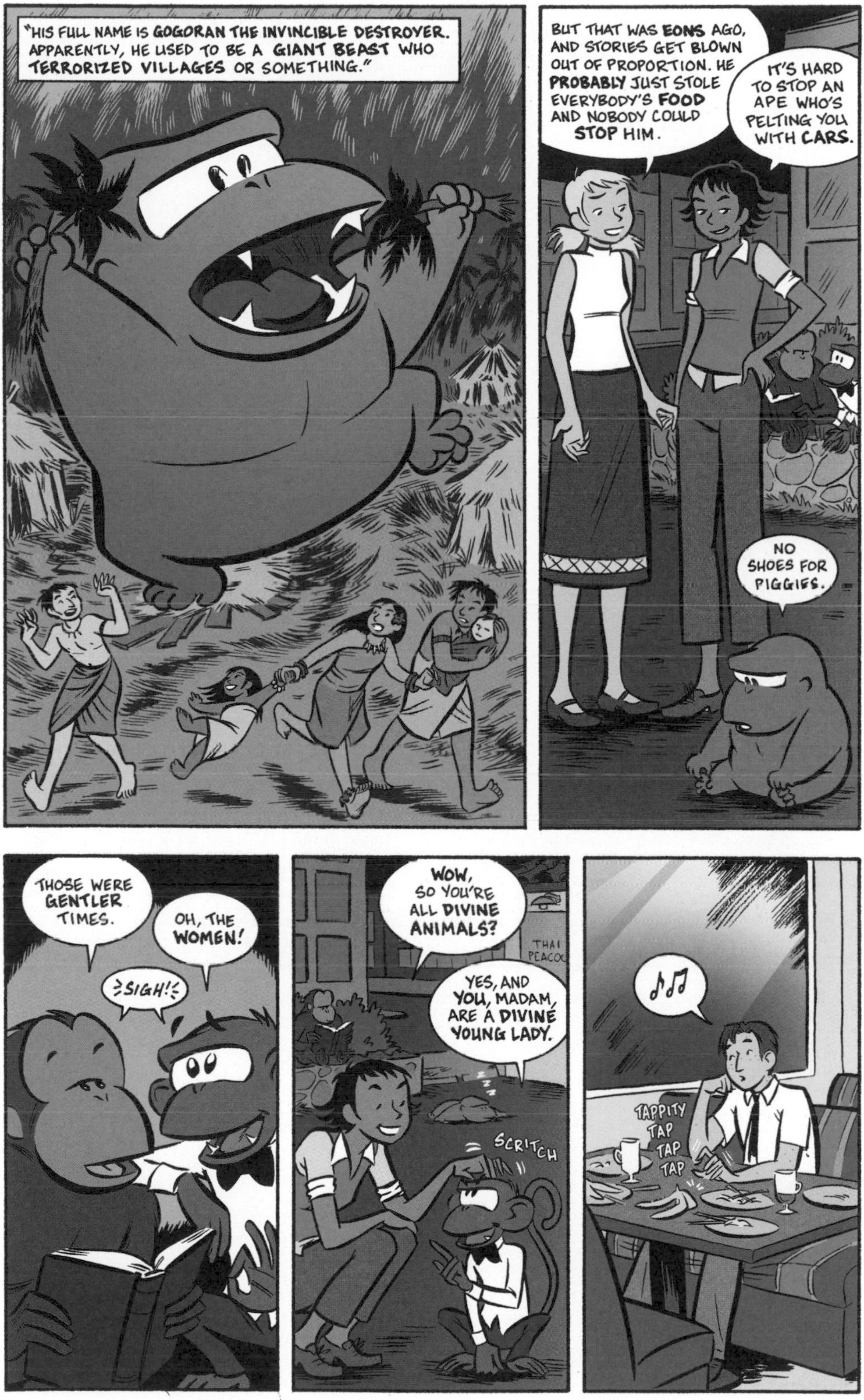
"HIS FULL NAME IS GOGORAN THE INVINCIBLE DESTROYER. APPARENTLY, HE USED TO BE A GIANT BEAST WHO TERRORIZED VILLAGES OR SOMETHING."
BUT THAT WAS EONS AGO, AND STORIES GET BLOWN OUT OF PROPORTION. HE PROBABLY JUST STOLE EVERYBODY'S FOOD AND NOBODY COULD STOP HIM.
IT'S HARD TO STOP AN APE WHO'S PELTING YOU WITH CARS.
NO SHOES FOR PIGGIES.
THOSE WERE GENTLER TIMES.
OH, THE WOMEN!
SIGH!
WOW, SO YOU'RE ALL DIVINE ANIMALS?
YES, AND YOU, MADAM, ARE A DIVINE YOUNG LADY.
THAI PEACO
SCRITCH
TAPPITY TAP TAP TAP

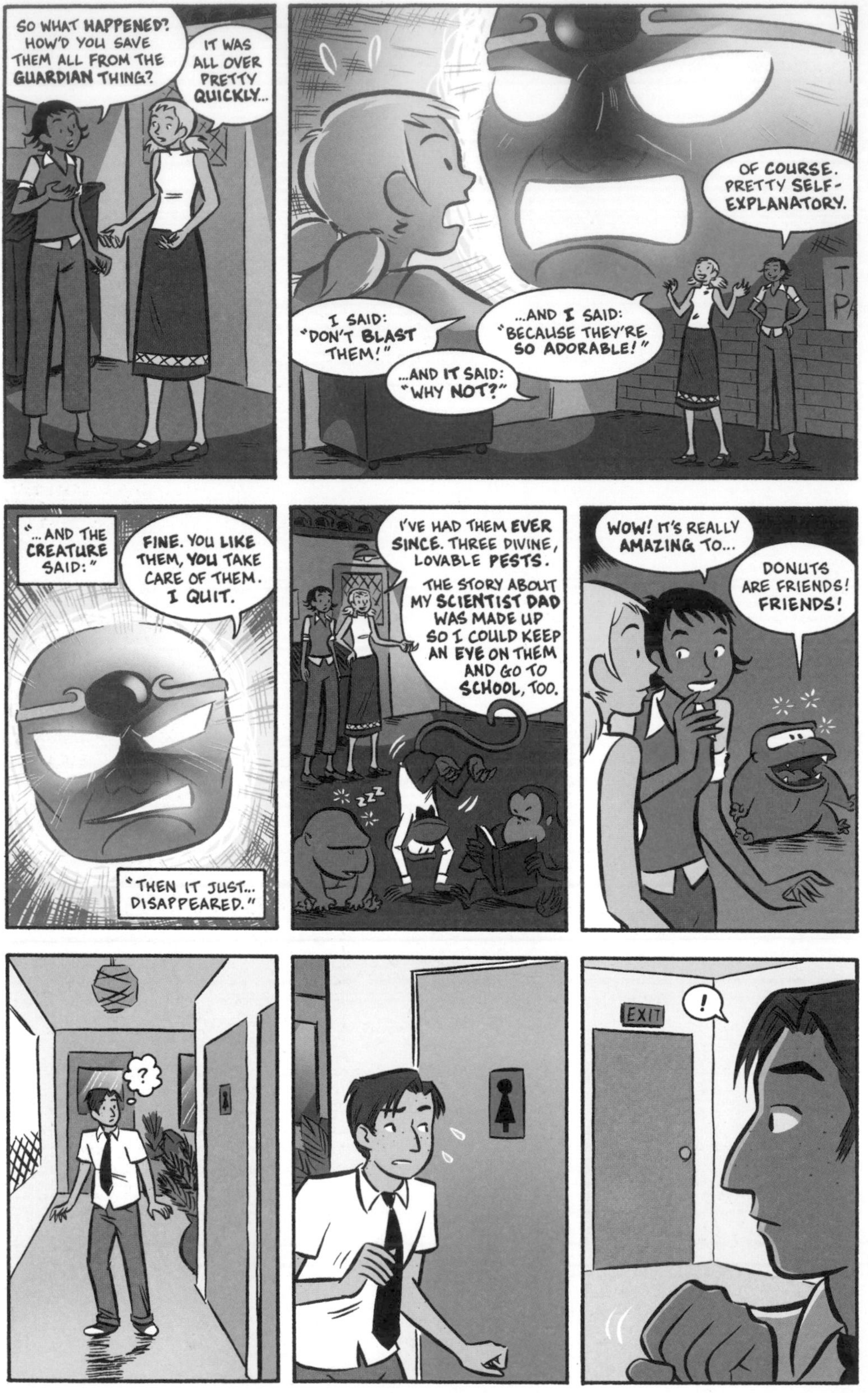
SO WHAT HAPPENED? HOW'D YOU SAVE THEM ALL FROM THE GUARDIAN THING?
IT WAS ALL OVER PRETTY QUICKLY...
OF COURSE. PRETTY SELF-EXPLANATORY.
I SAID: "DON'T BLAST THEM!"
...AND IT SAID: "WHY NOT?"
...AND I SAID: "BECAUSE THEY'RE SO ADORABLE!"
"...AND THE CREATURE SAID:"
FINE. YOU LIKE THEM, YOU TAKE CARE OF THEM. I QUIT.
"THEN IT JUST... DISAPPEARED."
I'VE HAD THEM EVER SINCE. THREE DIVINE, LOVABLE PESTS.
THE STORY ABOUT MY SCIENTIST DAD WAS MADE UP SO I COULD KEEP AN EYE ON THEM AND GO TO SCHOOL, TOO.
ZZZ
WOW! IT'S REALLY AMAZING TO...
DONUTS ARE FRIENDS! FRIENDS!
?
EXIT
!

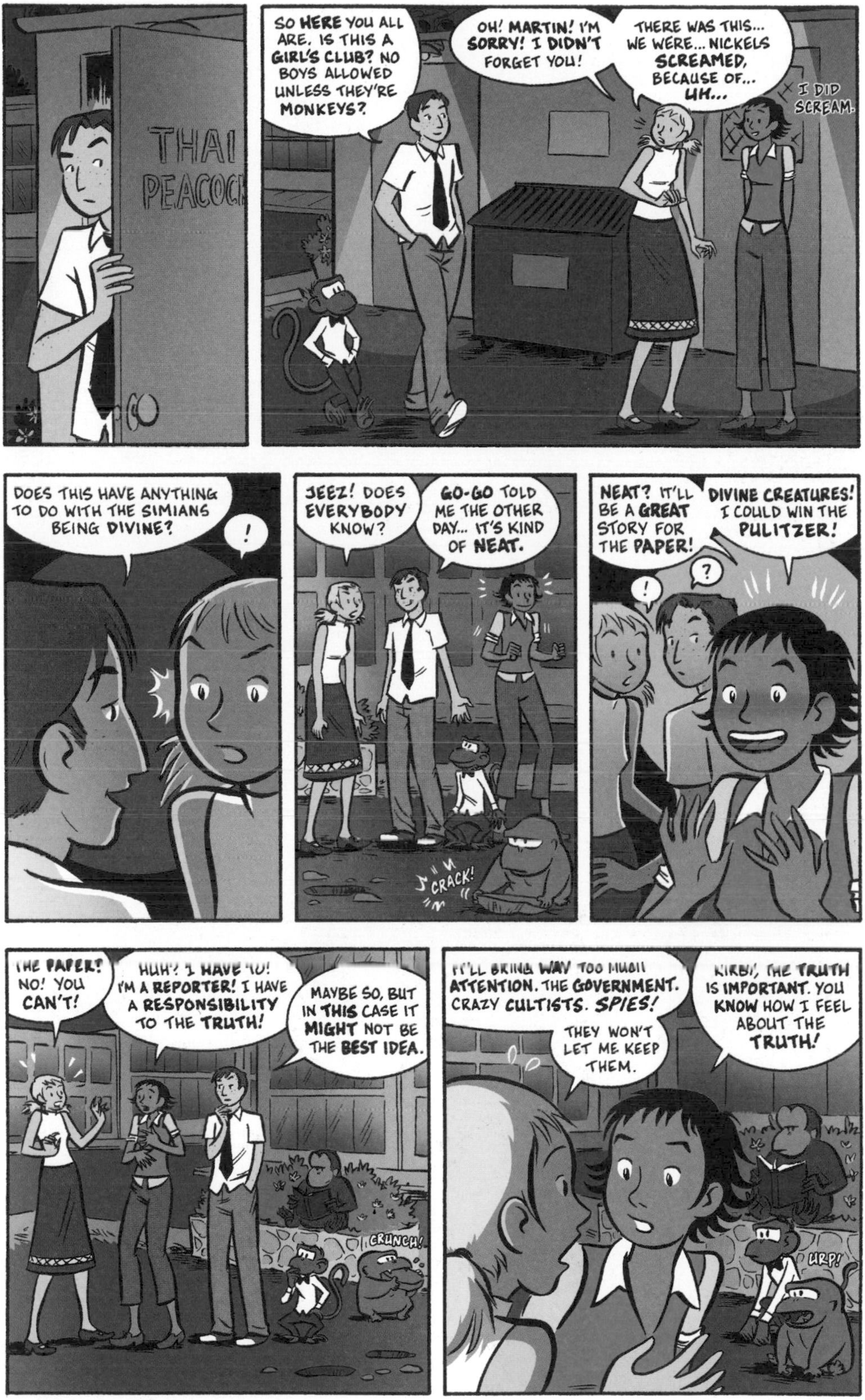
THAI PEACOCK
SO HERE YOU ALL ARE. IS THIS A GIRL'S CLUB? NO BOYS ALLOWED UNLESS THEY'RE MONKEYS?
OH! MARTIN! I'M SORRY! I DIDN'T FORGET YOU!
THERE WAS THIS... WE WERE... NICKELS SCREAMED, BECAUSE OF... UH...
I DID SCREAM.
DOES THIS HAVE ANYTHING TO DO WITH THE SIMIANS BEING DIVINE?
!
JEEZ! DOES EVERYBODY KNOW?
GO-GO TOLD ME THE OTHER DAY... IT'S KIND OF NEAT.
CRACK!
NEAT? IT'LL BE A GREAT STORY FOR THE PAPER!
DIVINE CREATURES! I COULD WIN THE PULITZER!
!
?
THE PAPER! NO! YOU CAN'T!
HUH? I HAVE TO! I'M A REPORTER! I HAVE A RESPONSIBILITY TO THE TRUTH!
MAYBE SO, BUT IN THIS CASE IT MIGHT NOT BE THE BEST IDEA.
CRUNCH!
IT'LL BRING WAY TOO MUCH ATTENTION. THE GOVERNMENT. CRAZY CULTISTS. SPIES!
THEY WON'T LET ME KEEP THEM.
KIRBI, THE TRUTH IS IMPORTANT. YOU KNOW HOW I FEEL ABOUT THE TRUTH!
URP!

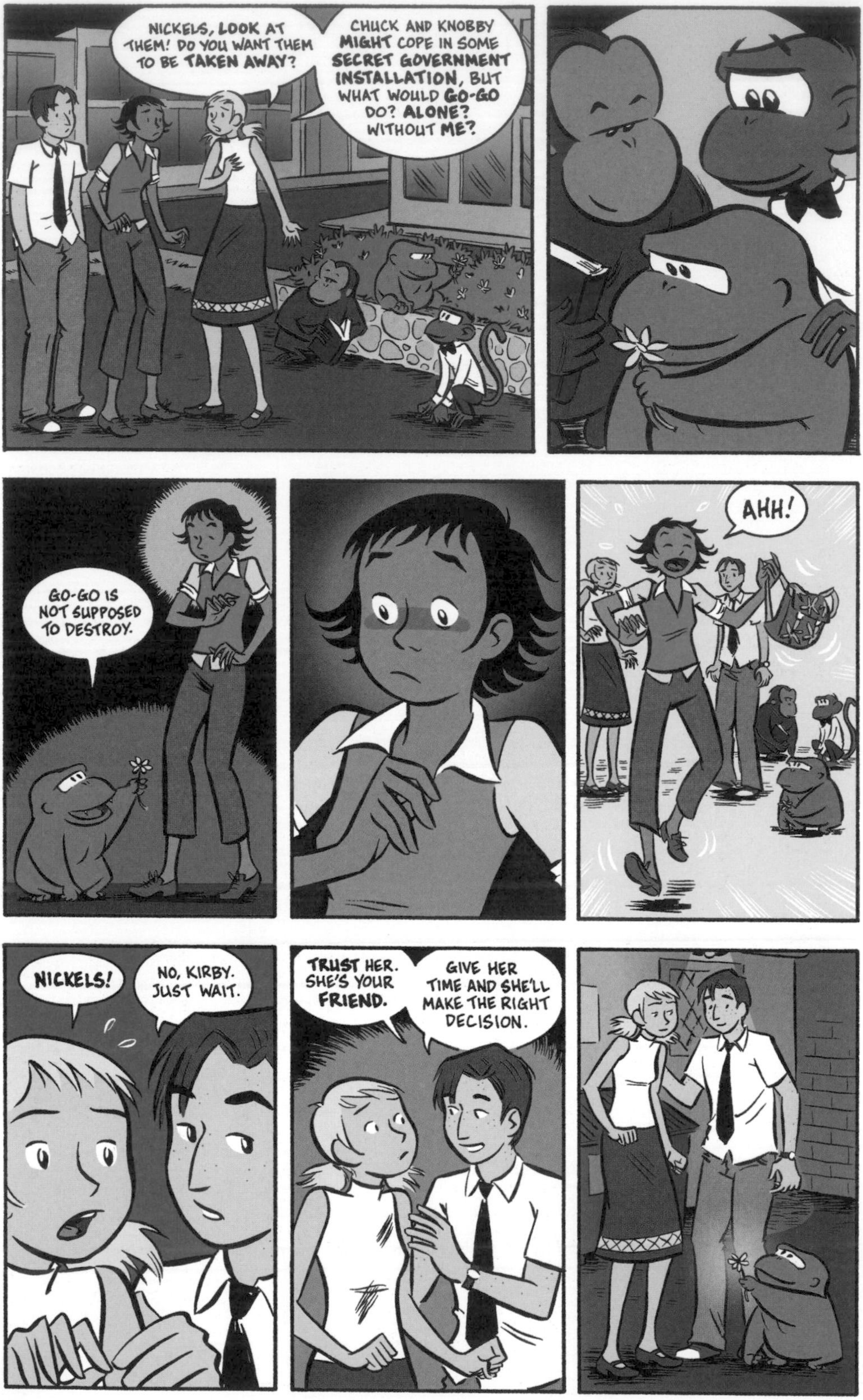
NICKELS, LOOK AT THEM! DO YOU WANT THEM TO BE TAKEN AWAY?
CHUCK AND KNOBBY MIGHT COPE IN SOME SECRET GOVERNMENT INSTALLATION, BUT WHAT WOULD GO-GO DO? ALONE? WITHOUT ME?
GO-GO IS NOT SUPPOSED TO DESTROY.
AHH!
NICKELS!
NO, KIRBY. JUST WAIT.
TRUST HER. SHE'S YOUR FRIEND.
GIVE HER TIME AND SHE'LL MAKE THE RIGHT DECISION.

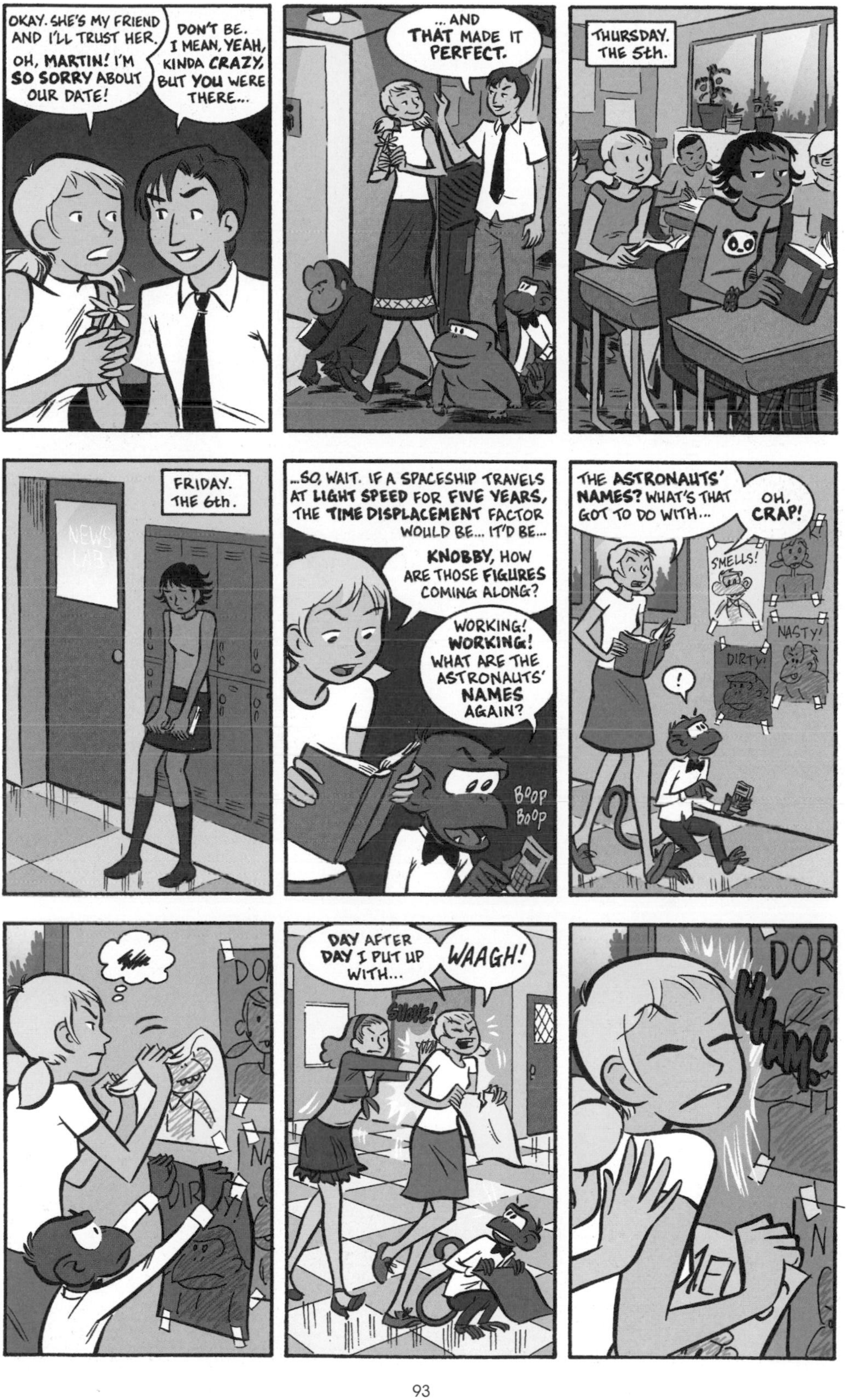
OKAY. SHE'S MY FRIEND AND I'LL TRUST HER.
OH, MARTIN! I'M SO SORRY ABOUT OUR DATE!
DON'T BE. I MEAN, YEAH, KINDA CRAZY, BUT YOU WERE THERE...
... AND THAT MADE IT PERFECT.
THURSDAY. THE 5th.
FRIDAY. THE 6th.
NEWS LAB
...SO, WAIT. IF A SPACESHIP TRAVELS AT LIGHT SPEED FOR FIVE YEARS, THE TIME DISPLACEMENT FACTOR WOULD BE... IT'D BE...
KNOBBY, HOW ARE THOSE FIGURES COMING ALONG?
WORKING! WORKING! WHAT ARE THE ASTRONAUTS' NAMES AGAIN?
BOOP BOOP
THE ASTRONAUTS' NAMES? WHAT'S THAT GOT TO DO WITH...
OH, CRAP!
SMELLS!
NASTY!
DIRTY!
!
DAY AFTER DAY I PUT UP WITH...
WAAGH!
SHOVE!
WHAM!

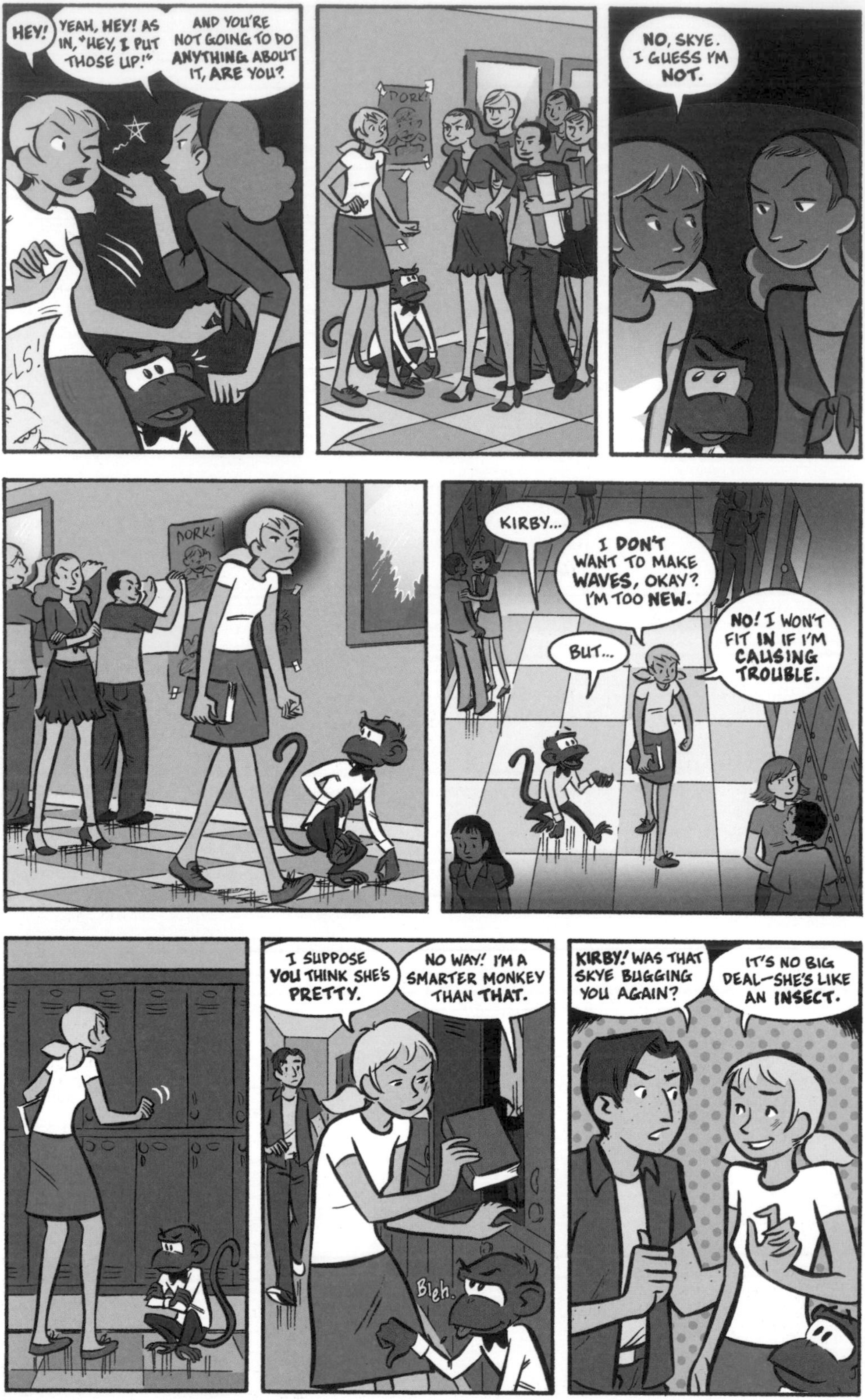
HEY!
YEAH, HEY! AS IN, "HEY, I PUT THOSE UP!"
AND YOU'RE NOT GOING TO DO ANYTHING ABOUT IT, ARE YOU?
DORK!
NO, SKYE. I GUESS I'M NOT.
DORK!
KIRBY...
I DON'T WANT TO MAKE WAVES, OKAY? I'M TOO NEW.
BUT...
NO! I WON'T FIT IN IF I'M CAUSING TROUBLE.
I SUPPOSE YOU THINK SHE'S PRETTY.
NO WAY! I'M A SMARTER MONKEY THAN THAT.
Bleh.
KIRBY! WAS THAT SKYE BUGGING YOU AGAIN?
IT'S NO BIG DEAL—SHE'S LIKE AN INSECT.

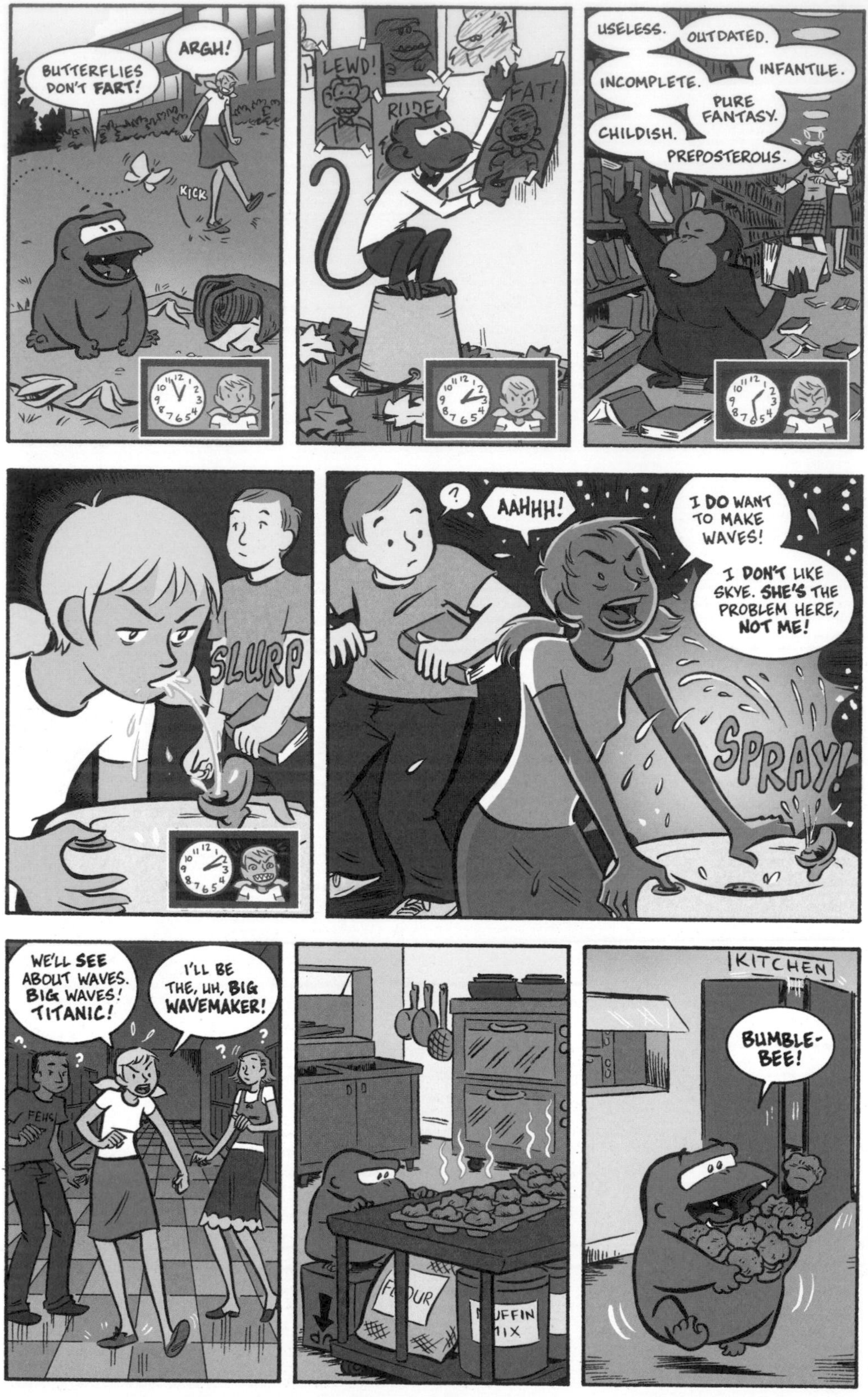
BUTTERFLIES DON'T FART!
ARGH!
KICK
LEWD!
RUDE
FAT!
USELESS.
OUTDATED.
INFANTILE.
INCOMPLETE.
PURE FANTASY.
CHILDISH.
PREPOSTEROUS.
SLURP
?
AAHHH!
I DO WANT TO MAKE WAVES!
I DON'T LIKE SKYE. SHE'S THE PROBLEM HERE, NOT ME!
SPRAY!
WE'LL SEE ABOUT WAVES. BIG WAVES! TITANIC!
I'LL BE THE, UH, BIG WAVEMAKER!
FEHS
FLOUR
MUFFIN MIX
KITCHEN
BUMBLE-BEE!

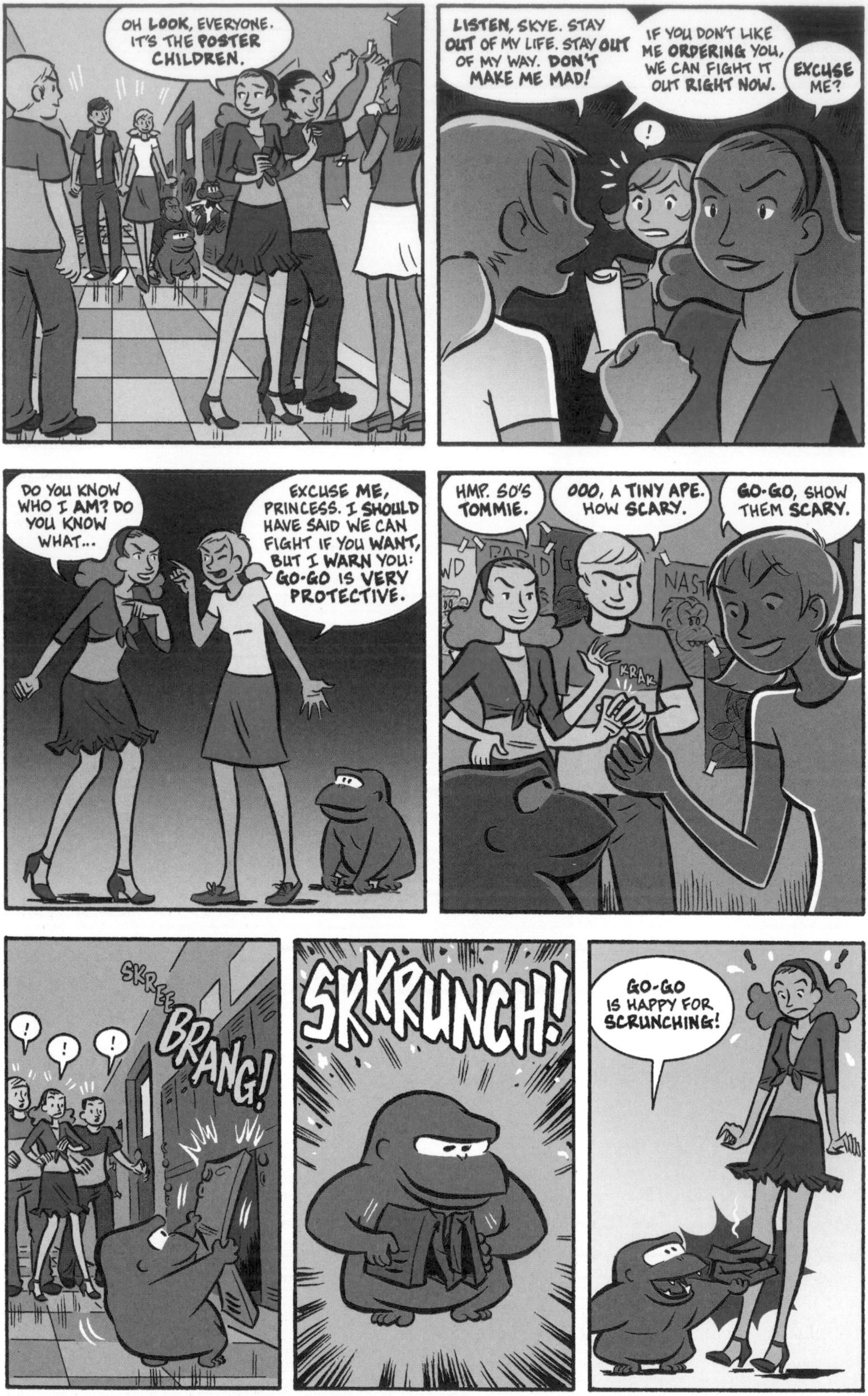
OH LOOK, EVERYONE. IT'S THE POSTER CHILDREN.
LISTEN, SKYE. STAY OUT OF MY LIFE. STAY OUT OF MY WAY. DON'T MAKE ME MAD!
IF YOU DON'T LIKE ME ORDERING YOU, WE CAN FIGHT IT OUT RIGHT NOW.
EXCUSE ME?
!
DO YOU KNOW WHO I AM? DO YOU KNOW WHAT...
EXCUSE ME, PRINCESS. I SHOULD HAVE SAID WE CAN FIGHT IF YOU WANT, BUT I WARN YOU: GO-GO IS VERY PROTECTIVE.
HMP. SO'S TOMMIE.
OOO, A TINY APE. HOW SCARY.
GO-GO, SHOW THEM SCARY.
KRAK
!
!
!
SKREE
BRANG!
SKKRUNCH!
GO-GO IS HAPPY FOR SCRUNCHING!
!
!

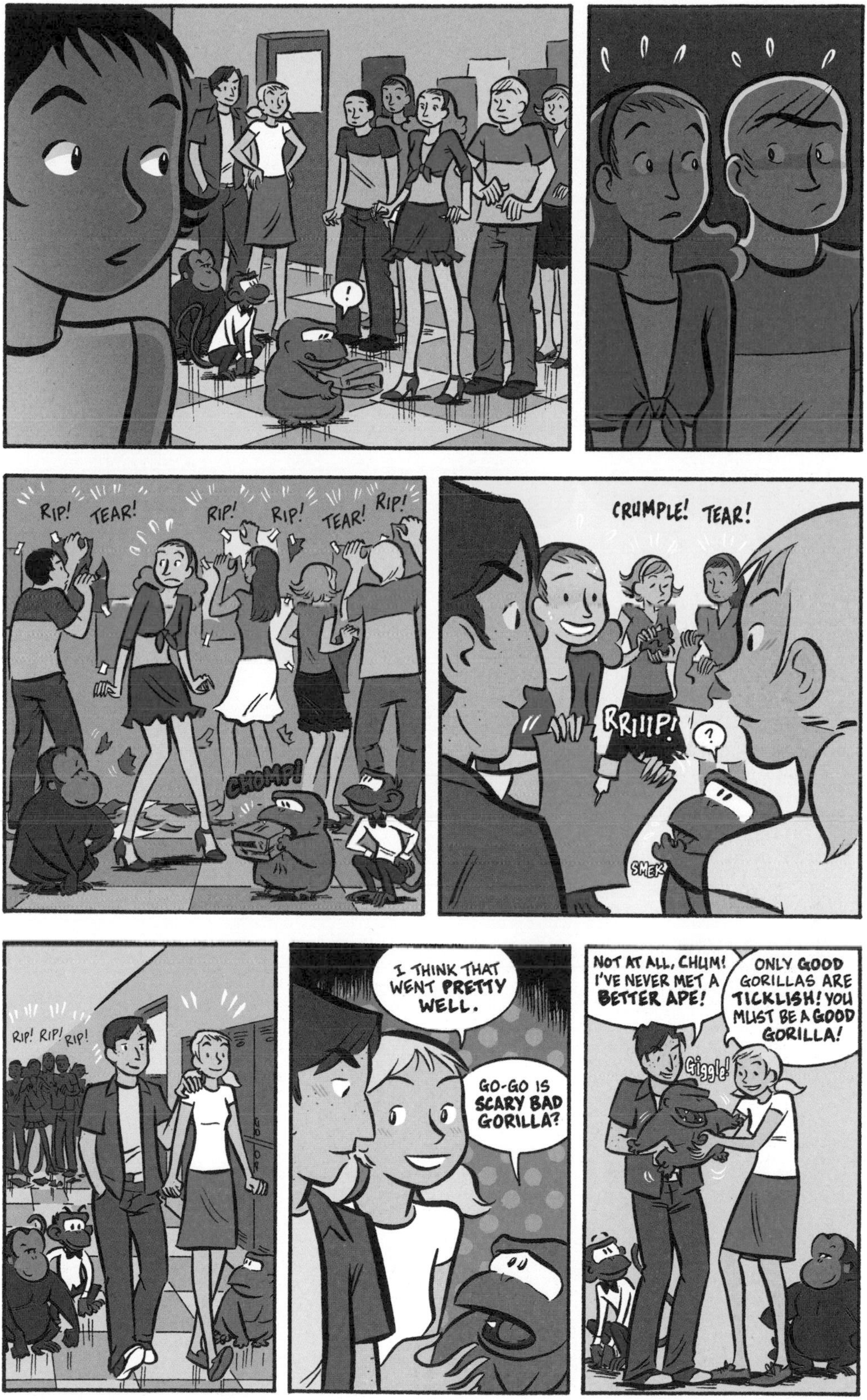
!
RIP! TEAR! RIP! RIP! TEAR! RIP!
CHOMP!
CRUMPLE! TEAR!
RRIIIP!
?
SMEK
RIP! RIP! RIP!
I THINK THAT WENT PRETTY WELL.
GO-GO IS SCARY BAD GORILLA?
NOT AT ALL, CHUM! I'VE NEVER MET A BETTER APE!
ONLY GOOD GORILLAS ARE TICKLISH! YOU MUST BE A GOOD GORILLA!
Giggle!

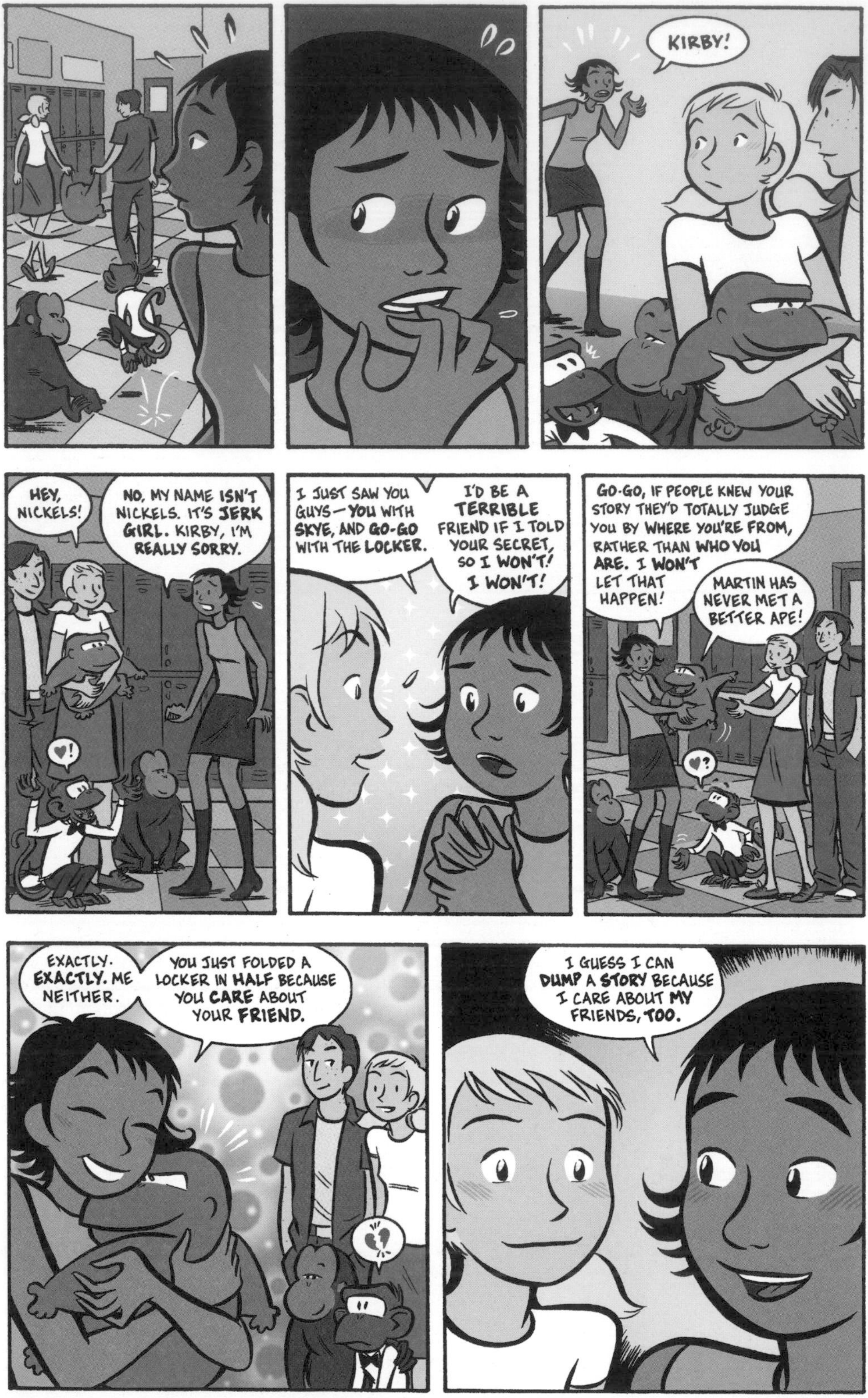
KIRBY!
HEY, NICKELS!
NO, MY NAME ISN'T NICKELS. IT'S JERK GIRL. KIRBY, I'M REALLY SORRY.
I JUST SAW YOU GUYS—YOU WITH SKYE, AND GO-GO WITH THE LOCKER.
I'D BE A TERRIBLE FRIEND IF I TOLD YOUR SECRET, SO I WON'T! I WON'T!
GO-GO, IF PEOPLE KNEW YOUR STORY THEY'D TOTALLY JUDGE YOU BY WHERE YOU'RE FROM, RATHER THAN WHO YOU ARE. I WON'T LET THAT HAPPEN!
MARTIN HAS NEVER MET A BETTER APE!
EXACTLY. EXACTLY. ME NEITHER.
YOU JUST FOLDED A LOCKER IN HALF BECAUSE YOU CARE ABOUT YOUR FRIEND.
I GUESS I CAN DUMP A STORY BECAUSE I CARE ABOUT MY FRIENDS, TOO.

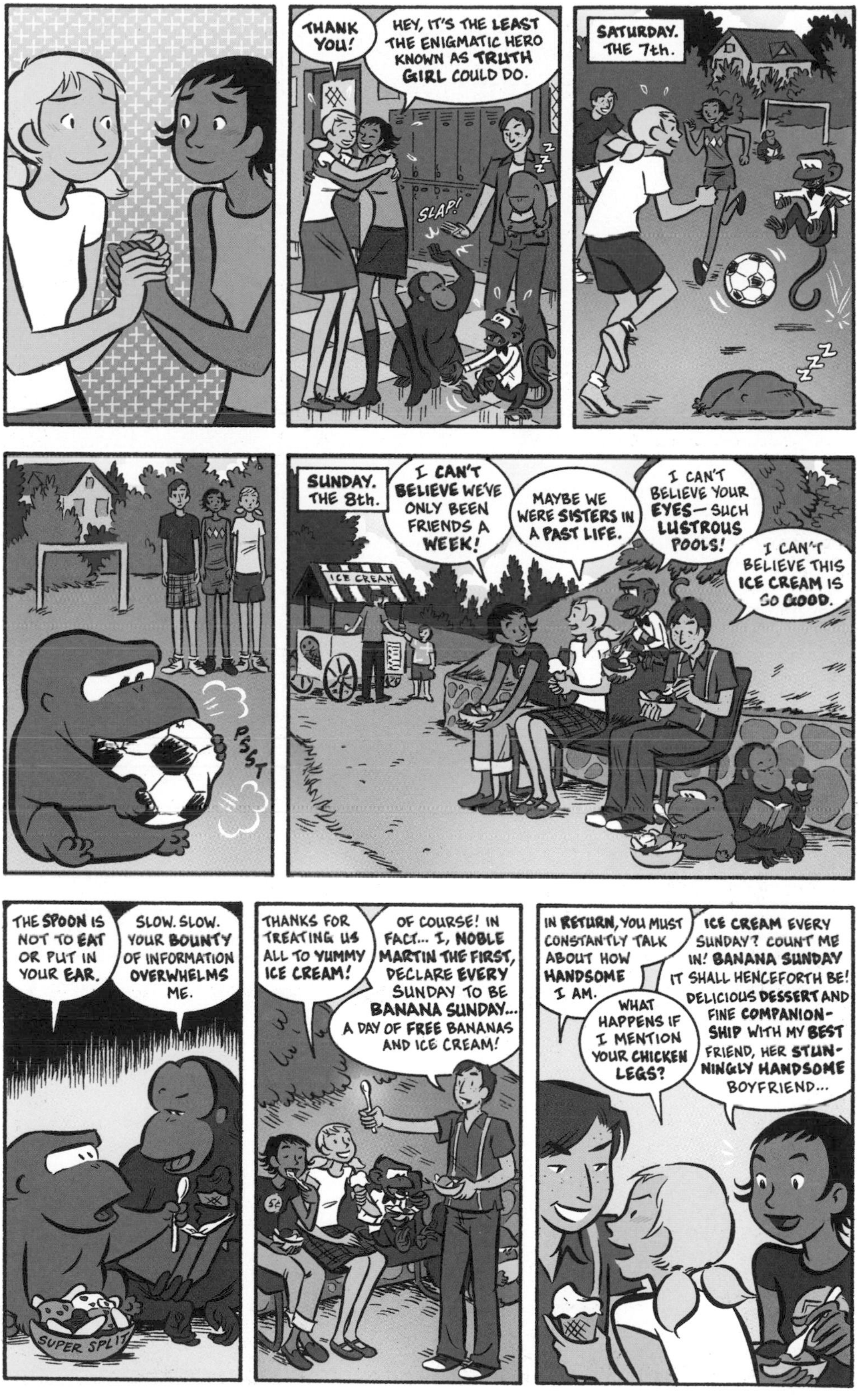
THANK YOU!
HEY, IT'S THE LEAST THE ENIGMATIC HERO KNOWN AS TRUTH GIRL COULD DO.
SLAP!
SATURDAY. THE 7th.
PSST
SUNDAY. THE 8th.
I CAN'T BELIEVE WE'VE ONLY BEEN FRIENDS A WEEK!
MAYBE WE WERE SISTERS IN A PAST LIFE.
I CAN'T BELIEVE YOUR EYES— SUCH LUSTROUS POOLS!
I CAN'T BELIEVE THIS ICE CREAM IS SO GOOD.
ICE CREAM
THE SPOON IS NOT TO EAT OR PUT IN YOUR EAR.
SLOW. SLOW. YOUR BOUNTY OF INFORMATION OVERWHELMS ME.
SUPER SPLIT
THANKS FOR TREATING US ALL TO YUMMY ICE CREAM!
OF COURSE! IN FACT... I, NOBLE MARTIN THE FIRST, DECLARE EVERY SUNDAY TO BE BANANA SUNDAY... A DAY OF FREE BANANAS AND ICE CREAM!
IN RETURN, YOU MUST CONSTANTLY TALK ABOUT HOW HANDSOME I AM.
WHAT HAPPENS IF I MENTION YOUR CHICKEN LEGS?
ICE CREAM EVERY SUNDAY? COUNT ME IN! BANANA SUNDAY IT SHALL HENCEFORTH BE! DELICIOUS DESSERT AND FINE COMPANIONSHIP WITH MY BEST FRIEND, HER STUNNINGLY HANDSOME BOYFRIEND...

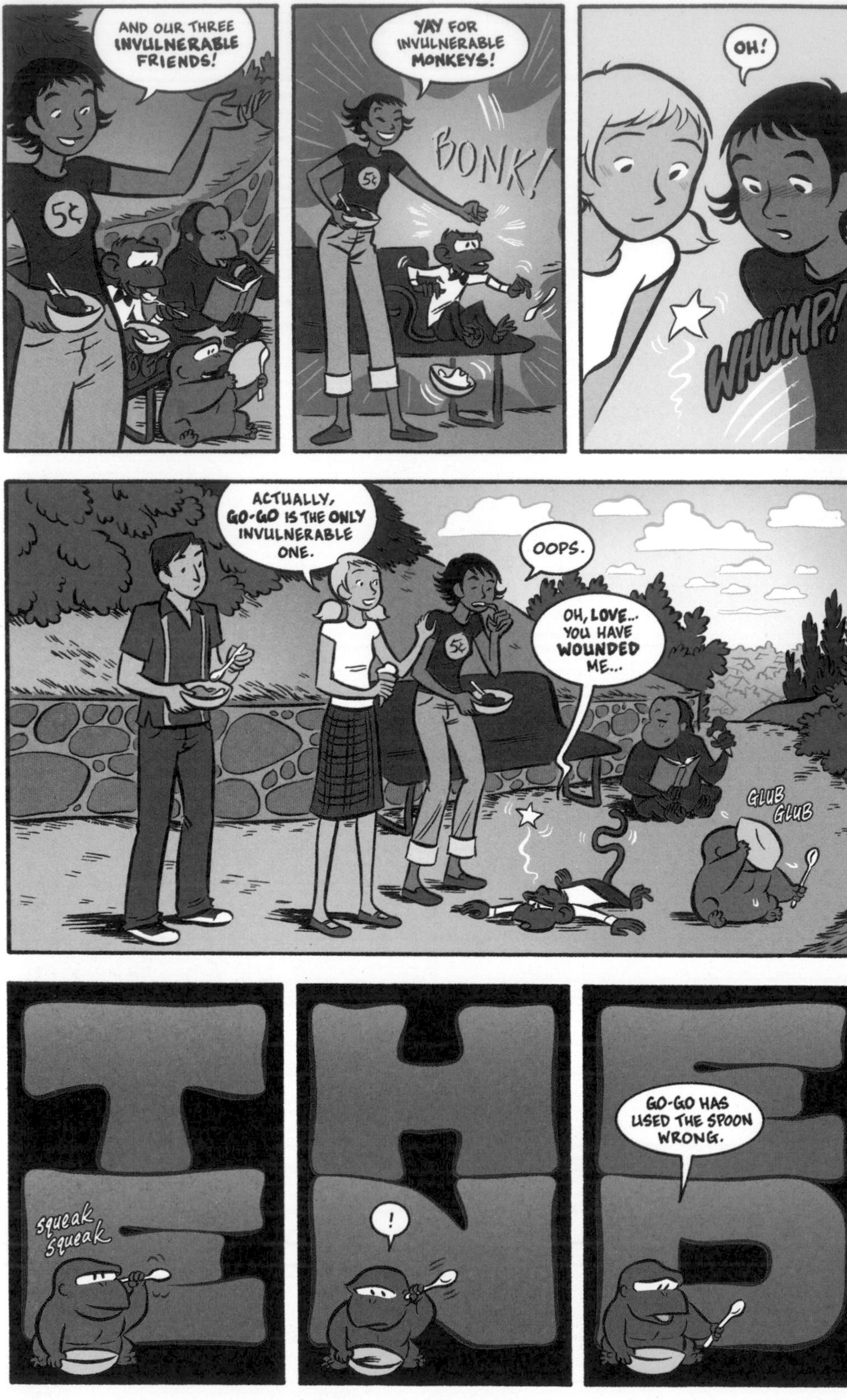
AND OUR THREE INVULNERABLE FRIENDS!
YAY FOR INVULNERABLE MONKEYS!
BONK!
OH!
WHUMP!
ACTUALLY, GO-GO IS THE ONLY INVULNERABLE ONE.
OOPS.
OH, LOVE... YOU HAVE WOUNDED ME...
GLUB GLUB
THE END
squeak squeak
!
GO-GO HAS USED THE SPOON WRONG.

BONUS MATERIALS

WATERCOLOR PAINTINGS

OF CHUCK, GO-GO, KIRBY, AND KNOBBY.

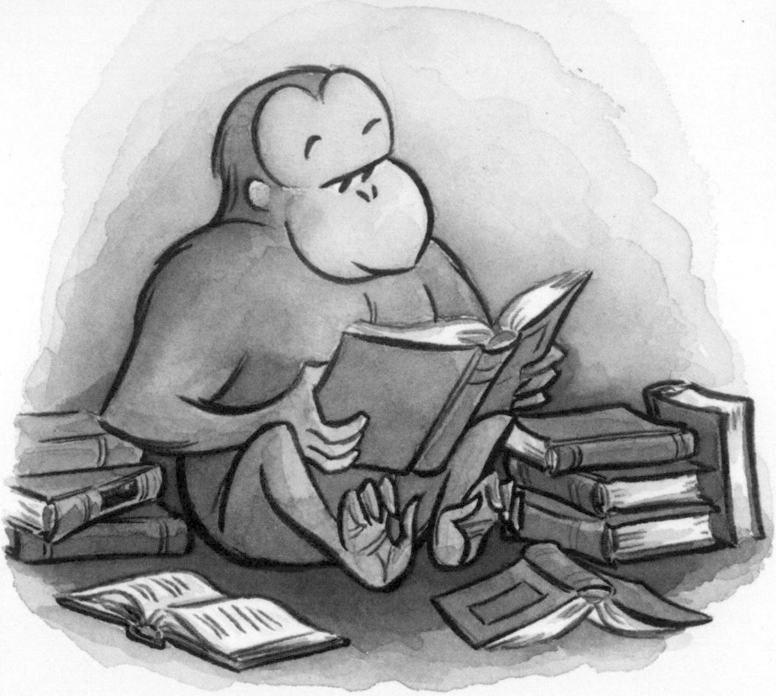

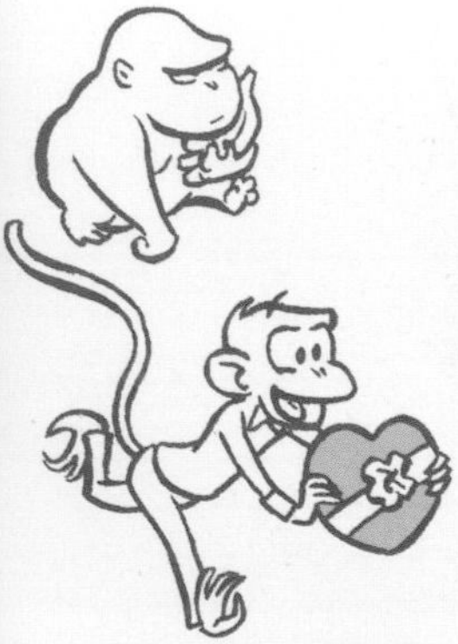

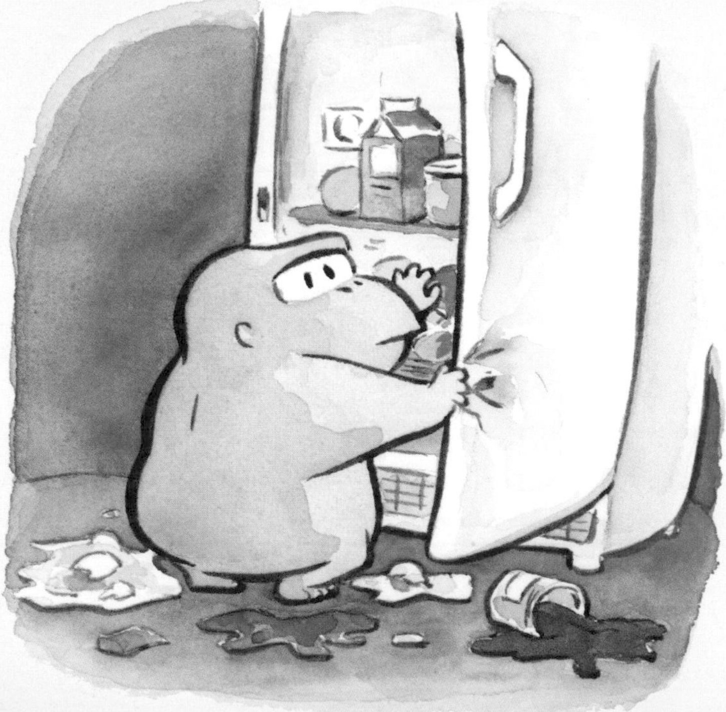

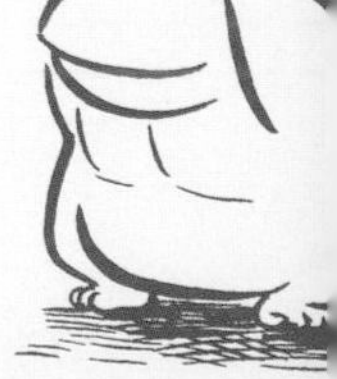

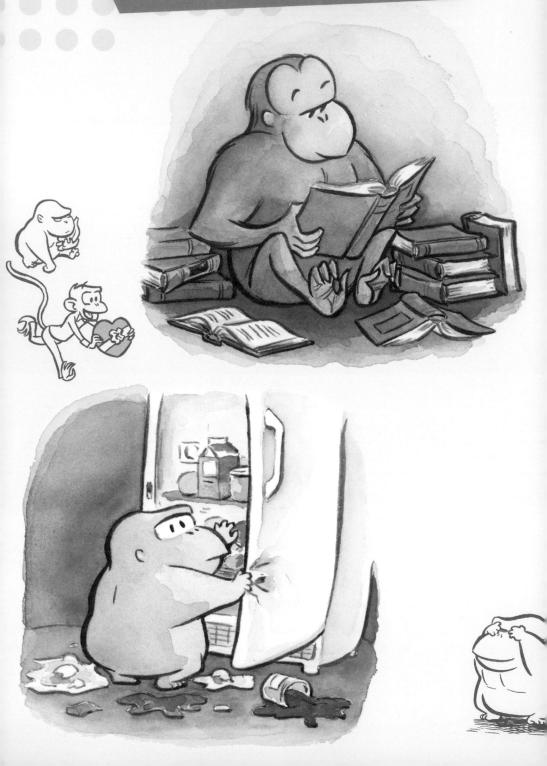

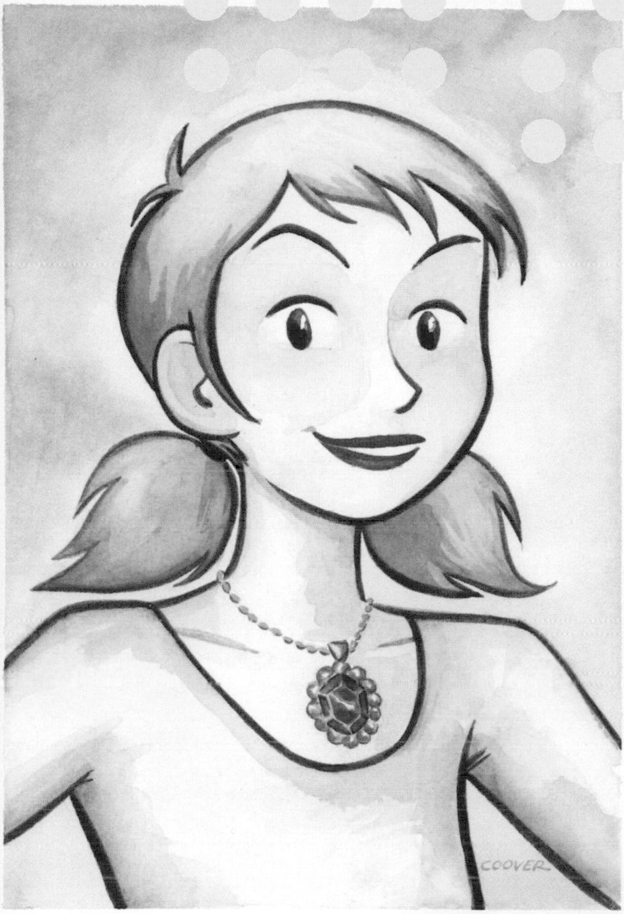
COOVER

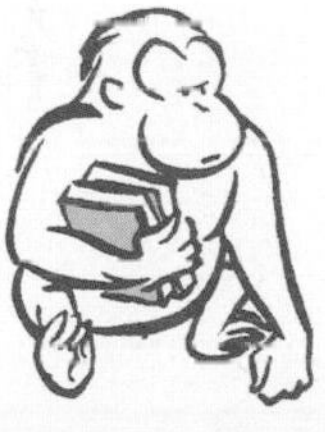

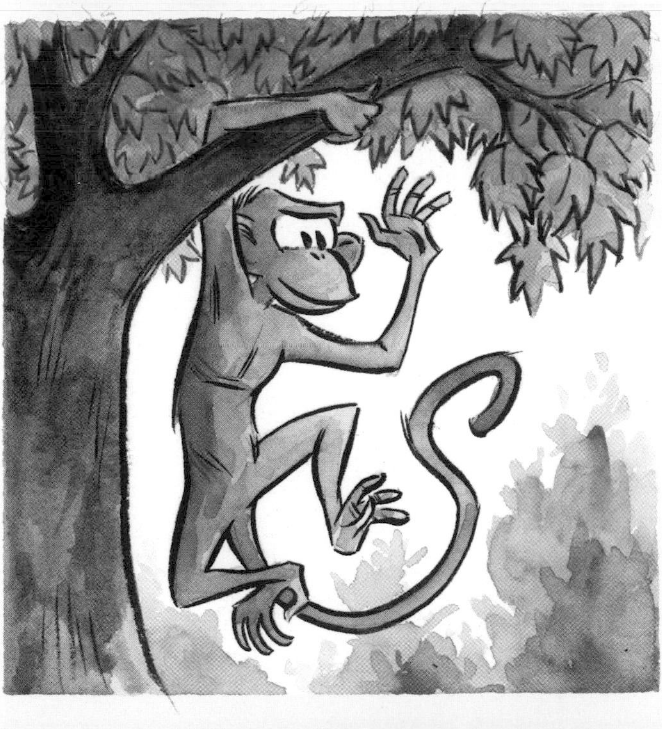

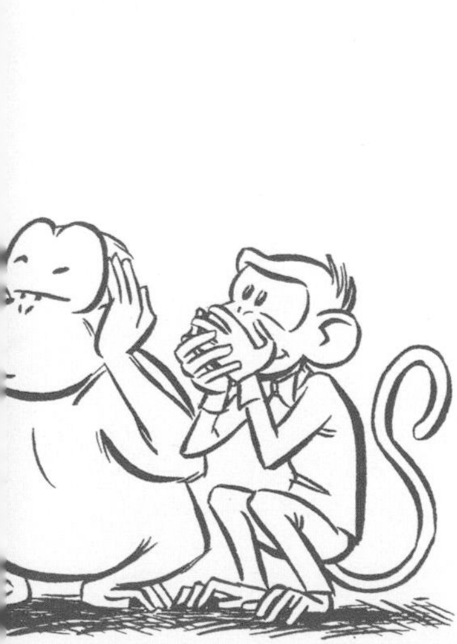

CHARACTER SKETCHES

IT'S GOOD TO DRAW CHARACTERS IN A LOT OF DIFFERENT STYLES AND POSES BEFORE DRAWING A WHOLE BOOK!

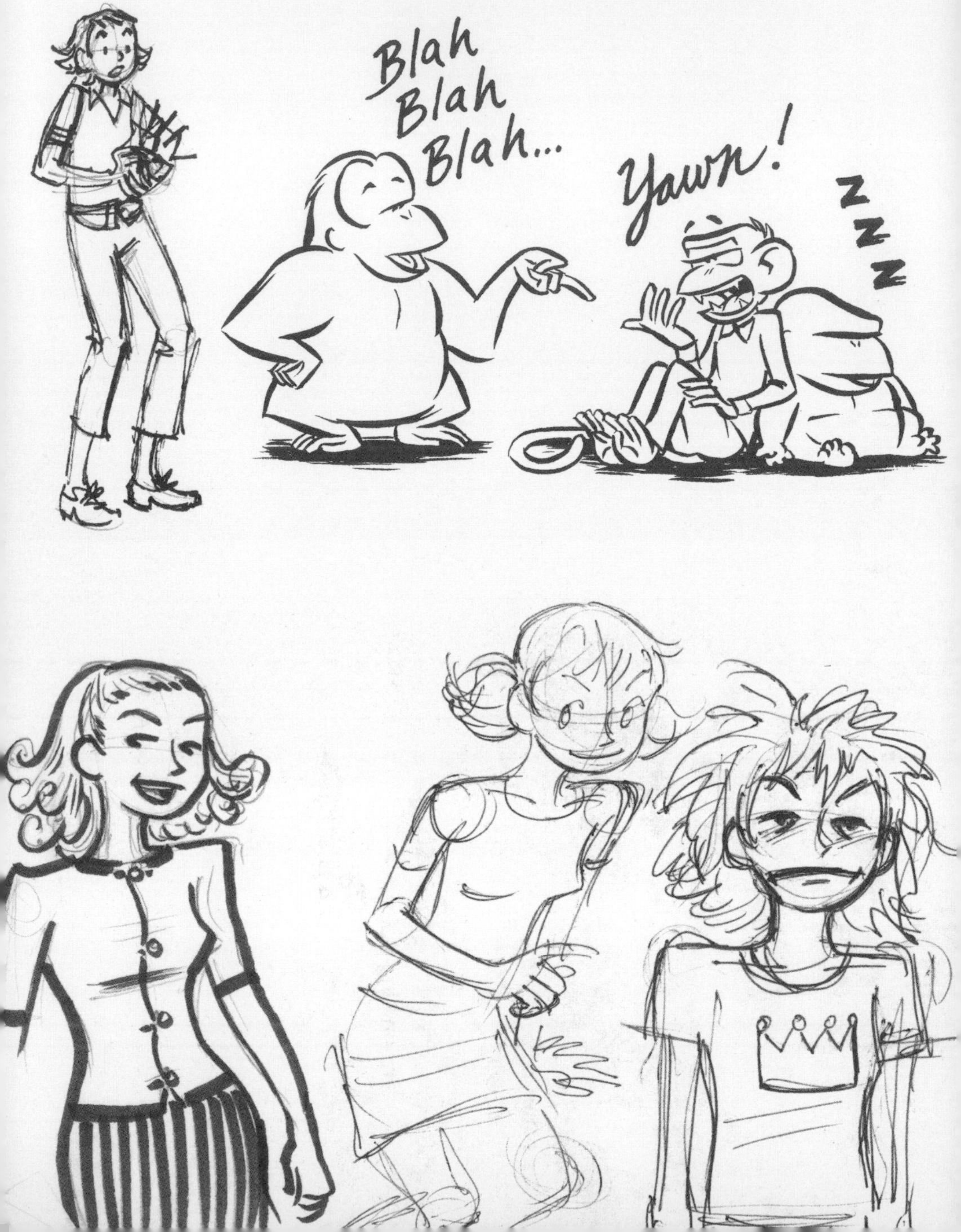
Blah
Blah
Blah...
Yawn!
Z
Z
Z

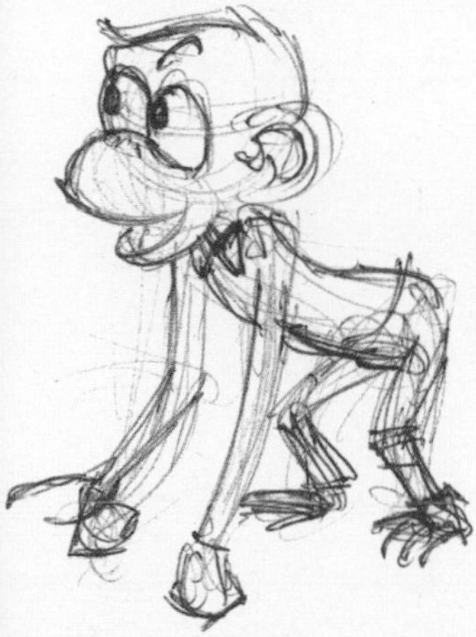

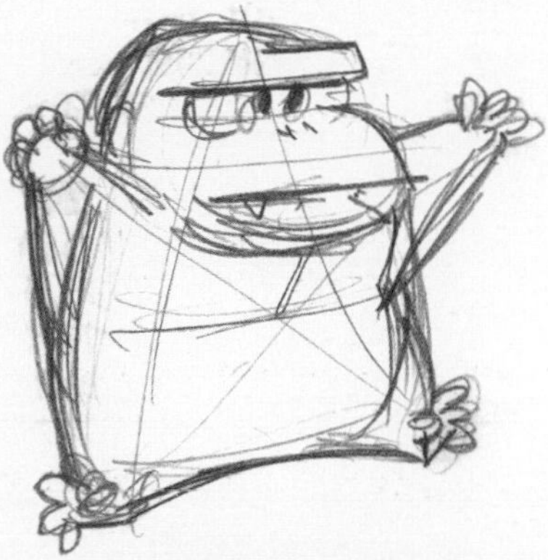

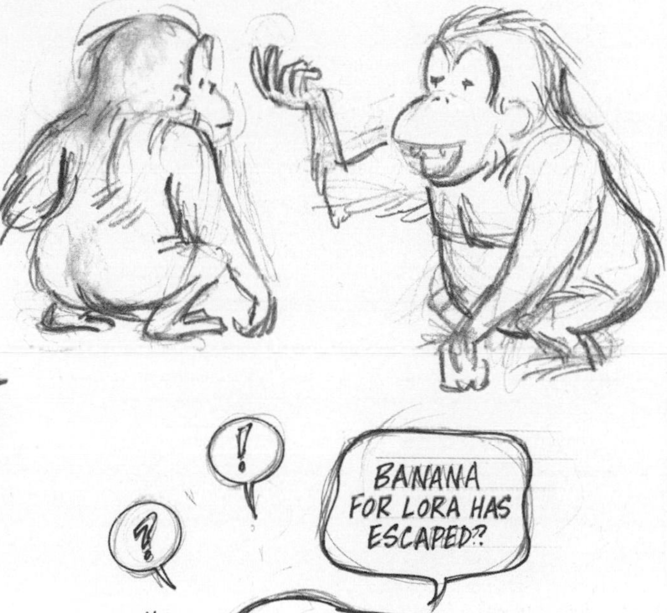

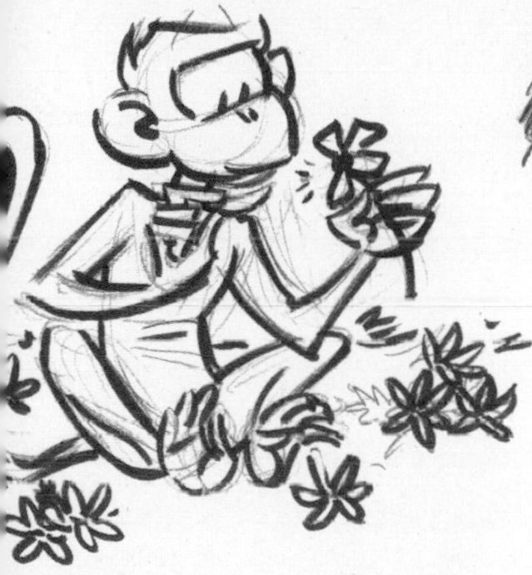

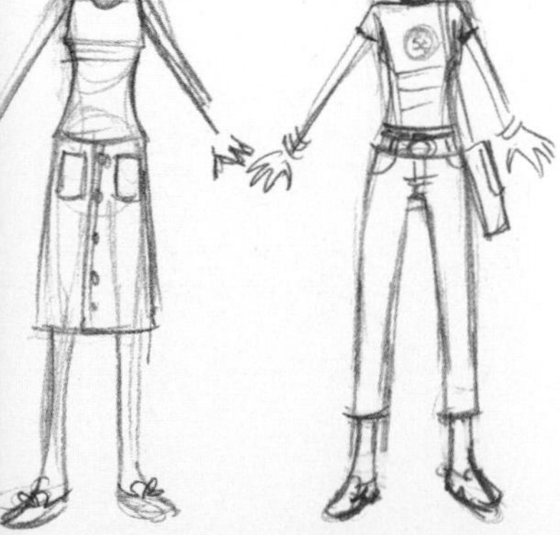

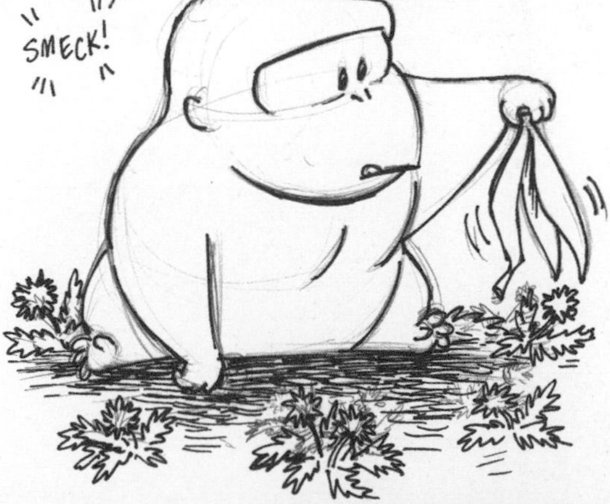
?
!
BANANA FOR LORA HAS ESCAPED?
SMECK!

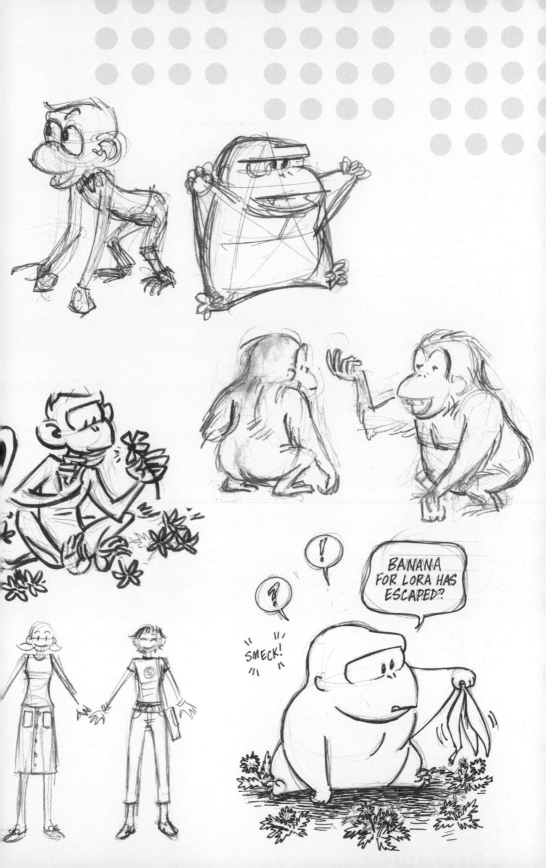

THE HAND-LETTERING PROCESS

ARTIST COLLEEN COOVER HAND-WROTE ALL THE DIALOGUE IN THIS BOOK! IT TAKES A LOT OF PRACTICE AND PATIENCE TO GET IT RIGHT.

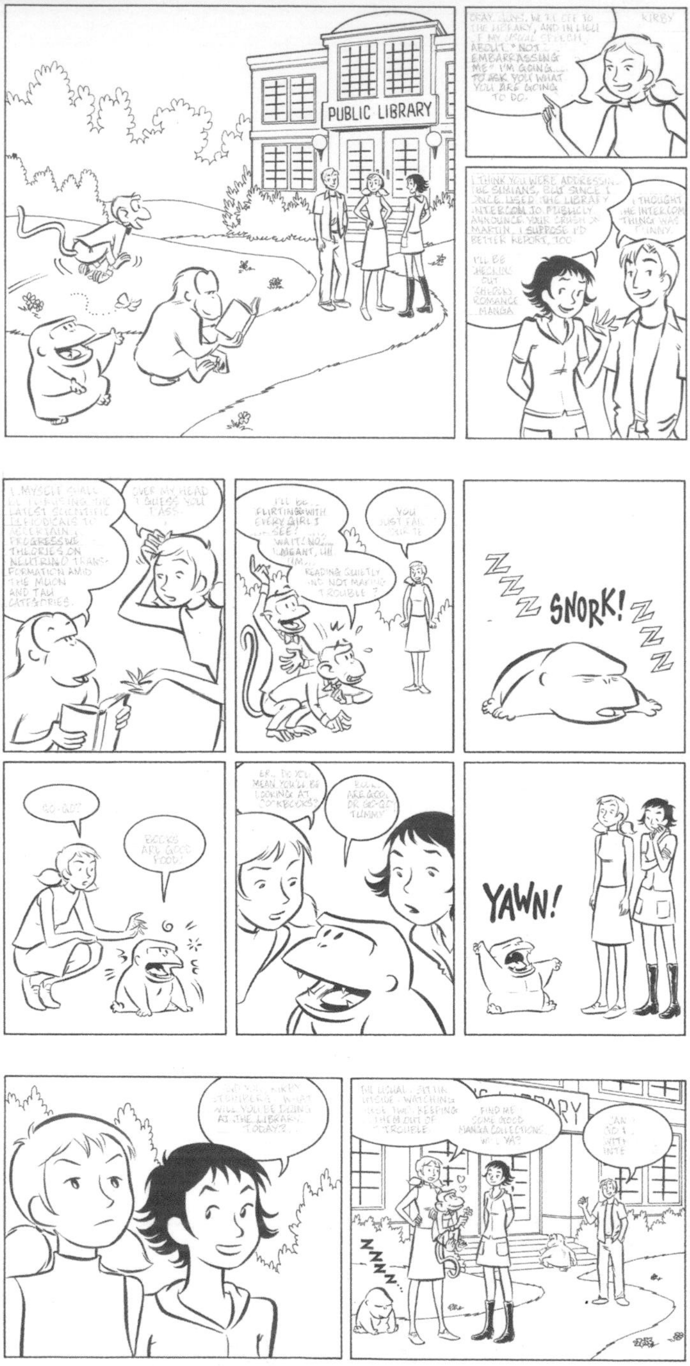
PUBLIC LIBRARY
KIRBY
SNORK!
YAWN!

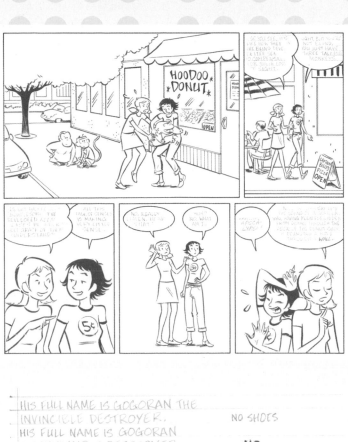

HOODOO DONUT
OPEN
CAPTAIN BILLY'S PIZZA OPEN
ALL THIS TALK OF SENSES IS MAKING VERY LITTLE SENSE...
HUH? NO, WHAT AM I...

HIS FULL NAME IS GOGORAN THE
INVINCIBLE DESTROYER.
HIS FULL NAME IS GOGORAN
THE INVINCIBLE DESTROYER.
APPARENTLY HE USED TO BE
A GIANT BEAST WHO TERRORIZED

NO SHOES

NO
SHOES FOR
PIGGIES.

HIS FULL NAME IS GOGORAN THE INVINCIBLE DESTROYER.
APPARENTLY, HE USED TO BE A GIANT BEAST WHO
TERRORIZED VILLAGES, OR SOMETHING.

OR SOMETHING.
HIS FULL NAME IS GOGORAN THE
INVINCIBLE DESTROYER. APPARENTLY
HE USED TO BE A GIANT BEAST
WHO TERRORIZED VILLAGES,

HIS FULL NAME IS GOGORAN
THE INVINCIBLE DESTROYER.
APPARENTLY, HE USED TO BE A
GIANT BEAST WHO TERRORIZED
VILLAGES, OR SOMETHING.

WOW,
SO YOU'RE
ALL DIVINE
MONKEYS?

BUT THAT WAS EONS AGO,
AND STORIES GET BLOWN
OUT OF PROPORTION. HE
PROBABLY JUST STOLE
EVERYBODY'S FOOD

WOW,
SO YOU'RE
ALL DIVINE
MONKEYS?

*Art pages are from an unfinished short story.

HOW A PAGE IS MADE

EACH PAGE GOES THROUGH A LONG PROCESS
ON THE WAY TO THE FINAL BOOK!

THUMBNAILS

PENCILS

INKS

COLORS

PAUL TOBIN is the author of the multi-Eisner-Award-winning *Bandette*, the Eisner-nominated horror series *Colder*, and the Eisner-nominated *I Was the Cat*, which is (spoiler) about a cat. His first novel, *Prepare To Die!*, was starred by Publisher's Weekly, and he is currently working on a series of middle grade novels, the *Genius Factor* series. He is the *New York Times* bestselling author of the *Plants vs Zombies* graphic novels, writes the weekly *Messenger* comic on Webtoons, and writes many more things while sitting in cafes, silently judging all those around him.

COLLEEN COOVER is an Eisner Award-winning comic book artist based in Portland, Oregon. She has been published by Oni Press, Dark Horse, Top Shelf, Marvel, and many others. She works with her husband, writer Paul Tobin, on the Eisner-winning series *Bandette*.

RIAN SYGH is a freelance comic artist and living enigma working out of Los Angeles, CA with his partner and two cats. He's done both illustration and sequential work with Boom! Studios, Diamond, HarperCollins, Oni Press, Valiant, and Z2 Publishing. He is the artist and co-creator of the Prism Award-winning comic *The Backstagers*. Which is pretty good, honestly.

READ MORE FROM ONI PRESS!

I WAS THE CAT
PAUL TOBIN
BENJAMIN DEWEY

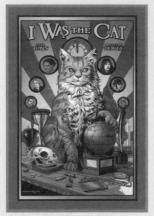

I WAS THE CAT
By Paul Tobin
& Benjamin Dewey
ISBN 978-1-62010-139-1

MATT GARDNER
RASHAD DOUCET
ALABASTER SHADOWS

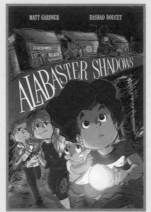

ALABASTER SHADOWS
By Matt Gardner
& Rashad Doucet
ISBN 978-1-62010-264-0

TERRY BLAS • MOLLY MULDOON • MATTHEW SEELY
DEAD WEIGHT
MURDER AT CAMP BLOOM

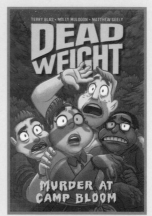

DEAD WEIGHT: MURDER AT CAMP BLOOM
By Terry Blas, Molly Muldoon,
and Matthew Seely
ISBN 978-1-62010-481-1

MERMIN
BOOK ONE: OUT OF WATER
By Joey Weiser

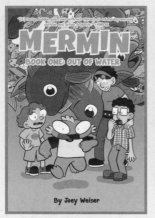

MERMIN BOOK 1: OUT OF WATER
By Joey Weiser
ISBN 978-1-62010-309-8

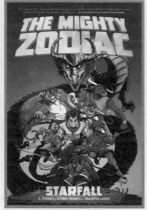

THE MIGHTY ZODIAC
STARFALL
J. TORRES • CORIN HOWELL • MAARTA LAIHO

THE MIGHTY ZODIAC: STARFALL
By J. Torres, Corin Howell,
and Maarta Laiho
ISBN 978-1-62010-315-9

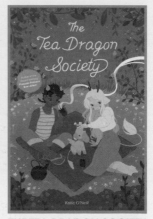

The Tea Dragon Society
Katie O'Neill

THE TEA DRAGON SOCIETY
By Katie O'Neill
ISBN 978-1-62010-441-5

For more information on these and other fine Oni Press comic books and graphic novels, visit www.onipress.com. To find a comic specialty store in your area, visit www.comicshops.us.

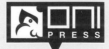